THE COLDNESS
OF NIGHT

THE COLDNESS OF NIGHT

A JACK PARIS THRILLER

GEORGE FONG

coffeetownpress

Kenmore, WA

coffeetownpress

A Coffeetown Press book published by Epicenter Press

Epicenter Press
6524 NE 181st St.
Suite 2
Kenmore, WA 98028

For more information go to:
www.Camelpress.com
www.Coffeetownpress.com
www.Epicenterpress.com
www.GeorgeFong.com

Cover design by Scott Book
Interior design by Melissa Vail Coffman

The Coldness of Night
Copyright © 2021 by George Fong

Previously published by Black Opal Books, Copyright © 2017

ISBN: 978-1-60381-785-1 (Trade Paper)
ISBN: 978-1-60381-786-8 (eBook)

Printed in the United States of America

To my dad,
the bravest man I know.

ACKNOWLEDGEMENTS

WRITING CAN BE A LONELY JOURNEY until you need something. A thought, and idea, or a piece of technical information to make the storytelling realistic. That's when you realize how many people help carry you through this journey. Thank you, David Corbett, Kirk Russell, Michael Connelly and Sheldon Seigel for your guidance and support in my desire to be a better storyteller.

To my literary agent, Kimberley Cameron of the Kimberley Cameron Literary Agency, who has never let me feel glum . . . at least not for long before encouraging me to keep writing. As always, thank you for your patience and tireless advocacy. To Joe Clifford for his editing, cutting, and sound advice.

And as always, to all the law enforcement officers I have had the honor of working with over my twenty-seven years as a federal agent. It is an honorable profession that should be proud of its successes but must learn from its failures.

And to my wife, Rebecca, for always being there, supporting my dreams as a writer. Some of life's journeys can be lonely. Rebecca has never allowed this one to be one of them.

"As a child, I never imagined that all of the real monsters in the world would be humans."

— Mobeen Hakeem

PROLOGUE

Today, before daylight:

I T WAS A TAPE.

More specifically, a cassette. It sat square, like a trophy on Jack Paris's living room table, perched on top of a stack of investigative case files. FBI policy was that files weren't supposed to be taken out of the office but Paris was never one for rules. Needless to say, late nights at the office weren't enough for him. He had to bring his work home. Investigations involving abductions and murders didn't come with set hours. For Paris, the work was all consuming, obsessive maybe. Hours bled into days that bled into weeks, into months. And when a case ended, there was always another. They kept coming and Paris couldn't help but look. Paris finally realized his addiction to his work took its toll: it stole away his personal life. Like oxygen slowly being sucked out of a room, he didn't feel his life suffocating until it was smothered out of existence. In this early morning hour, Paris sat alone in the dim light, staring at the stacks of case files, the last constant left in his world. But it was the new addition that made him uneasy.

Paris was a seasoned FBI agent with more years in his rearview mirror than he had looking forward. He had spent two decades tirelessly investigating violent criminals. When the cases came to an end, the murderers caught, the dead placed to rest, it was Paris who would be the one with the empathetic look and a comforting hand, telling others, ". . . in time. Everything gets better in time." This one was different. Paris knew he wasn't going to be the one offering consolation.

Not this time.

A stifling warm breeze cartwheeled through his bedroom window, the curtains loosely drifting like floating cobwebs. It was the end of summer but the heat certainly wasn't letting up. Even with the window open, the air felt heavy. Paris inhaled deeply, held it, and controlled a steady release. He hoped doing so would ease the anxiety he was feeling. It didn't. It had already been a week since the incident, the cause of his restlessness. There was a confrontation. Lives were lost and blame was being flung like seeds sown on a field. The details of that tragic night were still fresh in his head and Paris knew the cassette was the final piece of the puzzle as to why it all happened.

He made his way to the living room, fell onto his couch, and took a good look around. The place was a rental. The rooms were painted eggshell white, his furniture purchased from a local warehouse outlet. A price tag still dangled from one of the dining room chairs. Other than the framed pictures of his two children on the fireplace mantel, there were no reminders of a past life. The sparseness forced Paris to see and weigh the consequences of his decisions. One minute, comforted in a warm home with the ones he loved, the next, lost inside a photo of a missing child, the tears of a grieving parent, the explanation why someone wasn't coming home.

Those two worlds could never find harmony living in the same space. He hated having to choose one over the other, a choice that resulted in nothing but hurt feelings and broken promises. That was the reason Emily, his wife of nearly twenty years, asked for the separation. The nights leading up to the decision were filled with painful banter—he would say something, she would say something back, and, when there was nothing left to say, she would just end it with, "It's better this way." Just thinking about it made his bones ache.

Paris turned to the case files that decorated the stark room, like coffee table books. Except these books were filled with gruesome crime scenes, blood stained weapons, or someone no longer living. He could feel their energy. Like an electrical disturbance. They were waiting for his attention.

But the tape.

The tape, still sealed in its original envelope, was calling out his name from high on the glass table, demanding to be heard.

He stared at the unopened package. Originally it was left for him at the FBI office in Sacramento. Paris didn't want to open it in front of the other agents. Everyone knew what had happened. They just didn't need to know all the dirty details. So the envelope sat on his table for a week waiting for the right time. Like every night this past week, he thought about it.

It was time.

Paris leaned forward on the couch and nudged an empty crystal tumbler to the side, giving him an unimpaired view. He grabbed up the package, palpated it, and decisively slid a finger under the flap. Inside was a single cassette with a small yellow Post-It note. On it, scrawled by a woman's hand, were two simple words: *For You.* In today's world of digital media, the choice of cassette rang odd and poignant. He could only imagine the woman holding the microphone close to her lips, leaving her thoughts and memories on a lost medium. The message, he believed, would be deeply personal, even painful. Like family secrets, it was something everyone knew but was never spoken. He wished the tape didn't exist. But it did, and now he needed to hear it.

He pushed it into the portable player, hit play, and closed his eyes.

Her words broke the silence.

"My world ended the day my father died. The truth is, he didn't die—he was murdered. It took me a long time to admit that and, even after many years of finally having the courage to face that fact, it still causes my throat to swell.

"It was 1987 and I was only ten. It was a bright summer morning in my hometown of Vaughan, Mississippi. I remember how the day started, hot and sticky, even before I had a chance to step outside. I loved to play hard, like the boys in town. My hair was short, my temper even shorter. I never felt comfortable in a dress, opting for a pair of jeans and a white cotton blouse, the closest thing my mother could get me to wear to what she would consider minimally acceptable for a young Southern girl.

"Summer mornings always came early. The tall grass would bake dry, ropey strands of brown and gold straw under a blazing sun. The only sward saved from the drying heat were the patches shaded under the hundred-year-old magnolia and cottonwood trees. I can still see black crows perched on their branches like decorations, their eyes obsidian marbles, feathers glossy as crude oil.

"I remember that day. I had gotten up at dawn, hearing my father working in the barn around back, metal pipes clanking and the squeak of his wheel barrel. I slipped out the back kitchen door and skipped past the chicken coop. White feathered chickens the size of footballs scattered in mayhem, clucking their objection to my intrusion. The humidity was stifling, the air as heavy as my father's work boots. It'd only be a matter of time before the blistering sun would take control, turning the sky into God's oven. Mosquitoes clung to exposed skin. Still, mornings were as good as it got. The heat didn't sap away your energy quite yet. For me, this was my time to live in a world of pretend.

"On my way to the barn, I stopped to check on my rabbits. Kneeling beside the hutch my father made from scraps of wood and chicken wire, I smiled at the dozen or so bunnies huddled inside. My favorite rabbits were the biggest. Peanut Butter and Jelly. It wasn't until I'd taken the pair home that I realized Peanut Butter was a girl and Jelly a boy. I remember my father rolling his eyes when a pregnant Peanut Butter gave birth to a whole litter. He tried to look upset but his eyes softened when he saw how excited I was the moment my favorite rabbits became parents.

"I reached into the cage and pulled out Jelly, gently caressing him against my chest, stroking his long ears as they lay flat along his back. I would hum soft melodies, which relaxed him, and he would nudge his face into my stomach.

"'You're a good bunny,' I told him.

"Jelly's pink eyes glistened in the morning sun, his lower jaw rolling side to side, chewing on nothing. I placed him back in his cage and watched him scamper off into the thick haze of black and white fur.

"Heading toward the back of the barn where my father worked, I stopped. Beyond our stallions grazing, a cloud of dust rose over the horizon. I caught the boxy shape of a truck and thought it was too early for the mailman. I continued to watch until the trail of dust disappeared below the ridge that divided the edge of our property and the main road.

"I turned away and walked into the barn, jumping onto a stack of baled hay. An explosion of dust filled the air, catching rays of light as they danced their way back to earth. Minutes had passed, maybe more, when I heard the sound of a car door slam.

"I glanced out the barn doors. I could hear my father talking, low at first, followed by another man's voice. I pressed my body against the frame of the door, not wanting to interrupt.

"That's when I saw him.

"A large man with broad shoulders, wearing a starched white shirt with the sleeves rolled up to his elbows. I couldn't see his face since his back was to me and I was still far away, but I could see his hair was shiny and slick like he had just gotten out of the shower. He kept one hand behind his back, gripping a baseball bat. I couldn't make out his words but I remember my father's voice was calm. The big man said nothing, just nodded. Then the man stepped forward, closing the distance between him and my father. It was the first time ever I saw fear in my father's eyes. My father took a step back and covered his face. The man raised the bat high above his head and brought it down, hard. My father's head snapped to one side, as he fell to the ground. I froze, unable to force myself to move, to run. I didn't understand what was happening. I fell to the dirt, shoving my hand in my mouth, trying to stop myself from screaming. I bit down so hard I could taste blood. I watched helplessly as the man in the starched white shirt straddled my father's limp body, continuing to pummel him with that baseball bat. Every time he raised that heavy stick, I saw a stream of blood trail away in a thick crimson arc.

"I got up as quietly as I could, scrambling backward out of sight. I huddled into an alcove by a sidewall, deep in a dark shadow. I cowered in the corner, listening to the echo of the bat striking what had to be bone. I pulled my legs up to my chest and squeezed myself so tight, I could hardly breathe. I pinched my eyes tight and willed it to stop. When I found the strength to open them, I saw the man glaring over his left shoulder, looking at me. I froze, unable to move or breathe. Then he looked away, toward my rabbit cage. With the club still in his hands, he stepped toward the cage and took a powerful swing, like he was sweeping away trash. The cage exploded, the ground now imbedded in a blur of blood and ragged flesh. The man stood tall, his large frame blocking the rays of the summer sun. Shafts of blinding sunlight wrapped around his body and arms, giving him the look of a man on fire. I saw some of the rabbits sprint into the distance, searching for shelter. I looked to the side of the barn door and saw one hobbling, the one with a spotted black tail. It was Jelly. I saw terror in his eyes. He moved slowly at first, like he knew any noise would be his ending. Then he bolted into the tall grass beyond the horses, toward a tall oak tree, and he was gone. I began to cry, but not from sadness, elated Jelly was safe. Safe from the madman that was terrorizing my home, from the man that was hurting my father. I squeezed my eyes shut, wishing him safe. 'Run, Jelly,' I whispered, 'run to safety.'

"But suddenly, I wondered, was *I* safe? I couldn't disappear down a rabbit hole. I was here, alone, with a killer. I felt a shiver radiate down my legs before every muscle in my body hardened into stone. I suddenly tasted the salt from the tears that rolled down my face. I smelled the stench of sweat. I felt the hand of fear.

"I can't remember how long I hid in that alcove. It could have been an hour. It might have been the rest of the day.

"When the police finally came, the man was gone, my father dead, and my mother weeping over his body. I don't remember the police officer trying to speak to me but was later told I simply stared at the ground, repeating the same thing over and over:

"'Take me with you, Jelly. Take me.'"

The tape ended, the recorder clicked off, and Paris felt the crushing pain of his lungs void of air.

It was suffocating.

CHAPTER 1

Two Weeks Earlier,
Saturday Morning:

J ACK PARIS HESITATED.

Courage was never an issue but there was some amount of angst in stepping up any closer to the golf ball. He positioned himself just a bit behind it, taking in the stark white color, the perfect roundness, and the clear and unblemished dimpled surface. It was speaking to him. It was saying, "Hit me."

He zeroed in on the ball with a radar stare, his mind envisioning the swing, the flight of the ball. Zen-like. Golf is a mind game. That was always the mantra from his instructor. *'Hey, look at Tiger,'* he'd say while tapping a finger to his head. Then he'd take an easy swing with a five iron and land the ball on a carpet of green like a jet on a long runway. *'All in the mind.'*

He failed to mention the part about natural talent.

Paris settled his golf club, an over-sized Taylor-Made driver, right behind the ball. Jack Paris had been chasing kidnapers and killers for most of his career as an FBI agent but, at this moment, nothing gave him more uneasiness than that round white sphere.

He gave the ball a friendly nod, kind of like two adversaries coming to an amicable understanding, his hands searching to find a comfortable grip as he prepared to unleash fury.

"Hello, my little friend," Paris said under his breath.

"Why're you talking to the ball for?" The question—spoken in a thick

Boston accent—came from a member of his foursome. Special Agent Sean Patrick Dooley, but to those who had had the pleasure of being considered a member of his inner circle of friends, he was known simply as Dools.

Paris didn't look up, his attention still rapt on the golf ball. "Don't end a sentence in a preposition."

Dools displayed an indignant frown but acknowledged with a slight bow at the waist. "Fine. Why are you talking to the ball for, asshole?"

"That's better."

It was nine-oh-five a.m. on a Saturday morning, their regular tee time. Standing on the first hole at the Mather Golf Club in Rancho Cordova, California. Paris—along with his regulars, Dools, Daryl Gray, and Terrance O'Brien—was ready to tee off down a moderately wide fairway toward the green that was only a scant 388 yards straight ahead. The key word here being, *straight*. The course wasn't the best in town, didn't even have a nice bar. But it was the one they preferred. It was casual, comfortable, the greens, well-kept and forgiving. Above all, it was cheap. Paris gave the club a couple of wags. The head of his driver dwarfed the golf ball, taking on the size and shape of a medium size Buick. Moving slowly and premeditated, not unlike a predator shadowing its prey, he locked in on the ball, the contact, and ultimately, it soaring to the hole. Total focused concentration.

"You didn't answer my question, Jack."

Paris pulled back, losing his focus to the interruption. His eyes floated up to the open blue sky then toward Dools. He saw the other two smiling. Dools had an inquisitive look on his face, as if talking during a golf swing was sanctioned under the USGA Rules of Conduct.

Like he really cared.

"Well?"

"I'm just addressing the ball here."

"Eh . . . was that grammatically correct?"

"I'm just addressing the ball here, asshole."

Dools smiled. "That's better."

Paris stood board straight and began bouncing the club head on the perfectly manicured grass, giving his partner that *what for* look. "Mind if I tee off?"

Dools glided an arm across his body, hand open, palm up. For a big guy, he was a man of grace. "Give it your all."

Paris took the time to re-align his club, settling into a relaxed stance and then gave the fairway a last good look. Squared up, soft grip, steady breeze—

"So I don't forget to ask, you never told me whether you were going to help me with the Clarion investigation."

Again, Dools with the breach of etiquette.

This time, Paris unclasped his hands and let the driver fall. It made a muffled thud before knocking the ball off its tee. "For God sakes, Dools. It's our only day off."

For over a week, the Clarion investigation had been on his top ten list. The top ten list of things that bothered Dools, that is. The case—having been resolved and closed years ago—had new developments, and he called for it to be reopened.

The case was part drugs, part violent crime. The thing was, Dools didn't work drug cases. His whole career was slogging through the tsunami of violent crime cases that landed on his desk. The well-thumbed stacks of folders that rose like tiny skyscrapers and the marked-up boxes shoved along the walls of his cubicle could attest to the countless man-hours that seemed to have no ending. Yet, it never seemed like enough. Sometimes he felt as if the victims were peering at him through those files, asking, "What about me?"

And those old cases, they didn't just haunt. Every once in a while, they actually returned. Like this one.

Back in the day, Robert Clarion was well known to law enforcement as a successful drug dealer. But about five years ago, Clarion's eight-year old daughter was kidnapped and the case was "O and Aed," or opened and assigned to Dools. Based on his initial assessment, the snatching of Clarion's daughter was over a disputed drug debt. Go figure. In the height of the investigation, Clarion's wife, Barbara Lee Clarion, approached Dools and, in a haze of desperation, made a deal: Get back their daughter and she would get Robert Clarion out of the drug business—forever.

Long story short, Dools did just that. The daughter was recovered from a warehouse in West Sacramento and the kidnapper was killed in a shoot-out when he tried to escape. Score two points for the good guys.

O'Brien tapped Dools on his back then shot a thumb over his shoulder. "We got the next group waiting."

Dools waved a dismissive hand then turned his attention back to Paris. "Look, I spoke to Barbara the other day. She's really upset."

Paris looked over at the waiting foursome. One was staring at his watch, his face with the look of a person who had just sucked on a lemon wedge. Another slouched in his golf cart bouncing an anxious leg on the fiberglass hood. Paris lifted a hand and pumped it twice in a feeble attempt to apologize, indicating he was going to get the group moving.

"Well?" Dools asked.

"Well what?" Paris picked up his club, resetting the ball on the tee before squaring up, trying to get back to his concentration.

"You made a promise, Jack."

The promise.

Although it had been years, Paris did make a promise. During the course of the Clarion kidnapping, Paris and Dools got to know more about Robert Clarion and, more importantly, Barbara Clarion. At first, Dools thought of her as a potential informant, something the Director of the FBI mandates every agent should have—in large numbers. Her knowledge of the drug world would have been invaluable. But as they got to know Barbara, the two realized she wasn't at all interested in Robert's line of work. In fact, she had been trying to get him out of it for a long time. The kidnapping was her opportunity to force the issue with her husband, for them to make a clean break of the drug trade. Problem was there was a strong indication there were others involved in the kidnapping beside the one they killed. And that's what led to the promise.

Dools continued talking, like the waiting foursome had all the time in the world.

"You told her that if any of any other associate ever came back into their lives looking to settle the score, we would help her, keep her safe." Dools jabbed a finger forward. "Keep Rachel safe."

Admonition.

Paris didn't forget that part. Robert Clarion admitted his life as a drug dealer got out of hand. What began as sales of opportunity, snowballed into heavyweight distribution. Weight turned into power and power fueled his ego. As Clarion ascended into kingpin status, he thought he could dispute anything, including disagreements about monies owed. But he was wrong. A whopping $3,500 "discrepancy" led to his daughter's kidnapping. His daughter's life over three and a half lousy grand. It was then Robert Clarion knew he really screwed up. So, in exchange for the FBI's help, he agreed to work with Dools, testify against his supplier: Kevin Finch. A scenario that would have happened had Finch not been the one who died in the shoot-out with the FBI.

Daryl Gray joined in on the conversation. "If the supplier is dead, what's the problem?"

Dools faced Daryl and ardently said, "They're back."

Paris jumped in. "You don't know that."

"She's gone again, Jack."

Gone.

There was a moment of stillness by the group. The word hung heavy in the air. Paris added in a hesitant tone, trying to sound convincing. "Look, this isn't the first time she's run away."

Dools couldn't stop his jaw from tightening to the proposition. Since being rescued, Rachel Clarion had had a difficult time adjusting back to a normal life. The realization she was the daughter of a drug dealer, one that put her life in danger and nearly got her killed, was something hard to accept. The interesting thing was, it wasn't that her father dealt drugs. That, she admitted to her counselor, was something she could forgive. It was about trust. A father was to protect his children. At all costs. Robert Clarion didn't. Life became hard, she couldn't control her anger, and so, Rachel Clarion found her own way to deal with her anxiety. She ran away. Twice already, only to be located and returned home by the police. Paris was contending, this may be her third time.

But Dools was adamant. "This one's different. She didn't run away."

The way he said it wasn't argumentative. It conveyed concern. Real concern.

Paris pushed out both hands just above his waist, begging the question, "How sure are you?"

"Nothing's missing," Dools shot back, the words coming out like an approaching storm. "All her clothes are still at home, along with her school books and her backpack—"

Paris felt the words strike hard. *Classic signs of a suspicious disappearance.* He was unable to deny there could be something to what Dools was saying. He just needed more. "Was there a note left."

Ransom, that was what he was implying—anything that proved she'd been taken.

Dools choked back his barrage of factual points before expelling a sound of frustration. "No. No note."

"Excuse me—" This time the disturbance came from one of the players in the waiting foursome.

Again, Paris apologized.

Dools curled one side of his upper lip and harrumphed. Then he turned back to Paris and said it one more time—this time, with even more emphasis. "She's gone, Jack."

Paris had never doubted Dools's intuition. He was a smart investigator with the keenest of senses. If he said Rachel Clarion didn't run away then, in Paris's mind, Rachel Clarion didn't run away.

"One last question," Paris said. "Why now?"

Dools locked eyes with his partner. "Because revenge never takes a vacation."

Paris squeezed the bridge of his nose, a pain finding its way to his eyes.

Well?" Dools elevated his voice, loud enough so that everyone could hear.

"Okay, Dools. I'll help."

Dools smiled. He turned back to the waiting foursome and placed a finger up to his lips to indicate quiet. USGA Rules. His golf partner needed to concentrate. Paris squared his club to the ball, and everyone went quiet. Even Dools.

Focus, visualize, relax, control.

The club head dragged back in an even, smooth motion. The arc was perfect. The downward swing was a thing of beauty—like it was computer-generated. Contact, text book finish. Could have been on the cover of *Golf Digest.*

Dools, Terrence O'Brien, and Daryl Gray clapped. Golfer's clap. The back foursome didn't wait for the ball to land. They started pulling their clubs from their bags and made their way up to the tee box.

"Nice drive, Jack." Dools said.

They all stood, watching the trajectory of the ball as it ascended skyward.

Daryl Gray stepped forward as the ball glided onto the fairway, softly landing with a bounce and a roll to the right, coming to rest 110 yards from the pin. A perfect lay up. "Wonderful," he commented.

Paris looked at his friend and realized he wasn't interested in the shot. Gray was focused on other matters.

"What?"

"You gonna find that little girl?"

Paris tapped the head of his club on the short grass and looked over at the others in his foursome. They were quietly staring back in his direction, doe-eyed, obviously waiting for his answer. It was his only day off but it was apparent, Jack Paris's concentration wasn't going to be on his golf game. Whether he wanted it or not, right now his attention was going to be on the Clarion family—more specifically, their missing daughter,

Rachel, the girl he helped rescue five years ago. And, more importantly, what he needed to do to keep his promise. He was always going to make sure she was safe. Even if they had no idea where she was or what had happened. That was who he was.

Did they really have to ask?

CHAPTER 2

Monday morning:

CAPTAIN SHAWN DAVENPORT LEANED FORWARD on his desk at the Sacramento Police Department in downtown, his hands tented into the shape of a triangle. High-level brass liked to tent their hands. It made them show they were in control, look important, maybe even worldly.

"So, you think she's been kidnapped?" It was more of a rhetorical question before he added, "Again after five years?

No one said a word.

Paris and Dools sat square in front of Davenport's desk in a pair of matching brass-studded burgundy leather armchairs that looked like they came from a French museum. The desk was large and heavy, dark wood with a coordinating credenza and double book cases. The shelves were filled with books on management and leadership. The spines of the books looked like they had never been bent.

Davenport gently pushed away from his desk. "You think there were others involved in the original Rachel Clarion kidnapping? Ones that came back and took her again?" His eyes budged out. It appeared this time he was looking for a response.

"Yeah, I do," Dools said, his voice bold, busting confidence. "And so does he." Dools pointed a sharp finger at Paris.

Davenport turned toward Paris, one eyebrow arched.

Paris frowned, paused for a second, and nodded. "He's right. I do."

A soft voice was heard coming from the back of the room. "So do I."

Detective Valerie Calloway leaned against the wall with her arms crossed, a notebook wedged under her right armpit. Her head was tilted down and her eyes peering above a pair of jet-black reading glasses. Every head in the room swiveled over their shoulders and gave Calloway all their attention. Davenport didn't have to turn his head. From his desk, he had a direct shot to where she stood, like a target. He tapped a glossy blue fountain pen on a yellow legal pad, suddenly engulfed in silence.

"Well?" he said. "Enlighten me, Detective."

Calloway's green eyes bounced between Paris and Dools a couple of times before she pushed herself away from the wall standing in plain view of the group. She brushed aside a lock of red hair with her finger, tucking it neatly behind an ear, before tossing the notebook onto a vacant seat.

"Robert Clarion was like any other cocaine dealer."

"How so?" Davenport asked.

"He's cheap." Calloway walked up behind Paris and stood between him and Dools. The air suddenly filled in a soft fragrance, a result of her perfume reacting to the heat from her body. Everyone noticed. Except Davenport. "He never fronted any money for his drugs," she continued. "Everything was COD."

"What's your point?"

"His supplier—the one the FBI shot and killed?"

Dools smiled and gave a thumb's up to the group.

"Guy by the name of Kevin Finch," Calloway continued. "He was a known target of the DEA. After the shooting, I spoke with the agent at the DEA who was working Finch, and he said Finch never had two nickels to rub together."

Davenport's expression said he knew Calloway was right. Drug dealers were inherently cheap when it came to fronting money. Finch would've been no different.

Dools jumped in. "The agent told me that if Clarion owed Finch thirty-five hundred bucks, Finch owed his supplier at least three thousand of that. That supplier never got his money. Finch probably took the girl only because he was ordered by his supplier to do it. I doubt it was Finch's idea. He just got the short end of the deal."

Davenport looked unfazed. "Look even if Finch owed money to his supplier for the drugs given to Clarion, I would think three grand would be chump change. Whoever he is, why bother coming back after all these years to get back at Clarion now?"

Then it was Paris's turn. "We've been seeing a rash of homicides up

and down the coast. They appear associated." Davenport wasn't catching the implication. Paris opened a folder and tossed three photos on
Davenport's desk. Crime scene photos of bodies sprawled on sidewalks
and back alleys. Closed eyes and a lot of blood. "We ran the names of the
victims. They're all known drug dealers in their respective areas. They
shared the same drug supplier."

"Do you have a lead on their source?"

Paris hesitated. "Maybe. Phone records show a common number."
He paused for a second then added. "Same number Finch called on his
cellphone—when he was alive."

Davenport nodded silently, tent collapsed, hands now resting on top
of his desk. His fingers thrummed a quiet dance on his blotter sounding
like a muffled heartbeat. He stopped drumming, reaching for his coffee
mug and taking a long slow sip. He let the information soak in while his
eyes studied the crime photos that were fanned on his desk like a set of
playing cards, then said, "So you're saying Finch was dealing with the
same supplier as these dead suspects?"

Everyone nodded.

"DEA's MET team came through a couple of months ago and conducted a series of mass arrests," Calloway said. She stabbed a finger at
the photos. "These are the guys calling the ones DEA arrested. A check
on their phones showed they were connected to a common number
who I believe to be their supplier." Calloway again tapped at the photos. "These dead guys. They're the Finch's of the world. When the DEA
started rounding up their suspects, the money owed for drugs seized
never made it back to their suppliers. No money to the suppliers meant
no money moved up the food chain. And the big dogs at the top have to
get fed. And that's what may have started the killings."

"There's been a lot of chatter on the streets," Paris said. "Supposedly
a major supplier out there is very unhappy with his distributors not paying up on their debts, bust or no bust. DEA thinks he's trying to make
a point."

Davenport glanced from agent to agent. "What evidence do you have
that indicates this?"

"We got the common phone calls," Paris said. "More so, word is coming back from a number of CIs saying the same."

Calloway interjected. "I have to believe there's truth in numbers."

"It's not just the phone records and the CI statements that got us coming to this conclusion," Paris replied. "It's Barbara Clarion." He cleared

his throat and sat back in his chair. "We spoke with her yesterday and reviewed the original kidnapping one more time."

Davenport pointed his blue fountain pen at Dools, like an arrow leaving its bow. "Did we not get all the facts of what happened that night during the investigation?"

"Almost," Dools retorted.

"You were the lead, Agent Dooley," Davenport said. "Are you telling me you missed some important pieces of evidence that would have made a difference?"

Dools shook his head. "Nah. We got all we needed to get Rachel Clarion back alive. And we killed the bastard that grabbed her; that's a fact."

Davenport raised both hands, palms up. "Then what?"

"We investigated this like any kidnapping case," Dools said. "What we should have done was follow up on the drug angle." He looked at Paris and then back at the captain. "We left a thread loose by not apprehending the man who put the plan in motion. Finch's supplier—"

This time Paris tapped a finger at the photos. "Whoever is their supplier, he's come back for his money. And those who won't pay end up like these guys." He turned to Dools, as if admitting he was right all along. "With Robert Clarion, he not only didn't pay, he called the FBI. I think this is no longer only about a collection. This is also about being disrespected. And that lasts forever." He gave the closing remark a moment to sink in. "Rachel Clarion didn't run away this time," he said before giving it a final summation: "She was taken."

Davenport shook his head as he tried to mentally assemble this puzzle, his hands now twirling the expensive fountain pen. "I think you boys at the FBI have an active imagination. That's a real stretch." Paris opened his mouth to respond but Davenport cut him off. "Serial drug debt vendetta killings . . ." He gently put down his pen and pursed his lips, pushing both index fingers—back in the tented position—up to his chin. "Even if I go along with the theory that these dead drug dealers did have a common supplier and that they did owe money and that the supplier was sending out a message, what solid piece of evidence do you have that makes you think this ghost supplier has come back for Clarion's daughter after all this time?"

Paris and Dools turned their heads and stared at each other, as if to see who was going to respond to Davenport's question.

"Why now?" Davenport repeated.

Dools leaned forward, resting his forearms on Davenport's massive wooden desk. The desk creaked, as if absorbing all of his energy and determination. "Because Barbara Clarion called us."

"And?"

Dools didn't break his stare at Davenport. "Someone's been watching their house."

CHAPTER 3

Monday evening:

BARBARA CLARION FIDGETED on her living room sofa, holding onto an unlit cigarette. She played with it, nervously rolling it back and forth between her fingers without any intentions of lighting it up. Smoking was something Barbara gave up right after the kidnapping, part of the pact she made with God, or maybe to herself. Either way, it was a good excuse to quit.

Robert Clarion stood up from his recliner and walked over to the front window. The television was on but neither one of them seemed to be paying much attention to it. He pushed aside the custom drapes, opening not more than a two-inch slit to peer out. Outside, he stared at the perfect row of streetlights burning bright against the darkness, as they did every night. The pavement was wet from a summer rain an hour earlier and the quiet street went on until it didn't. Large Italian Cypress cast shadows across the grass and swayed slightly from an intermittent breeze. That was the only movement he saw. No strange cars or lurking figures. Secretly, he wished there was. Then at least, he knew what he would do.

Barbara spoke softly as she placed the unlit cigarette to her lips. "He's not there anymore."

Robert kept quiet as he continued his gaze out the window with the same dull stare he had fixed on the television screen two minutes prior. Eventually, he let the curtains fall back into place before returning to his recliner. He knew she was right. Whoever had been watching the house was gone.

Since the kidnapping five years ago, both Robert and Barbara had felt age chasing them down a lot faster than time itself. They were both in their late thirties, in good shape but had never really fully recovered from the scarring that came from Robert's life as a drug dealer, from their daughter's near-death experience. It was something that Barbara still held Robert responsible for, something he would be consciously aware of for the rest of his life. Barbara had a slim figure with nice curves that she worked hard at maintaining. Her backside still drew the admiration of every man within eyeshot when out to dinner or at one of Rachel's school functions. Her legs were as elegant as long stem roses. She said it came from her rigid daily workout routine but Robert knew she was born with it. Her blonde hair was shorter than when they first met, cut just above her shoulders, giving her face a look of timeless grace. And Robert was still the handsome man she met in High School. Five-eleven, one hundred seventy five pounds, still mostly muscle. He had a full head of hair that lay across his scalp like one of those models in a fashion magazine with a brush of gray at the temples.

Barbara stood up and walked over to a small liquor cart near the fireplace. She poured a splash of Scotch from a crystal decanter, and handed it to Robert, who accepted the offer with a weak smile, before setting the drink on the armrest of his recliner.

She placed a hand on his shoulder, gave it a gentle rub. "I saw him there this morning," she whispered. "He wasn't there long. This time."

"Are you sure he wasn't there all night?"

Barbara shook her head then heaved a long deep sigh. She didn't know for sure.

Robert's thoughts immediately went to Rachel and he stared down the hallway.

"Where is she this time?"

His question wasn't for Barbara. It was a statement made out of frustration, helplessness. Robert was asking a higher power. It was clear in Robert's few words: she didn't run away.

Barbara felt the sting run through her spine. "I'm worried, Robert. This one feels different."

He sank deep into his recliner and covered his eyes with both hands.

"Why is this happening?" Barbara forced her voice to soften but it was still filled with anxiousness. "Isn't there anything you can do?" She maneuvered around the chair, knelt next to Robert and looked up into his eyes. He didn't—or couldn't—look back. "Can't you just give them their money?"

Money for Rachel. It's not that simple. Robert shook his head and frowned. "They don't care about the money. They care about making a statement. Besides, I wouldn't know who to pay and they sure as hell haven't introduced themselves."

Barbara remained silent.

"I'm sure they didn't like the fact the FBI got involved. Like we flipped them the bird." Robert tapped his wedding ring against the crystal tumbler that was now tightly gripped in his hand. Barbara waited for him to come up with a solution, an answer. He always did. His inability to do so now spoke volumes.

"You need to talk to Agent Dooley," Barbara said. "You must tell the FBI what's going on." She paused, not wanting to show any signs of deception in her eyes. What Robert didn't know was that she had already told the FBI about the suspicious car, about the dark figure. She told Agent Dooley of the stranger showing up at Rachel's school. She even mentioned the telephone calls that ended up with nothing more than silence on the other end and then a hang up. The calls, not even Robert was aware of. And mostly, that Agent Dooley had come to the house, checked out Rachel's room, saw what was left behind, what was not taken. Even Agent Dooley believed this didn't look right. "Did you hear me?"

Robert nodded, keeping his eyes on his drink. "I hear you. I'm just not so sure I want to talk to the FBI quite yet." He massaged the space between his eyes. "I need to think."

Think? Barbara was stunned. They were talking about their daughter's life and he wanted to think? Why? This time was different, not like the past. This time, she didn't run away. "She was taken, Robert."

There it was, the word finally said, what they both knew to be the truth: *Taken.*

"I've got some people I know who owe me. They may be able to help me resolve this without involving the cops."

Barbara felt the blood drain from her face. She was barely able to keep her balance. She looked at her right hand, saw it was shaking, and reached over with her other. Squeezing tight, she rubbed, as if it was the cold that was causing her to shiver. "Look, Robert, I heard on the news there have been a string of murders that the police think are related to unpaid drug debts." That was a bold-faced lie. She didn't hear it from the news. She heard it from Agent Dooley. "Money like Kevin

Finch owed." She touched Robert to get his attention. "Those that don't pay up, they kill."

"You don't know that."

"You don't know that it's not." Her voice cracked.

Robert looked up and caught Barbara's tear-filled eyes. "Okay, okay. I'll talk with the FBI. Just give me a couple of days to see if I can take care of this myself. Just a couple of days, please."

Barbara nervously fumbled with the string of pearls around her neck, the ones Robert bought her when times were good, money was flowing. After a few seconds, Barbara begrudgingly agreed. "I want my daughter back."

Robert held still.

"A couple of days, Robert. That's all. Then you will get help from the FBI."

Robert forced himself to look in control, that all would be fine. "Promise," he said.

Barbara held back words she wanted to say, how all this was his making, that their lives had been forever changed, all for easy money. His fault. Instead, she decided to stay quiet.

But Robert had changed. He realized the mistake he made, the consequences of going into business with those where money trumps all and violence could always be justified. He left that world after Rachel was kidnapped. And to his credit, he never looked back.

Barbara felt Robert reach out and touch her on the arm to say everything was going to be all right. She manufactured a false smile as she left the room.

THE ROOM FELL QUIET, THE TELEVISION still being the only distraction glowing in the background. Robert chewed on his thumbnail, thinking about what he needed to do. There was no doubt in his mind that whoever Kevin Finch's supplier was, he'd have to know about Robert's role in the operation. Learning about the recent string of drug-related murders, Robert had become convinced his wife was right: his life and that of his family's was in grave danger.

He pushed in the leg-rest on his recliner and placed the glass on the coffee table. Walking into his home office, he clicked the light switch on and sat at his desk. The lamp on the corner lit up, bathing the desk in a low and subtle hue, while the rest of the room remained gray and without shadows. He pulled a key from his pocket and slid it in the bottom left-hand drawer, one of the few he kept locked, an agreement that he made with Barbara after bailing from the drug business. No more secrets, he promised. But this drawer was the exception, one he was allowed to keep for himself.

"My job, Barb," he said no louder than a whisper. "My job to fix."

Robert slid the drawer open. A handful of papers lined the drawer, bank statements and Certificates of Deposits. That wasn't why he'd come here. On top of the stack sat his gun, a nine-millimeter Walther's PPK, stainless. Picking it up, he felt the cold steel against his palm, perceiving its purpose and power. He thought about the day he purchased the gun, for protection in his new line of work. Less than a decade ago, he'd made the call to enter the drug trade. The move was nothing but a means to make a little money for his family, get them on their feet. A home, a car, a good school for Rachel. That's all he wanted. But over time, his success offered opportunity to expand his territory. To do so, meant someone had to give up theirs, and that made him enemies. Enemies who took such a slight beyond money and business. Now it was personal.

Rachel had been just like any other child. Like most kids, she had lived a carefree life, without major worries or fear. She loved being read stories, and unconditionally believed in Santa Claus, the Easter Bunny, and the Tooth Fairy. Mostly, she took grown-ups at their word. Trusted them implicitly. But since the kidnapping, she had changed.

He saw it in her eyes. These days Rachel studied her surroundings with a dutiful awareness. No longer curious of unfamiliar things, she was instead skeptical of details outside the norm. She could no longer fall asleep alone and required a nightlight. The backpack she carried to school now included her phone with the GPS map constantly on. She didn't like being alone, and new adventures were no longer exciting. They had stolen that from her. They had scarred her.

Now they have taken her again.

Their actions crossed beyond the line of reason, giving him no choice but to respond in kind: By physical force.

His moment of silent thought broke when he caught sight of a shadow at the door. A dark figure, small and still, partially hidden behind the wall. He knew who it was but that was impossible. She was missing, he knew it, but everything in his mind wanted it to be true. He wanted it to be Rachel.

"Are you coming up?" The ghost's voice was soft but demanding.

Robert slid the gun below the desk, out of sight, and smiled, forced himself to believe Rachel was there at the door. Something he needed to keep his sanity. "You bet, sweetie. In just a minute."

The ghost of Rachel gently kicked at the carpet with her bare feet, looking as if she was considering waiting for her dad to escort her up.

"Go on, Rachel," Robert said in a coaxing voice. "I promise to be up in less than a minute."

He watched the vision of his daughter turn and walk away, disappearing like a fine mist at sunrise. Whether or not a figment of his imagination, his daughter left him again, and there was nothing he could do to stop it. Robert felt a devastating pain in his heart.

Looking down he saw the gun still tightly gripped in his hands, resting on his lap. He started seeing flashes of his daughter's face, fear being the constant theme. In a heartbeat, he felt his face heat up. These images were more than enough to convince him of what he needed to do. And the weapon in his hands was giving him the directions. He shoved it into his jacket pocket and patted it twice, as if he was putting it to bed. Then he turned off the light and quietly walked out of the room.

CHAPTER 4

THERE WERE THREE STACKS OF PAPERS on Detective Calloway's desk: the in-stack, the out-stack, and the I-don't-give-a-shit-stack. That one was naturally the tallest.

Calloway was hunched down over her keyboard, typing out a report when Jack Paris walked up to her office and knocked on the doorframe. She continued typing for a few seconds before hitting the send key and raising her stare toward the door. She seemed to be looking right through him at first, or maybe considering her options, before waving a hand inviting him in.

Paris had known of Calloway for several years but only learned more about her from his recent conversations with Dools since the whole Clarion case re-emerged. She helped out as a patrol officer during the initial kidnapping and was now the detective assigned to the new case. Calloway was slender, five-five with deep green eyes and ginger hair. She never wore makeup—at least not at work. She had a youthful appearance about her, athletic—someone you wouldn't take for being a street cop but more like a college student.

When she first joined the department, the rank and file would bust her chops for being what they described as less than threatening, but they quickly discovered she was more than the sweet kid next door. One night during a shift in midtown, Calloway and her partner rolled up on a major 415—a drunken street brawl. In the commotion, one of the drunks shoved her partner to the ground. A second later, patrol officer Calloway hauled off with a snap kick that landed square in the perp's family jewels, dropping him to his knees. Calloway grounded his nose into the pavement and cuffed him from behind his back.

That was end of the altercation. After that, there were no more cheap shots taken at the rookie officer.

"Got a minute?"

Calloway smiled, pushed back in her chair, and crossed her arms. She was wearing jeans and a crisp white cotton blouse. She shifted in her chair and, when she did, her top button popped, splaying open and revealing a view of her neckline blending to a smooth collarbone. A thin gold chain followed the curve of her neck, maybe a pendent hidden within the fold of her shirt collar. Paris couldn't help but look, his eyes following the contours, feeling half-guilty for the prolonged regard. He cleared his throat before forcing himself to meet her eyes, fumbling to cover up his awkwardness: "Thanks for backing us up on the Clarion case." Smooth comeback.

Calloway straightened, fidgeting with the button, discovering the reason for his distraction. For a second, he thought Calloway was blushing. "I just want to help." She reached across her desk and dug through a stack of papers, pulling out a one-inch handful. Toll records from Meridian PCS Cellular phone service, the pages dog-eared and marked up by a yellow highlighter. She tapped a finger on the top page. "I checked on a common number that was being called by those dead drug dealers." Removing a top sheet along with a few attachments, she handed it to Paris. "Here's a summary of what I've determined."

Paris moved closer and studied the report including a flow chart linking suspect telephone numbers. The diagram looked like a wagon wheel with a couple dozen cell numbers, all pointing to a center hub and number. He pointed at the middle. "I recognize that one. It belongs to our UNSUB who we think is ordering the killings."

UNSUB stood for unknown subject, and that was exactly the problem. Meridian PCS, like any cell company, was in the business to rent phones, no matter who you were. Those needing anonymity. That included drug dealers, child molesters, and murderers. As long as they paid their bill, they had phone service. In any name, true or fictitious. That was what our UNSUB did. The phone that Calloway had tracked was subscribed to a John Smith. How original.

Calloway nodded. "I've been pursuing this guy for years."

Paris was puzzled. "This phone number's been good for that long?"

"No, this guy, whoever he is, has been slinging dope for a long while.

I've been trying to get him ID'ed, trailing him from one cell phone number to another. He'd dump a phone and move on. I thought I lost him until the Clarion kidnapping reemerged. When your partner started pulling tolls in an attempt to ID your kidnapper, I noticed the numbers were the same as the ones calling my guy. That's when I began looking into this cell." She pointed at the stack. "I believe the guy *really responsible* for the Rachel Clarion kidnapping is the same guy I've been chasing for the past five years."

Paris placed the pile back on Calloway's desk. "Why didn't you bring this to our attention sooner?"

Calloway bit down, her jaw muscles flexing as she mindlessly moved the papers around on her desk then looked away.

She was clearly agitated, maybe even a bit embarrassed. "I wanted to work this out myself before bringing anyone else in." She grabbed the toll records and shoved them inside her desk drawer, as if she regretted her decision to open up.

From what little Paris knew of her, it fit her personality. Dools had told him Calloway was a good cop but a loner.

A loner. Just like Paris.

What followed was an uncomfortable silence, as she had somewhat backed herself into a corner, and he could see she was looking for a way out of the conversation. He didn't want to alienate her any further, especially since they had a common goal.

"Totally legit," he offered.

Time seemed to slow as he waited to see how Calloway would react. She sat up straighter in her chair, studying Paris before sucking in a deep breath. The gold necklace glided straight into a V, the pendant disappearing below the top button and beyond his view. Once again, he caught himself, looked up, and decided to recover her trust. "Tell you what. How about I get everything Agent Dooley has on the Clarion case and bring it to you for you to look over. Help identify this guy who may be your drug supplier." He stuck out a hand, hoping to find a way back into her good graces. The room went quiet. "I got a missing girl, Detective. Mother thinks she's been kidnapped for the second time. I think it would be in both our interests to find her," he said. "Deal?"

Calloway glowered at Paris for a few seconds, silently, then at his hand that was intimating a gesture of collaboration but now appearing to be hanging in the air uncomfortably long. She let out a breath, relaxed a bit, and took his hand. "Deal."

DOOLS SHOOK HIS HEAD LIKE A dog shaking off water. "Oh, Jack. What have you stepped into?"

"What?"

Dools smiled and wagged a scolding finger. "You don't remember, do you?"

"Enough with the questions. Just tell me."

They stood in the middle of the bullpen alone. The rest of the squad was out covering leads. Dools pushed his chair over in front of Paris's desk and took a seat. His large neck contorted his tie, twisting it off center. It had to be Tuesday because he was wearing the blue tie with the red stripes. Dools owned five ties, all blue. Tuesday's tie had the red stripes. And he always wore the obligatory white shirt. Dools subscribed to the headquarters' credo that an agent always wears a white button-down. If not white, the only other option would be Oxford blue. To him—and of course, J. Edgar—no self-respecting agent would be caught dead when called up to the director's office on the seventh floor in anything but a suit, tie, and a white shirt. Dools had a closet filled with white shirts. For Dools, his idea of casual Friday was loosening the knot on his tie.

His shirts sleeves were rolled up just below his elbows, exposing thick forearms that he folded across his chest. "Do you remember when we worked the Briggs murder?"

Paris said he did, took a seat too, with his eyes rolling skyward. This was going to take a while.

"As you recall, Noel Briggs was a wealthy enough guy."

"And?"

"And some people have said that maybe Briggs didn't make all his money on the up and up. Some might say he was making a good chunk of his wealth from his not so legal activities early in his development." Dools stopped mid-explanation to play with the paperweight on Paris's desk, tossing it between his hands like a baseball. "Guess who came up with this theory?"

Paris took the paperweight from Dools and returned it to his desk. "Let me guess. Calloway."

Dools formed his hand into the shape of a gun, pointed at Paris, and let the imaginary hammer fall. "You know, on *Jeopardy*, all your answers are supposed to be in the form of a question."

"Fine, 'Who is Calloway?'"

This time, Dools responded without a break in the dialogue. "I'll tell you who. She's the one trying to link every murder, kidnapping, and robbery to this phantom drug dealer for the past three years. Ever since she became a detective. Like she was trying to prove something. The lady doesn't give up."

Paris mulled over the accusation. "Maybe she's on to something."

"Maybe she's a nut job."

Dools, the compassionate one.

"Have you had a chance to look over her analysis?" Paris reached into a black ballistic bag and pulled out a roll of papers, the rubber band around the ream squeezing it into the shape of a jelly-roll. As part of their new-found relationship, Calloway had an amiable moment and decided to give up some of her investigative analysis. The papers landed with a thud on Paris's desk, rolling toward Dools.

He eyed the bundle suspiciously, before turning his attention back to Paris, and shrugged. "No, I haven't."

"Well, there you go." Jack edged the cylinder even closer. "Give it a look. You never know. Maybe there's a young, hard-working, female detective out there who knows something you don't."

Dools forced himself to consider Paris's last remark while he moved the papers back and forth with two fingers. "I'll give it a look, all right." Still attempting to distance himself, but clearly drawn in, he sighed. "And if I think she's right, then I'll be happy to run with her on this case."

"Yeah," Paris said sarcastically. "You, being a mentor and all."

Dools looked sideways at Paris. "Funny."

Paris leaned away, fighting back a grin. His eyes returned to the Calloway papers, now opened and splayed on his desk. Dools was pushing them around, peeling out a page or two then slapping a sticky tab near a phone number or an address that he found interesting. Squeaky wheels were spinning in Dools's head.

"Tell me what you know about her?" Paris asked.

Dools's gaze lifted above the coiled pages. "What? You're not interested are you?"

"Eh, I'm married, remember?"

Dools shook his head. "Separated."

"Whatever."

"What do you want me to say?" Dools raised both his hands in mock surrender before his voice drizzled down to a tone bordering on contempt. "Look, like I told you before, I've got friends over at the PD and they tell me she's a lone wolf." He pushed off with one foot, his chair gliding back a few feet. "Came onto the force six years ago, worked patrol in Del Paso Heights and then around Oak Park. She asked for the crap areas of town."

Paris waited for more.

"They said she was a good patrol officer. She worked hard and made it known she wanted to work dope."

"Moved up quick?"

"Yeah, the HIDTA task force was looking for a female UC to do dope buys, play the part of a girlfriend."

Paris knew it often started out that way.

"You know the type. Anyway, she did real well so the team asked the brass if she could come over permanently and they agreed."

Paris drummed his fingers on the desk. He recognized the signs of a young aggressive officer making a move to get what she wanted—a detective's position. It wasn't at all unusual and, in fact, Paris admired her zeal. The problem was she lacked experience. Paris's gut told him he could work around that.

He looked back at the reports. Much of the data was stale and in need of updating. Renewing an old investigation didn't bother him. It was the variables that concerned him. One being, Detective Valerie Calloway. Dools didn't hold back on what he thought of the detective. Most of that was just personalities, like two bull dogs staking out the same fire hydrant.

"So, she likes to keep to herself," Paris said. "Nothing wrong with that."

Dools raised an eyebrow. "Call it the way it is. She doesn't play well with others."

"Maybe she just hasn't found the right partner."

"Boy, Jack, you're really becoming the social worker lately. Wasn't it Freud that said maybe a tunnel is nothing more than a tunnel? Or maybe there's a train coming down it to run you over? The answer is simple: Detective Calloway just doesn't like people."

Paris gave it a thought. Dools could be right, then again, he hoped not. Paris twisted in his chair and pulled the Clarion kidnapping case files off his desk. He flipped through the serials, glancing over the PD reports that were authored by Calloway.

He really didn't know what he was looking for but thought just reading how she wrote may give him some insight on the detective.

"You think she actually identified this kidnapper/supplier?" he asked.

"Possible," Dools forced himself to confess. "She's worked out a couple of good leads." He went to his notebook, flipped through a few pages, and landed a finger in the middle of the book. "She's conducted a series of surveillances in San Francisco. Got a guy who is moving moderate weight."

"Is that her target?"

Dools shook his head. "Nah, don't think so. I went out with her on a couple of days when she was short-handed. She told me the guy we were watching may be her primary target's distributor."

"Like Finch."

"Yeah, like Finch."

"What's the status on the guy you were watching?"

Dools scratched his head then ran a hand through his hair, referred to the notebook again before saying, "Well, from what I understand, their target has gone quiet."

"In what way?"

"The surveillance team hasn't seen him for a couple of days. They're contemplating putting a pole cam on his residence. They're keeping a watch in case there's movement."

"This target of hers, he got a name?"

Dools stood up and pulled out a five by eight photo from his briefcase. He tossed it on Paris's desk. It was a black and white DMV photo. The picture was grainy because it looked like it had been Xeroxed at least a dozen times. Dools touched the face.

"Target's name is Kennedy, Peter James. Thirty one, no 'crim' history."

Peter Kennedy wore a dark suit, light shirt and tie. His hair was neatly cut, stylish with a wave that would fit in *GQ Magazine*. Paris stared at the picture. Didn't fit the look of a drug dealer. He looked more like an up and coming stockbroker.

"What was the car that Barbara saw out in front of their house?"

"She couldn't tell. Said it looked like a Chevy Camaro or Pontiac Firebird. They all look alike to her."

"So, does Kennedy, Peter James have a Camaro or Firebird registered in his name?"

Dools shook his head. "But that doesn't mean anything. He's a drug dealer. Probably has cars registered under several aliases. He's nothing more than a pretty boy, isn't he?" His tone was sharp, maybe with a bit of jealously. "Besides, like I said, I believe Calloway thinks this guy Kennedy isn't your kidnapper. This guy, Kennedy is one step down. You need to find his supplier."

"Okay, Dools," Paris said as he leaned forward across his desk, picking up the phone. "Let's give Detective Calloway a visit and see if she's willing to play nice in the sandbox. Maybe together, she'll identify who's supplying Mr. Kennedy and we'll know who may have Rachel Clarion.

CHAPTER 5

PETER KENNEDY STARED AT HIMSELF IN a full-length mirror, adjusting his silk tie. He gave it a few tugs and pinched the double Windsor until it was perfectly centered.

His apartment sat twelve floors up in his high rise, a growing affluent area of San Francisco known as Rincon Hill. Something he would describe to his friends as *posh*. He was the kind of guy who liked to use the word posh.

His bedroom window offered a panoramic view of the Bay, framing the Golden Gate Bridge with the Pacific Ocean as the backdrop. His was a place few were able to afford. Despite his young age, Peter Kennedy enjoyed the financial resources to live in one of the most expensive areas in the country.

Kennedy was strikingly handsome. Suits—which he wore every day, even when he didn't have a reason to—were his trademark look. He was one of those guys who could roll out of bed, throw on whatever was lying on the floor, and look like he was ready for a photo shoot. Six years ago, Kennedy was in his Stanford University dorm, studying Economics. Already in his junior year, he started to have doubts about his declared major. Economics was one of those degrees that landed you a job in the business and finance industries. Or worse, a government position. He didn't really want to use his analytical and mathematical skills, unless it meant being his own boss. He wanted to make money—his own money. And so, he made a number of inquiries through his closest of college friends and came to know an entrepreneur who ran a retail sales business. That would be one that sold weed. High quality weed. Kennedy spent the last three years of his college days developing a lucrative distribution network that rivaled most compensation packages offered to partners in major law firms. Graduation was a bonus. By that time, it was the drug business that made him financially successful. From weed, he advanced to coke. Lots of coke. The move to a higher level of drugs was his graduation present to himself.

A gym bag stood next to his feet, the dark canvas bag, square and heavy. Kennedy cast a glance of indifference before turning back to the mirror. He took in a somber breath and let it seep out slowly as if everything he did was just a chore. With a gentle tug, he grabbed the straps of the gym bag and slung it over his shoulder before heading out the door.

KENNEDY PULLED HIS '68 BRITISH RACING Green Jaguar XKE off onto a side street in Chinatown and squeezed it between a large box van and a Ford Focus. He glanced down at his watch, a Patek Phillippe Calatrava Platinum. It was an exquisite watch, one that exuded the image of wealth and prominence. To Kennedy, status outweighed any form of practicality. If money could seep from his pampered pores, it would glisten with the luster of a Patek Platinum.

He was just a few minutes early for his meeting. When he opened his car door, the smell of rotten garbage from the nearby Chinese grocery store wafted in, spoiling the soothing smell of fine British leather. The sun was bright but there was a crisp breeze blowing down the street sending a slight chill down Kennedy's back. He pulled his Armani suit jacket tight across his body as he waited for his associate to arrive.

Cars flew past and people rushed by, none of which were the people Kennedy was supposed to meet. As the minutes progressed, he watched with increased intensity, examining each passing vehicle, trying to memorize the make, model and the faces inside. He was good at that. It's what kept him out of trouble. A seemingly innocuous car circling the block one too many times would draw his concern. That would be the police.

A fast moving Cadillac pulled up the street and decelerated in a hurry, causing the front of the vehicle to pitch toward the pavement. The car rocked for a moment before coming to rest. The backup lights came on and the Cadillac slowly maneuvered into a tight parking space. Kennedy watched the car parallel park, wondering how the hell the driver was going to put a vehicle the size of a small country into a space that barely qualified for a compact. A moment later, all four doors swung open and large men in dark suits bailed out. The front passenger exited the car and stretched. His head swiveled from side to side before catching sight of Kennedy looking in his direction. It was the leader, Ramone Santiago. He smiled, focusing all his attention on Kennedy. That made Kennedy uncomfortable. He watched Santiago say something to the driver, then to the back passengers, causing them all to look in Kennedy's direction. They were monoliths in dark wool jackets. Their eyes were hidden behind dark shades. It wasn't difficult to know what they did for a living.

Kennedy raised a fidgety hand, waved, and then let it drop to his side. Santiago nodded and the four made their way over. Kennedy nervously bounced on the balls of his feet, like a child waiting for the ice cream man. It only took the men a matter of seconds to span the distance, standing abreast just inches in front of Kennedy. He instantly stuck out a hand and the leader of the group took it.

"Hey," Kennedy said, trying to gather his courage. "I was wondering if you were coming, Mr. Santiago."

Santiago pulled off his sunglasses, exposing dark pupils. They were pinpoint. Without saying a word, his eyes sharpened on Kennedy's forehead, as if he was thinking what a bullet would look like lodged in that particular spot.

"I mean, I knew you were coming—" Kennedy said, clearing his throat and adding, "I must have come a bit early."

Santiago remained unforthcoming. Voiceless, he pointed at the gym bag that sat next to Kennedy's leg before scrutinizing him again with a raised eyebrow.

"Yeah," Kennedy said. "That's for you."

One of the men reached down and took possession of the bag.

Kennedy hadn't been dealing with Ramone Santiago for very long. He was referred to him by an associate. This was the obvious next step up in his distribution operation and Santiago was going to get him there. Already with three significant-sized deliveries under his belt with Mr. Santiago, Kennedy had scored a ton of money. That was a good thing. Then he learned that Mr. Santiago was known in the underground world as one who never let an opportunity pass him by, unless that opportunity left in a body bag, especially if they disrespected him. That was a bad thing. But for Kennedy to make it big, he had to deal with those who made him a bit uncomfortable. That was the risk of getting a chance to play in the big leagues.

"There's fifteen in the bag," Kennedy said, pausing for a second as a sharp cold breeze hit him in the face. Then he added, "That'll be three hundred G's."

Santiago smiled then jerked his chin in the direction of the car, telling the man with the thirty-three pounds of cocaine to take the gym bag to the car. The man turned and jogged across the street. The only thing Kennedy could do was watch.

He raised a finger then used it to scratch the side of his head. "Ah, why don't you just give me my money and I'll be on my way, Mr. Santiago?"

Ramone Santiago shook his head, grinding his teeth loud enough for Kennedy to hear the tension in his jaw.

"No. I don't think so this time, Pete."

Kennedy's whole body stiffened and he stared at the man, bewildered. "I don't understand, Mr. Santiago. Haven't I always given you what you needed and on time?" He was about to try and sound tough, threatening, but then thought the better of it.

Santiago pretended to pout and nodded, as if he was agreeing with Kennedy. "Always."

"Then why? What have I done to piss you off?"

Santiago walked closer to Kennedy, close enough to feel the warmth of his breath on his face. He gently tugged at Kennedy's suit lapels, smoothing them out from the breezy weather then patted him on the chest. "Today, Pete, we are changing our relationship."

"How's that?"

Santiago smiled as his two associates flanked Kennedy on both sides before they took a strong hold on his arms.

"I think today we're taking control of your business."

Kennedy felt the blood drain from his face.

"I assume you have more?" Santiago intimated in the direction of Kennedy's car, presumably indicating more than the fifteen kilos he had provided.

Kennedy grappled to find the words. "Yeah, sure."

"At your home?"

He nodded.

"Good. Then let's go get them."

One of Santiago's henchmen led Kennedy back to the Jaguar but, this time, Kennedy was shoved into the passenger's seat. Not being able to think of a reasonable solution out of this predicament, his head started to swim. His empire was about to take a major step-back but that was the least of his worries. Kennedy didn't know whether or not by tomorrow, he was going to be lying on his Posturepedic California King-size bed or in a dirt hole. He watched Ramone Santiago slowly walk back to his Cadillac where he swung it around, trailing close behind the Jaguar, back to Kennedy's twelfth story high-rise flat with the unforgettable view of the Pacific Ocean.

CHAPTER 6

V ALERIE CALLOWAY STOOD OVER THE DESK across from Jack Paris's because it was empty and no one seemed to mind her being there. She played with a corner of the desk calendar, for no particular reason other than to show her uneasiness.

Paris saw it in her posture too. He looked down the bullpen alleyway and saw Dools pulling reports from stacks of folders piled on his desk, every so often, stealing a glance at Calloway then over at Paris.

Eyes closed, shaking his head, Dools was reaffirming his opinion about the detective. Hiding his feelings was not one of his strong points. After a few grunts, he took a moment, grabbed up his papers, and headed over.

Calloway saw Dools dragging a chair in their direction. She waited for him to arrive before sitting down.

"So what's the plan?" Dools asked both.

Paris checked with Calloway, waiting to see if she was going to respond. She caught Paris's gaze and shrugged.

"The way I see it," Paris said, "we push on two fronts. The first is to set up a surveillance on the Clarion residence. Maybe we'll get lucky and see someone come by, leave a note," he offered, referring to a ransom note. "And we set up a telephone trap and trace as well as CCTV."

Calloway and Dools both nodded.

"The other is to try and get a buy into this group, Kennedy's group. Make a series of those, along with phone tracking, we might be able to identify the supplier."

"And find Rachel," Dools interjected.

Calloway concurred.

"Either one of you got someone that can buy dope from these guys?" Paris asked.

Calloway jumped in. "I spoke with my contact at the DEA. They got one in custody willing to cooperate. Another is on the fence."

"Which has the best opportunity to help us nab the supplier?"

Calloway placed a hand on the edge of the desk and slowly rocked back in her chair. Impatient. Ill at ease. High-strung. All the adjectives fit. "Unfortunately, the one on the fence."

"Figures," Dools muttered.

She opened her notebook and flipped through a couple of sheets of paper, stopping on one with a color photo clipped to it. She pulled it out and read.

"Guy's name is Enrique Soto. He's a moderately small-time dealer but was reliable in getting whatever he needed. DEA did him on the last go-around for about three ounces of powder. They took him into State court."

"I think we need to have a conversation with Mr. Soto," Paris said.

"I tried to set up a meeting with the DDA," Calloway said.

"And?"

"The state isn't interested in working off Soto's drug charges. Thinks it would send the wrong message to the community."

"What message is that? Saving face is worth more than saving lives?"

She shrugged.

"I say we give it another try," Dools said, pushing his way into the conversation.

"Agreed." Paris looked over at Calloway. "Can you call over to the DA's office and find out who's got the ticket on this case? Then let's go pay him a visit. Maybe we can get the ADA to reconsider."

"Sure," Calloway said, a wry smile on her face as she looked over at Dools.

Paris could see that Detective Calloway enjoyed stirring the pot.

"That's how we roll here on the VC squad," Dools said, his Boston accent transitioning to LA gangster.

Calloway tried to suppress a quiet laugh. That was the first time Paris had seen a lighter side of her. He liked how it felt.

Paris picked up the telephone and called Assistant United States Attorney Casey Andrews. He has brought her most of his cases because she was one of the better prosecutors. Never gave up without a fight and an appeal. The phone rang only once before Andrews answered.

"Good afternoon, Counselor."

"What do I have to do now?" Andrews responded, not bothering with a hello.

Her tone made Paris grin. "It's complicated but the short of it: I will be sending you a court order for a pen register and trap and trace."

"Simple enough," she said.

They talked about the order and the case, the dual objective of identifying a drug dealer and finding a missing girl.

"You think they're one in the same?"

"I got a detective here that thinks so," Paris replied.

"What about this guy, Enrique Soto?" Andrews asked. "You think you can get the DA's office to work with you in cutting him some slack if he cooperates?"

This time, Paris hesitated merely long enough to foresee the outcome. "I'll do what I can to make him understand that a young girl's life may depend on it."

He hung up the phone and caught Calloway and Dools both giving him a pessimistic stare.

"Okay, Valerie, how about putting in that call to the DA? I think we should get going on this as soon as possible."

She spun her chair and walked over to an empty desk, leaning a hip against the edge. It caught Paris's attention, which caught Dools's attention. Which caught her attention.

Calloway picked up the phone and dialed a number, waiting for the call to connect. Paris turned to Dools who was hunched over, pretending to study his shoes.

A moment later, Calloway was speaking with someone on the line.

"Get some buy money from the draft office," Paris instructed Dools.

"How much?"

"For two buys, let's go with twelve grand."

"No problem." Dools shot up and left.

Things were starting to move. Paris wondered if the plan would come off. More so, if it could be done in time to make a difference.

CHAPTER 7

A T A SMALL TABLE AT THE STARBUCK'S just off the freeway in downtown Sacramento, Robert Clarion listened as Roy Torrington spoke. Torrington kept still, head hung over a Grande decaf, the steam encircling his face like a ghostly shroud. The coffee shop was mostly empty. Just a few employees scraping at canisters behind the counter, but Clarion could see, everyone could feel tension in the air.

"I don't know if I can help you, Robert."

Clarion sucked in a short breath, lips puckered. He didn't look up. "I understand."

Torrington pulled his hands away from his coffee, palms up. "Look, Robert, it's just too dangerous." He hesitated, as if he was gathering his thoughts to justify his last remark. "Even if I try to make contact with Finch's old supplier, he's going to want to know who it's for. If I mention your name, he'll most likely chop off both my legs just to make a point."

Clarion's head bobbed in feigned understanding. But he wasn't paying much attention to Torrington's excuses. He was thinking about what he was going to say next, what he needed to say to get Torrington to make contact, to set up the deal, to say yes. No wasn't an option. Clarion needed a deal that would lead him to the supplier, then up the next rung, so he could put the threat to his family to rest.

"Robert, you know who you're asking me to buy from, right?"

Clarion squared his shoulders. "Pete."

"Yeah, that's right. Pete." Torrington lowered his voice and leaned in. "The people that Pete deals with aren't the kind that forgive and forget, if you know what I mean."

"You don't have to tell him it's me, Roy. You just have to say it's for a reliable friend of yours. I'll pay top dollar. Even give you a bonus. An extra grand if you can make it happen by tomorrow."

Torrington sat back, his left eyebrow arching, as he tried to make sense of Clarion's anxiousness in doing something he swore years ago, he would never do again. "What's going on, Robert? Why are you getting back in the business? Wasn't that last fiasco enough?"

Clarion leaned forward, pushing Torrington's coffee cup to the side of the table so that there was nothing between them. "You ask too many questions, Roy. My reasons for getting back in aren't any of your business. You're supposed to do what I ask you to do."

Torrington slid low in his seat, turning to the window toward a fountain in the courtyard, the water spilling sideways from a heavy gust. The gap between the glass doors whistled from a burst of cool air while Dean Martin crooned "Volare" somewhere in the background.

Clarion's right elbow was perpendicular with the table as he jabbed a sharp finger in Roy's direction. "You owe me."

Torrington's demeanor changed at the unveiling of what he knew to be true. Chewing on his lower lip, he kept silent, forcing himself to keep his attention out the window.

"I could have turned you in to the cops when Rachel was kidnapped. Told them all about just how close you were with Finch. It would have been you they would have focused on."

Torrington raised his hands above his heads, shook them to concede. "I get it, all right?"

But Clarion kept pushing. "I held back, even though I knew you could have helped get my daughter back. I didn't do it because I knew you weren't involved in what Finch did. But I knew you could have helped. I was protecting you." He paused for one last explosion. "My daughter, Roy!"

Clarion pulled back a bit, spying a couple of new customers in the Starbuck's giving them uncomfortable dirty looks. Clarion, determined to bring him around, leaned closer to Roy. "Look, I'm asking you for a little help, that's all. Just set up the deal and I'll make it worth your while." He reached in his pants pocket, pulled out a wad of cash, and, without concern, peeled away at the bundle. "Here, a thousand to start. Take it and call me later. Let me know when you get a hold of your guy. I want this done by tomorrow, Roy. Tomorrow."

Torrington stalled, waging a battle in his head, then accepted. He slapped his hand over the cash and dragged it to his side of the table.

Clarion stood, walked over to Roy, and rested a hand on his shoulder. "It'll be all right."

Torrington didn't budge, didn't even look up. Clarion turned and made his way out the door, leaving Torrington sitting next to a cold cup of coffee and a wad of cash securely grasped in his fingers.

CHAPTER 8

PARIS LOCKED EYES WITH ENRIQUE SOTO, neither saying a word, the only sound coming from the buzz from the overhead florescent lights. The pre-arranged meeting was taking place in a small conference room at the Sacramento County lock-up. Soto was wearing the customary orange jumpsuit, off-white socks, and clear plastic jelly shoes. He squirmed in a wood chair. His hands were cuffed in the front, the metal restraints scraping the table every time he made a gesture. Calloway sat next to Paris, Dools on his other side. Casey Andrews from the United States Attorney's Office was also there, standing along the back wall, talking to Soto's attorney. Their voices were low but the banter sounded like a running gun battle. Andrews had spoken to the ADA assigned to the state case, who said he didn't have time to make the meeting personally. But he had granted Andrews the authority to work out a deal. Soto studied the faces in the crowd. Why had so many had come for such a small amount of drugs?

Eventually, Soto's attorney sighed loudly, shook Andrews's hand, and made his way to a seat next to his client. He shoved a handful of papers in front of Soto and tapped at a line at the bottom of the top page.

"Okay, Enrique, just sign here."

Soto dragged his hands across the table, took the pen, and scrawled a shaky line as his signature. He didn't even bother reading it, trusting his attorney had done the right thing.

Paris had opened his notebook, ready to get some background information about Soto, when Calloway leaned forward, stabbing a pen toward Soto's face. "I want to know how sure you are you're going to be able to set up this buy."

Soto remained unfazed. "Yeah, I can."

"What about the fact that you've been arrested? How are you going to explain your release?"

Soto smiled. "No one knows I've been arrested."

His attorney jumped in. "You guys picked him up while he was in Yuma, Arizona. He's been sitting in a local lock-up out there for the past week waiting to be extradited. He just got here and hasn't seen gen pop."

Soto's smile disappeared, being replaced with a frown. "They tossed me in AdSeg."

Gen pop was general population, and AdSeg stood for administrative segregation. Which meant Soto was telling the truth. He'd been isolated, making it unlikely anyone knew he was here.

"What about your contacts outside?" Paris asked.

Soto shook his head, his nervousness now visible. "No, no one knows."

Soto's attorney interjected. "He's a long-haul truck driver. Gone for weeks at a time. As far as anyone is concerned, he's still on the road."

"You owe your supplier any money?" The last thing Paris needed was another bad debt and a dead distributor.

"No. The three ounces I was picked up was paid for. I didn't get jammed up until long after that deal."

Calloway's mouth opened, ready to launch into more questions but Paris placed a hand on her arm. "Let's back up a moment."

The room went silent.

"Enrique, before we get going, I need to know: who is your supplier?"

One more time Soto's head spun around searching the faces assembled in the room, his expression indicating surprise, like he thought everyone knew. "Pretty-boy Pete—Peter Kennedy."

According to Calloway, Kennedy hadn't been seen coming or going from his apartment for several days. But other cases needed attention, too, and surveillance had been sparse. Kennedy's Jaguar was still in its designated parking space. Besides a few phone calls, his cell had been quiet. Paris wasn't giving out more information than he was taking in, and that included telling Soto whether they knew who Peter Kennedy was.

"Are you sure he's still selling dope?"

"Yeah," Soto said. "If he ain't been picking up, he's still slinging." He opened his mouth to say more, but suddenly reconsidered.

"What?"

"Pete moves weight, more than what I normally buy." He winced slightly at the idea of it. "We go way back, but me buying anything more than a few ounces at a time might look suspicious."

"But you can do it, right."

Soto rolled his shoulders. "I'll try."

Calloway made a fist and gave the table a solid thump. "No trying, Enrique. This is all COD. If you don't deliver, you don't pass Go. You go straight to jail."

"I said I can do it," he said, his attitude taking a quick turn, trying to sound convincing. "Fuckin' piece of cake. Just get me out of here."

Calloway continued to pelt questions at Soto, most of which Paris was going to ask anyway so he didn't interrupt. A couple of times, the questioning got heated, Calloway raising her voice and Soto cowering like a turtle trying to find shelter inside a hard shell. The attorneys would intervene, counter, object, and then in the end Calloway would get her answers. Another hour and the interview was over. Dools was on his way to the district attorney's office to begin the process of getting Enrique Soto released and into their custody.

Calloway and Paris gathered their things and walked out to the parking lot. The sun was high in the sky, hot, but there was a breeze cutting between the buildings, refreshing after being inside so long. Paris slid on his Ray-Bans, Calloway just shaded her eyes with a hand. The two meandered slowly as they talked.

"I figure we get him out and get him a phone," Paris said. "Start putting in calls to Kennedy. We set up the first buy, follow him back, hopefully to whoever he has to pay, and then do it again."

Calloway nodded. "I can get another team to take away the person Kennedy meets with. Hopefully, it will lead back to the supplier and, if we're lucky, to our target." Paris ran through the plan in his head but remained silent. Calloway looked at her watch and Paris knew what she was thinking. "I'm going back out to Kennedy's residence," she said. "If I leave now, I can be out there in two hours."

"You want some help?"

She quickly shook her head, as if she didn't need time to consider the offer. "I'll call you if it looks like there's activity."

One-man surveillances were high risk. Getting spotted was the last thing any investigation needed, and without a change-out every so often, the person outside became a long-term fixture that people start to wonder about.

"I'll be fine, really." She held up a hand as if she was taking an oath. "I'll call if I get anything."

Although he didn't feel comfortable about her being out there alone, Paris gave in, not voicing any objections. They were still away from their cars when the conversation lapsed into silence. He took the opportunity to speak candidly, hoping to get an understanding of their working relationship.

"I appreciate your enthusiasm." The words sounded odd and somewhat disingenuous when he said them.

She kept her look straight ahead but he noticed her jaw muscles tighten as they continued to walk. "What are you trying to say?"

"I'm trying to stop someone from hurting a young girl, and you're trying to capture a major dope dealer, I get it. We both have an agenda but I want to make sure we're together on this."

Calloway's posture abruptly changed and her pace quickened with more determination. "Don't worry, Agent Paris. You tell me what you learn and I'll do the same."

This wasn't the direction he was hoping for.

"Valerie, I don't want to just update you. I want us to work together." Paris waggled a finger back and forth between the two of them, then flared both hands as if to say, *Well?*

"Yeah," Calloway replied. "That's what I meant."

The high voltage tension wasn't getting them anywhere. Paris decided it was time to shift the conversation elsewhere.

"I'm going back to the office and get the money for the buy. Should be ready to go first thing in the morning. By then, Enrique will be waiting to be picked up. Dools and I are planning to work out our Ops plan for the buy."

Calloway nodded, but didn't seem to have any interest in joining in on the planning.

Couldn't say he didn't try.

By the time they reached their cars, Paris could tell Calloway wanted nothing more than to get into hers and leave.

"Call you if I see anything," she reiterated, her tone flat, automatic.

Paris couldn't help but feel pissed, wondering how the conversation had disintegrated so fast. Keys in his hand, he watched Calloway get into her car and pull out of the lot before he even opened his car door. She never looked back, and she never said goodbye.

CHAPTER 9

Traffic to San Francisco was moderate for most of the way with the exception of where Highways 80 and 580 converged, forcing you to choose between the San Francisco's Bay Bridge and the city of Oakland. Hordes of vehicles from the 580 freeway, coming from Contra Costa County, poured onto the intersection without any concern of oncoming traffic from the 80 freeway, causing brake lights to flash in bright red bursts and the front hoods of overweight SUVs to dive toward the concrete highway. Several times, Calloway lay hard on her horn, the most egregious drivers getting the finger when she passed.

Exiting off the Bay Bridge, she had made her way to Kennedy's building and found an open parking space just down the street, shaded under a tree. A cool ocean breeze from east to west kept the fog over the bay for the time being. Calloway angled herself low in the seat and rested an elbow just outside the open car door window. She was far enough away not to draw attention but close enough to make out the faces of those leaving the building. As far as surveillances go, this was as good a spot as it got.

She keenly scrutinized the front of the building. Just to the right was a large rollup door that led to the underground parking. Driving in, she hadn't seen a back exit. To the best of her assessment, the door and garage offered the only ways in and out of the apartment. She watched cars and people come and go for over an hour but there was no sign of Peter Kennedy.

Another thirty minutes passed, and Calloway's back started to feel like a knot. She stepped out of her car and decided to take a walk around the building, maybe sneak a look inside the underground parking garage to make sure Kennedy's car hadn't slipped past her. She locked her doors and slowly headed toward the building. There was no one to notify she'd stepped away, no one to relieve her on point. She was by herself. Even though one-person surveillances were damn near impossible, Calloway preferred solitude to the congestion and noise from a large team. Colleagues as well as friends had tried warning her of the dangers of going it alone. To her, though, teamwork came with too much baggage. Being unaided, no matter what happened, made her responsible to only one person: herself. That was the way she liked it. Truth was, she just liked flying solo.

As she approached the garage door, her cell phone vibrated in her jacket pocket. Calloway pulled it out, studied the screen, and recognized the number. Her chest tightened and she turned away from the building toward a quiet spot where she could take the call. She pressed the answer button and braced herself before speaking.

"Hi." There was silence from the other end. "How's she doing?"

Calloway could hear Nurse Selma Rodriguez clear her throat, sounding like she was ready to give a prepared speech. In a way, she was.

"Not well. She had some good days in between the bad days, but now there are more bad days, and they are worse than ever . . ." Selma let the last sentence hang, waiting for Calloway to respond. But she had nothing to say. "It won't be too long before she won't be able to recognize anyone, let alone speak coherently," Selma continued. "Once that comes about, you will have lost her forever." The nurse paused, then spoke slowly, focused. "You won't be able to tell her goodbye."

Calloway's arm felt like as if filled with lead, and the simple act of holding the phone to her head had become a struggle. She dragged her free hand to the bridge of her nose, pinching hard and squeezing her eyes tight to fight back the tears, trying to keep steady, composed. "Is she in pain?"

Selma grunted, a frustrated sigh. "Good Lord, Ms. Valerie—"

"Okay, okay, I'm going to come. I promise."

"Don't promise me, she isn't *my* mother."

"I know." Calloway's words were laced with guilt. Over time, she had become the un-attentive daughter, finding excuses not to visit. Mostly involving her work. In essence, Nurse Selma Rodriguez was a better daughter.

"She asked about you today," the nurse said.

Calloway felt like she was suffocating. When she tried to speak, her words were barely audible. "What did she say?"

"She wanted to know where you were. Asked if her little girl was home from school."

The nurse's chiding was sharp and uncomfortable. Despite Calloway's best efforts to stop them, the tears started to fall. She found a bus bench and sat down next to an elderly woman clutching a small cart filled with groceries. The woman looked over at Calloway, and her eyes dropped, as if she could feel her pain. Calloway turned away and combed a hand through her hair, pushing it back and out of her face. Quickly, she wiped away the tears and tried to compose herself. "Yeah—yeah, okay. Would you tell her I came home? Tell her I'm outside playing and that I'll come in in a minute."

"Okay. I'll tell her, Ms. Valerie." Another moment of silence followed. Calloway had nothing to say, Selma nothing to add. "She's not in pain," she finally said.

Calloway smiled. "Thank you, Selma."

"Just come as soon as you can. You need to see her."

"I know."

The called ended and Calloway sat quietly for a few minutes to gather herself. Endless buildings lined the street, city hills swallowing them up, dropping them out of sight. It was like the entire city was teetering, sloping toward the expansive, hungry Pacific. A bus pulled up and the doors opened. The elderly woman sitting quietly next to her hesitated for a second, gave the sad girl next to her one last pitiful look before getting on the bus.

As the bellow from the bus engine faded into a rumble of conflicting background noise, Calloway's cell phone vibrated again. Her shoulders dropped and her head tilted toward the open blue sky. She let it ring, considering on letting it go to voicemail. There was only so much she could deal with. She reconsidered and forced herself to glance at the screen. She shoved the phone to her ear and concentrated on trying to sound calm.

"Hello, Jack. What's up?"

"Been watching Kennedy's pen register. There's been a slew of telephone activity recently."

Calloway wiped away her last tear and eyeballed the building. "I got nothing here. Give me a minute. I'm going to try and see if his vehicle is still in the basement."

"Okay." Then he added, "The tech guys are telling me the calls are coming from your area. He's got to be there in his apartment or really close by."

She thanked Paris for the information, ended the call, and walked toward the building. A car pulled from around the corner, slowing in front of the garage doors. Calloway froze. She recognized the car, a black Cadillac sedan, tinted windows, gold emblem. She waited for it to come to a stop, watched as the driver rolled down the window, and pushed a button on the call box. It gave Calloway a chance to get a clear look at the driver. He was a large man with a square chin, sharp cheekbones, and shaved head. Tanned, almost bronze. The face of a pit bull. It was Alexei Mogilevich, a henchman-for-hire.

"Shit," she muttered, ducking under a row of trees so that Alexei didn't get a chance to spot her. Not only did she know Alexei, Alexei knew her.

Calloway held still while Mogilevich crept the Cadillac forward. The roll-up door raised and the vehicle disappeared into the darkness of the garage. The door remained open for a split second and then started down, gears engaging in a heavy rumble. Calloway gave it a few beats, then sprinted, full tilt toward the opening, slipping under just before the gate came to rest. The air smelled of car exhaust and she could feel the reverberation of an idling engine. Outside noise from passing cars and buses drowned out in the background, muffled from the concrete and steel foundation. She took a minute to gather her bearings. To her right, she detected the glow of brake lights. Slowly she filtered between parked cars, spotting the Cadillac pulling into a space twenty yards ahead. Alexei Mogilevich stepped out of the Cadillac and walked toward a set of glass doors that led to a bank of elevators. As soon as Mogilevich entered the elevator, Calloway ran to the double glass doors and checked the numbers on the panel as the lift ascended. The one that Mogilevich took crawled upward before stopping at ten, two flights below Kennedy's.

What the hell?

Calloway pushed the button for an elevator and apprehensively waited for one to open. She reached for her cell phone and scrolled to Jack Paris's number. She paused for a moment, closed the phone and shoved it back in her pocket.

"Not yet," she said in a whisper.

The elevator bell dinged and a door opened. Calloway stepped in and punched at the buttons. As the elevator door closed, Calloway reached to her waist, touched her pistol and extra magazines. She shook her hands, trying to get rid of the tension. The mechanics of the lift groaned, jerking upward. Fifteen seconds later, the elevator came to a stop on floor number nine.

CHAPTER 10

THE FOLLOWING DAY, PARIS CLEARED A ROOM at the Sacramento Field Office to begin the calls to Pete Kennedy. Dools brought Soto over early so Paris could work out any last-minute issues. Like any dope investigation, nothing ever went exactly as planned. Today was no exception.

One of Paris's hands was resting flat on the table, the other drumming anxiously. He was feeling agitated. For the past thirty minutes, Soto had come up with a handful of excuses about why he shouldn't ask Kennedy for the drugs directly. Paris was also having no luck reaching Calloway, adding to his aggravation.

Soto's head bounced like one of those bobble-head sports figures, eyes bulging out at Paris, acting as if they were in agreement.

"Right? Am I right? If I start asking for dope right away, Pete's going to know this is a set up."

"Wasn't it you that used the phrase, *piece of cake*?"

Soto alternated between wringing his hands and cracking his knuckles. "Yeah, more or less."

"You said you could do this." Dools was standing over Soto's back, a hand resting—more like squeezing—Soto's shoulder.

Soto flinched then sank in the chair. "Yeah, I can but not like this. Give it a couple of days. I'll call him, talk shit, find out what's going on—"

"Enough," Dools barked. "I've heard enough out of you, you little shit." He slid a hand under Soto's armpit, hoisting him high out of the chair until his legs wobbled under him. "You're done. I'm tossing you into general pop, and this time I'm going to make sure you get a roommate. A real nice one."

"Wait!" Soto raised both hands in the air. "All right, I'll call, I'll call. Just give me a minute to think of how I'm going to ask him."

Dools looked at his watch then at Soto. "Time's up."

"Okay." Soto paused, pulling on his shirt to smooth out the wrinkles, trying to regain his composure. "Okay, I know what I'm going to say."

Dools smiled. "Like you said, Kiki, piece of cake."

Over the next hour, Soto placed four phone calls to Kennedy, all of them going directly to voicemail. Each time, Soto left him a message, asking Kennedy to call back, saying it was important.

By the time he got to his last message, Soto sounded irritated, insulting Kennedy about how disrespectful it was not to return his call, how Soto had been such a reliable friend, why couldn't he be the same? During the break between calls, Paris continued trying to get a hold of Calloway without any luck.

"Maybe she's on sick leave?" Dools said sarcastically, knowing Calloway never got sick and never went on leave.

"Who do we have out at Kennedy's place?" Paris asked.

Dools held up his right hand, bending back a finger every time he rattled off a name. "Hoskin, Cohen, Marquez, and some new kid, just transferred in. I just spoke to Hoskin. Said they will be there any minute now."

Dools kept his hand in the air, four fingers curled down, one pointing up. The middle one. Dools pushed it closer into Paris's view.

"This one—it's for Val—"

"For Christ sakes, Dools."

"She doesn't play nice in the sandbox, Jack." Dools kept the middle finger extended like it added to his pronouncement, shoving it even closer toward Paris's face.

Paris reached up and placed a hand over Dools's, forcing it down. "I get it."

Paris wasn't in the mood to get into an argument about Calloway and her lack of cooperation, her inability to share, and, most of all, how much Dools just flat out didn't like her. Instead, Paris shifted the conversation back to the case. "How long before the guys are on point?"

Dools grumbled, cleared his throat. "Soon. Hoskin says he'll have eyes on the front door of the building probably in fifteen. The others are close to arriving and will scout the area, watching for cars and foot traffic."

"Good. Go check with Harrington and see if there's any activity on Kennedy's cell phone."

Dools cast a sideways glance at Paris, letting him know he'd changed the subject. He was trying to decide if he wanted to let it go.

"Everything will be fine, Dools."

"Yeah, okay," Dools replied. He turned and headed out the door.

It was not uncommon for everything to be in place, buy ready to go down, only to be knocked off track by something as simple as not being able to get a return call from the bad guy. In the world of drug investigations, that's reality.

Paris tapped a finger on top of the digital recorder. "You ready to try again?"

Soto sat up.

Paris noticed an unlit cigarette dangling from Soto's lips. "No smoking in a government building."

Soto shook his head. "Not smoking." He pulled it from his lips and held it out for Paris to see. "It's not lit. Just a nervous habit." He put the cigarette back in his mouth and picked up his cell phone, getting ready to punch in Kennedy's number. "Here we go again, you fuckin' *puto*."

Before Soto finished keying in the number, his phone started to ring, playing the theme song to *Miami Vice*. Suddenly, he looked annoyed.

"Who the hell is this calling me?" Before he could answer the call, Paris handed an ear bud to Soto. The other bud was already in Paris's ear so he could listen in on the conversation.

"Stick it in your ear. No calls unless it's recorded."

Soto rolled his eyes but took the piece and shoved it in place. He pressed the answer button.

"Who's this?" There was a long pause and Soto wasn't sure if his caller was still there. "Hello," he barked into the phone. "You there?"

"I'm returning your call."

Soto had a puzzled look on his face. "I called you?"

"No," the caller replied. "You called Pete."

Soto sat up, leaned over the table, and tapped his pencil on a pad of paper. He drew a question mark then pointed at it. "Who are you?"

"Friend of Pete's. You said you needed something."

Soto hesitated for an instant before answering. "Yeah, well, where's Pete?"

"He's tied up. He asked me to call you. So what is it you want?"

"How can I trust you?"

The caller didn't have to think about his response. "I guess you can't. See ya."

"Wait." Soto strained to hear if the caller disconnected. "You still there?"

There was a frustrated breath, then, "Last chance. What is it you want?"

"I need a few," Soto said.

"How much?"

"A few. I can take up to half a pound."

The man gave a smug chuckle and Soto could picture him shaking his head. "That's it? I don't have time for this."

"Wait a second. I've been dealing with Pete for years. He's never complained about giving me what I need."

There was a moment of silence, like he had to mull over Soto's contention. Then the man said, "Okay, let me talk it over with Mr. Kennedy."

Mr. Kennedy? What are you, some kind of an assistant?

The man didn't give Soto a chance to respond. The call was over.

Paris pulled out his earpiece and let it fall to the table. "Well, that went well," he said, his observation weighted with sarcasm.

Soto glared at Paris. "What do we do now?"

"We wait."

CHAPTER 11

ROBERT CLARION LEANED HIS ARM against the driver's side window, his cell phone pressed tight against his ear as he sped through traffic. Cars honked, people pulled over, and old men in big cars yelled something in Chinese. It didn't sound friendly but Clarion didn't care.

"Come on, pick up," he pleaded to himself.

Clarion was ready to hang up when he heard a click, then a voice. "What's up, Robert?"

"You know why I'm calling, Roy. You get what I need?"

Roy Torrington sounded anxious, as if he wanted to please Clarion. "Yeah. I told you I would."

"How much?"

"How much weight or what did it cost?"

"I'm not in the mood for games. How much?"

"Half a pound."

Clarion calculated the amount in his head. "So about six grand?"

"Six and a half," Roy said.

"I assume the *half* is your fee?"

Roy paused a second. "Yeah, well, business is business."

"Fine." It wasn't an issue for Clarion. He wasn't doing this for financial profit. "You pick it up already?"

"No, was waiting for you."

"Good," Clarion shouted. "Don't get it yet."

Roy's voice raised an octave as he stuttered in frustration. "Yesterday you were chomping my head off to get everything together right away. Now you want me to wait?"

"I still want it, just hold off until we meet."

"I'm confused."

"You want the money, don't you?"

Dead air. Then, "Yes."

"Wait until we get together."

They made plans to meet in Chinatown. Clarion hung up and pushed the gas pedal harder. A throaty growl emanated from the exhaust pipes of his BMW 540 as it launched over a low dip in the road. More car horns and screaming, fading expletives lost in the cacophony of the city.

Clarion concentrated on getting to the location early. Like a high-speed train on rails, he maneuvered tight turns and narrow side streets, in and out of traffic, eyes drifting down toward a paper bag wedged between his leather seat and the center console. Bundles of hundred dollars bills flowered out the top. Clarion reached down and nudged the bag aside, uncovering what he was looking for: his Walther PPK. He grabbed it by the grip and cradled it, as if to make sure it still fit his hand. As quickly as he found comfort in the gun, Clarion resolved to have it close, within easy reach. He shoved the gun into his jacket pocket before returning both hands to the steering wheel.

The traffic had begun to lighten up but there were still cars double-parked, trucks dropping off produce, the elderly shuffling across the street, carting bags of groceries. If a bullet could sway, that's how Clarion drove on his way to his destination. Speed was his partner, the brake, rarely touched.

Time ebbed too slowly in his mind but ten minutes later he found his cross street, slipping the BMW between a '75 Pinto hatchback and a Toyota Prius. He sat still for a moment, staring straight out the front windshield, trying to gather his courage.

Courage.

That was what he thought what he needed but deep down inside he knew it was more than that. It was the desire to fix the mistakes of his past. To save his family, he needed more than courage. He needed to believe in himself. He needed to accept whatever measures taken were justified. Because what he was about to do might require him to kill.

His entire world was coalescing into a single thought as he

unconsciously chewed on his thumbnail, thinking of Barbara, of Rachel. In a split second, it all became clear. His mind was made up, all apprehension extinguished. Robert Clarion had all the justification he needed.

TORRINGTON DIDN'T CARE ABOUT PUDDLES OF murky water. He cut through an alleyway behind an endless row of Chinese restaurants and butcher shops, rank with the smell of discarded fish parts and rotting meat. Commercial dumpsters cluttered uneven pavement in a zigzag pattern, and wooden crates, crammed with wilted remnants of cabbage and bok choy, towered against rear doors. But Torrington barely perceived the pungent smell, his mind focused on getting to the location where he knew Robert Clarion would be waiting. He clutched the small canvas bag slung over his shoulder, making his way out the alley to a busy street filled with tourists. Torrington scanned the street, hoping to see Clarion's BMW. The sun was dipping in his line of sight, causing Torrington to shade his eyes with his right hand. He came to a halt, checked a row of cars, bumper-to-bumper, none of which resembled a BMW. Torrington glanced at his watch, pulled out his cell phone, and speed-dialed Clarion. Two rings and Clarion answered.

"Where are you?"

"I'm coming. Don't do anything until I arrive."

"Geez, Robert. I told you I would wait for you. What's got into you?"

There was a pause. "Nothing. Sorry. Just a little nervous."

"Listen," Torrington said, his voice now more relaxed, "You think I should just get your stuff so I can be on my way?"

Silence.

"I got another thing to do today."

"A *thing?*"

"Yeah, a thing." Torrington's tone was defensive. "I got things to do."

"Cool your jets. I'm right around the corner."

Torrington lowered the phone and caught movement from across the street, in the alley. He walked toward the moving figure. The bright, low sun made it difficult for Torrington to make out the person, shafts of light wrapped the approaching body like a blanket. It wasn't until the individual was deep into the alley that Torrington was able to see it wasn't Robert Clarion.

He was a big man, wearing a long, dark wool overcoat, the kind found on business executives—or mob guys.

Torrington froze. The man in the coat fixed his sights on Torrington then lowered his gaze toward the puddles of water, and continued walking.

Torrington heard a familiar voice from the other end of the alley. He turned and caught sight of Clarion, standing next to a half opened door. He had come through a Chinese pastry shop via a back delivery entrance.

"Good, you're here." Torrington walked toward Clarion, pulling the bag off his shoulder, before barking out a command: "Hurry up and fill it."

Feeling irritated at Torrington's tone, Clarion paused for a fraction of a second to exhale his desire to bite back, knowing it would do no good. He reached inside his jacket and pulled out the small paper sack with the money.

He shoved it into the bag with angry force and tossed it back at Torrington.

"Count it if you want."

Torrington shook his head. "Known you too long not to trust you, Robert."

No one moved. An unnerving game of chicken, each one waiting for the other to say something, to get this going.

Clarion balked first. "What's next? You going to call the guy?"

Torrington nodded, pulled his phone, hit the speed dial.

A familiar voice answered. "You ready?"

"I've got the money. Where do you want to meet?"

"We already have."

Torrington was caught off-guard. "What are you talking about?"

"Never mind. My guy will be there in thirty seconds." The phone call abruptly ended.

Torrington slammed the phone shut. "Shit."

"What?"

"My guy said he's already here. He'll meet me in thirty seconds."

Clarion pulled back into the doorway and gave a hard look down both sides of the alleyway.

"What's wrong?"

"I don't want this guy to see me. Last thing we need is him to recognize me and decide to kill the deal."

Torrington understood. "Get the hell out of here!"

Clarion gestured at Torrington as he rolled back inside the pastry shop. "Call me as soon as he leaves."

Torrington didn't say a word, just nodded his response.

Clarion disappeared, leaving Torrington standing alone in the rank alleyway. A few seconds later, Torrington spotted a figure making his way down the alley, gait slow and laid-back.

As the man came into focus, Torrington recognized the long, dark wool overcoat.

"You got something for me?" the man said.

Torrington took a step back. "Yeah, I got it." He handed the bag over to the man. "Go ahead and count it."

The man continued to smile. "That's all right. If my boss sees it's short, you'll be hearing from us."

Torrington felt a shiver electrify through his body, wishing he'd taken Clarion up on his offer to count the money first. "Pete's never questioned me before." He looked at the man for a second, a funny feeling coming over him. "You do work for Pete, don't you?"

The man didn't respond, just gave Torrington a dead man's stare.

"Don't worry," Torrington said. "It's all there."

The man started to back away and turn to leave.

"W—Wait," Torrington stuttered. "H—How'd you know where I was?"

The man shrugged. "That's what I get paid for." He picked up the pace and quickly blended into the foot traffic at the end of the alley.

"Hey," Torrington barked, trying to sound tough. "How long before you bring me back my product?"

The man didn't bother responding, didn't even flinch. He just kept walking.

Torrington kept his eyes on the man until he disappeared into the crowd. He exhaled a tense breath, perspiration soaking into his collar. "That went well, I guess." He felt his phone vibrate, pulled it from his pocket and hit the answer button. "Yeah?"

"It's me, Robert."

"The guy came and took the money. Fuck, Robert, this guy—"

"Which way did he go?"

"What?"

"Dammit, Roy, which direction did the pick-up man go in the alley?"

"Grant. Toward Grant Street, why?"

"What was he wearing?"

"Hell, I don't know." A pause then stammered words. "B—Black slacks, hard shoes, a dark g—gray winter overcoat. Why?"

"Nothing. Just sit tight and wait to hear from me."

"What the hell is going on?"

Torrington waited for a response but, after a few seconds, realized he was the only one on the line. He closed his phone, took a deep breath, and sighed in confusion.

CLARION SHOVED THE PHONE INTO HIS JACKET POCKET and sprinted toward Grant Street. He wedged behind an elderly couple, blading his face so that whoever came around the corner would not be able to see him, scanning the sidewalk the next block over. The crowded street was overrun with tourists snapping pictures, locals running errands. A small patch cleared near the middle of the block along a row of parking meters.

A tall man wearing a dark-colored winter overcoat crossed the street. Clarion saw the moneybag slung over his shoulder.

Clarion followed, dodging an old station wagon clunking down the busy commercial street. He kept at least a half block behind, following in hopes of seeing the man meet with the boss. Clarion strained to keep his sights locked on his target he now labeled, Gray Coat. He wasn't a cop but even he knew doing a one-man surveillance was damn near impossible. Slowing his pace, Gray Coat cut across several streets, eventually pushing through the glass doors of a small business before disappearing from sight. Clarion's heart raced. He ran up to the door, slowed, then glanced in as he walked past.

King's Bakery was painted in red outside the glass window. It was dark and crowded inside, but he could make out two tall white men, one of them Gray Coat, talking to a young Asian with jet black hair slicked back, leaning against a glass counter. Clarion crossed the street and leaned on the hood of a parked car, holding still and hoping this would be a short wait.

CHAPTER 12

E NRIQUE SOTO SAT IN THE PASSENGER SEAT of Paris's surveillance car, a cobalt blue Acura TL. Tugging at his collar, Soto peeked down, inside the front of his shirt where the small recording apparatus was taped to his chest.

After an hour of trying to get Soto to understand how he needed to set up a drug delivery with Peter Kennedy—or his assistant—Paris knew this wasn't going to be as easy as Soto led them to believe during their first meeting at the jail. There was a lot of explaining and re-explaining. In the end, Paris came to only one conclusion that described Enrique Soto. He was an idiot.

Soto fumbled with the mic. "So what if the guy, like, wants the money up front?"

Paris leaned forward and knocked Soto's hand away from the wire. "Leave it alone. The more you think about it, the more conspicuous it becomes."

"What's conspicuous?"

Paris pointed at Soto's chest. "The mic."

"No," Soto said. "What does conspicuous mean?"

"Just leave the microphone alone."

Soto nodded as if he understood, before quickly growing confused again. "But what if he wants the money?"

Paris thought about the question. Not long after their initial call with the supplier, Soto got a return call. The supplier agreed to deliver the half-pound of coke, payment due on delivery. But the scenario was contingent on Soto then requesting another half immediately upon the first delivery. That would give Paris and his crew the ability to follow the supplier back to the stash house and, hopefully, to the man really in charge. The one who was actually supplying Peter Kennedy. Paying for the first half pound was a given, but fronting money for the second half was iffy at best, especially not knowing who this guy was. Paris wasn't interested in the drugs. He wanted Kennedy's supplier.

To this end, fronting the money was a risk Paris was willing to take. Would the middleman be so accommodating? That was the question. And Paris had no choice but to roll the dice.

"You think you can trust this guy?" Paris asked.

Soto turned his head and spat out the car window. "I trust Pete but I don't know who this guy is."

"Okay. If it becomes a deal breaker, give him the money. But you make sure he gives you a definite delivery time for the second half."

Soto remained silent, nodding he understood, then without thinking, started fiddling with the wire.

Paris slapped his hand away again. "Get over to the meet location and wait there. As soon as you two separate, call out over the microphone, discreetly, where he's headed, what he's driving. Got it?"

Again, Soto nodded, but now sweat had started on his upper lip and forehead. He swiped a sleeve across his mouth. "Lots to remember, eh?"

"Just relax. You'll be fine." Paris placed both hands on Soto's shoulders and squared him up, eye-to-eye. "Now tell me, what's the signal if things go bad?"

Soto raised both hands above his head until they could go no higher. "Like this."

"And what do you say in case we can't see you?"

"What do you mean *in case you can't see me?*"

"It's just another verification if you're in trouble."

Soto paused, staring into Paris's eyes. "Don't shoot?"

"That's right, Enrique. *Don't shoot.*"

Paris took the time to explain, again, what Soto was supposed to do and how, if given the opportunity to travel with his contact to pick up the drugs, to go. Soto said very little, which was unusual for him, just a lot of "uh-huhs" and head bobbing, as if he understood, but Paris knew most of his instructions were lost in the empty space between Soto's ears. Paris handed Soto a small brown bag containing six thousand dollars, the amount negotiated for the first half pound of coke. Paris handed him a second bag with another six for the second half, to be used only if need be. Soto shoved the bags inside his coat and smiled. Now it was obvious. This part, he had done before. One last nod and Soto stepped out of the vehicle. A cool gust of ocean breeze blew in from the Bay. Soto headed down the street, toward the intersection of Grant and Pacific. Paris watched him slowly trudge along the busy artery, cross over, and slouch onto a Muni-bus stop bench.

In twenty minutes, the supplier would hopefully arrive with the half pound. If things went right, Soto would order the second half, forcing the contact to meet the supplier who would then travel to the stash house, maybe make some phone calls, which Paris could ID. A pen register had already been set up to track Peter Kennedy's phone.

There were a few agents from the San Francisco division sitting on Kennedy's apartment as his team was called to support the buys. A lot could be learned, leads generated from this transaction.

That's if Soto did his job right.

The receiver monitoring the wire crackled, a lot of background noise, interference from the cars on the road, even the wind cutting past Soto's body. From where he sat, Paris could see Soto slouched on the bench, picking his nose while softly catcalling at young women walking down the boulevard. Paris turned down the volume.

His cell phone vibrated. He answered it without taking his eyes off of Soto.

It was Dools. "What's happening?"

"Nothing much," Paris said.

"I see him." Dools chuckled. "Remind me never to shake his hand."

"Is our surveillance team in place?"

"I got the area boxed in with an additional two agents on foot in case the target starts diving into the local shops."

Two on foot, four in vehicles. That didn't include the four Sacramento PD detectives, which brought the number to ten. "How about the SFPD detectives?"

"I got them spread out with our guys."

That was good. The San Francisco PD detectives knew every inch of their city. Too many small alleyways and dead-end streets to keep law enforcement guessing. "I gave Soto the second six grand."

"You do like to live dangerously."

"Just make sure everyone knows to keep an eye out for two bags of money being exchanged."

Paris hung up and glanced at his watch, noting the time. Fifteen minutes before the target's arrival. He looked over and spotted Soto, who was no longer sitting but now standing next to a tall, slender man, with wispy gray hair on the side, bald on top, wearing what looked like a navy blue pea coat.

The man was listening to Soto, who was very animated, waving his arms, coming close to raising both in the air.

Paris could see Soto wasn't in danger, just nervous. Paris cranked up the volume and tried to listen in on their conversation. Soto was rambling, talking at a quick pace. The bald slender man said nothing.

Paris got on the Bureau radio. "Heads up. Our guy's meeting with someone." Paris gave a quick description. Because of the subject's slender build, Paris designated his subject "Skinny," as a means of referencing him to the surveillance team. "Did anyone see where he came from?"

"No," Dools said. "Just as we hung up, I saw him walk up from the north. Didn't see him get out of a car."

The radio traffic started to buzz, everyone checking in, confirming their location and their readiness to take the target away from the meet. Paris strained to listen to the conversation but it was muffled and scratchy. Skinny said something, stuck out his hand, and Soto placed one of the brown paper bags in it. Skinny then pointed to the trash bin next to the bench. Over the wire, Paris heard him say, "Your product is in there. Better get it before a vagrant finds it first."

Soto told Skinny to wait as he walked over to the trash bin and retrieved a black plastic bag, tightly wrapped and taped into the shape of a brick.

Soto strode back to the man and started talking. Again, Soto spoke rapidly and Paris had a hard time making out what he was trying to say. Then he heard Skinny raise his voice over the wire. "You want another half?"

Soto had put in the second order.

Paris saw Skinny shake his head, heard him say, "No guarantees. I'll call you if I can get it today."

"Cool," Soto replied. "I'll wait to hear from you."

"I got it," Dools transmitted over the radio. He began directing surveillance agents to start moving in on their target.

Soto stuck out his hand but Skinny just gave him a smirk before turning and walking away.

CHAPTER 13

"We're moving!" Dools shouted into the radio.

The rest of the crew acknowledged, vehicles closing behind their target.

Paris hesitated, deciding not to start up his car. He wanted to see if Skinny was going to continue walking. Soto turned away then glanced over his shoulder, hoping to get a direction. Paris got on the radio. "I'm going on foot."

He didn't wait for a response. He grabbed up the HT radio, shoved in the earpiece, and jumped out of the car. Skinny was still traveling north on Grant Avenue, keeping his eyes to the ground. Paris crossed the street and jogged until he was within a block. The radio traffic picked up, the surveillance team boxing him in front with Paris bringing up the rear. The two other agents on foot were hanging loose and away, knowing Paris was taking point.

Wasting no time, Skinny made it to the end of Grant and curved right onto Broadway, traversing at a good clip. His jacket lifted above his waistline when he ducked past a low hanging sign. That's when Paris saw it: a pistol wedged along Skinny's right side. It was only exposed for a second but Paris saw it was an automatic. Skinny cut the next corner hard, disappearing into a crowd of pedestrians. Paris ran up and made the bend, searching deep into the throngs of bodies. Skinny had dissolved into the chaotic mix.

"Shit." Paris keyed up his HT, picking up the pace, punching through the crowd that pushed against him from the opposite direction. "I lost him."

Radio chatter exploded, all eyes searching for their target. Dools's voice cut through the static. "I'm heading your way. If he's between us, we'll box him in."

Paris made his way up Columbus Street, peering into every window and entrance as he darted past businesses and storefronts on the busy street. Restaurant patrons and dry cleaner customers crowded sidewalks and doorway, but Paris saw no skinny white male wearing a navy blue peacoat. By the time Paris made it up to Vallejo Street, four minutes had past, more than enough time for Skinny to have cleared the area. Paris turned around, looked back at the route he had just taken. Nothing. Then, Dools came over the radio.

"I'm right in front of you."

Down the next block on the other side of the street, Paris spotted Dools, his large body and light Irish skin standing out in a crowd of dark-haired Asians. Paris motioned him forward. Dools acknowledged with his chin then hastened to a slow jog.

Paris felt his stomach turn. It only took a split second for a plan to collapse and, he thought, that was direction this one was going. He had already begun formulating a back-up strategy. The best he could hope for was to re-engage Skinny when he appeared with the second delivery. Maybe then, they would be able to see him go back and meet up with his supplier. But that could take time and a lot of luck. In a last attempt, Paris scanned the bustling crowd. Suddenly, he saw two white males coming out of a small business. The first one, a large guy, stopped and retrieved something from his pocket before turning away from Paris. Pulling on a wool cap, he hunkered low in a worn bomber jacket as he walked away. As he stepped off the curb, Paris was then able to see the other man.

Skinny.

He was forcing his way through the streaming foot traffic and waving at a slowing taxi. Skinny darted out into the street and ducked into the back seat of the cab. On the other side of the street, Dools waited for the cross traffic to clear. Paris keyed up his mic. "Get over here! I got Skinny in a taxi about to leave."

Dools jumped off the curb and sprinted across heavy traffic. Car brakes squealed and horns blared, drivers screaming, offering hand gestures that could be deciphered in any language. Dools jumped back and waved an arm at a car turning through the intersection, moving in their direction. One of the surveillance vehicles sped up next to Dools, slamming on its brakes, stopping inches from where they stood.

Dools turned toward Paris and screamed, "Get in!"

The taxi was already making its way across the next intersection and the light was coming close to changing color.

"The taxi," Dools said from the passenger's seat, pointing out the windshield. "Follow the taxi."

"Which taxi?" the agent driving yelled. "There are at least six!"

"That one!"

The vehicle launched forward, swerving past double-parked cars, commercial trucks, and a slow moving mini-van. By the time he reached the intersection, the light had turned yellow and there was a car directly in front of them.

"Don't stop," Dools commanded.

The driver gunned the engine and leaned heavy to the left. The car swayed into oncoming traffic, nearly clipping the front bumper of a '68 Plymouth Fury station wagon before swaying back into the right hand lane and flying through the intersection. Paris leaned to the right and scanned the cars in front, spotting their taxi.

"There! The one making the right."

The driver grabbed up his radio mic and called in the coordinates to the other surveillance agents. Dools tried to relax. Paris pulled himself forward to keep a close eye on the cab.

"No problem, guys," the driver said.

"Yeah," Dools. "Just like Soto says. *Piece of cake*."

The cab continued south on Columbus Street while Skinny reclined in the back. Within minutes, the rest of the surveillance team fell in line, shadowing through Chinatown until the taxi finally stopped near a bank parking lot on Stockton Street.

"He's out," Dools called out on his handheld.

Paris watched Skinny bail from the cab and wander under an overhead canopy in front of the Bank of America entryway. He reached in his pea coat, retrieving a pack of smokes. He shook one out and shoved it between his lips.

"He's waiting for someone," Paris said.

They remained at an idle for a few minutes, watching Skinny leaning against a wall. A few cars stuck behind them honked their disapproval before swerving around. They were a rock in the middle of a moving stream. "I can't keep the car here for much longer without drawing attention," the driver said.

Paris pulled on the door handle and the chilled wind filled the interior.

"Where're you going?" Dools asked as he tried to look back over his seat at Paris.

"I'll try to keep an eye on our boy from across the street. Stay close by in case he gets into another car."

Dools tossed a salute as Paris slammed the door shut and jogged across to the other side of the road. He stopped in front of a Muni bus stop and sat down in the open-glass seating area. He had a good view of Skinny, who continued leaning against the outside of the building, puffing on his cigarette, smoke clouding his face. Ten minutes rolled by. Aside from incidental movement, a glance at his watch, drag from his cigarette, Skinny did not move.

Then Paris saw Skinny pull his phone from his pocket, listened without saying a word, shook his head, then put the phone back into his pocket.

"I think we've got movement," Paris said to the other surveillance members. "Looks like he's leaving."

The street bustled but Skinny was taller than the rest, making it easier for Paris to keep an eye on him. He followed him down to Stockton Street where Skinny quickened his pace, angling toward Grant. The light turned green and he crossed over, turned left, heading north. Halfway up the block he slowed and stepped into a Chinese bakery.

"He's in a business."

A surveillance agent called out on the radio. "I see him. I'm on it."

A few moments later, Paris spotted the agent walking past the bakery. He slowed briefly, trying to get a good look inside before pushing on. The agent lingered next to the business where he dropped a quarter into a newspaper stand and pulled out a paper.

The radio crackled from the surveillance agent on foot, who spoke in a low voice. "I see him inside, talking to an Asian male behind the counter. Skinny has the moneybag he got from the CI on the counter. Asian male looking inside it. The business is King's Bakery. Pretty small. Can't go in without being noticed."

"I got the back alleyway covered," another surveillance member chimed in.

Paris found another Muni bench across the street, sat down, stretched his legs out in front of him and folded his arms across his chest. Skinny was boxed in and, unless he could fly, he wasn't getting out without Paris knowing. The problem was, Paris could only speculate what he was up to.

CHAPTER 14

ROBERT CLARION REMAINED DOWN THE STREET from King's Bakery, concentrating on the person sitting at the Muni-bus stop. It didn't take more than a minute to realize the man was a cop—and a cop he knew.

He recognized Special Agent Jack Paris from his daughter's kidnapping case. Clarion glanced over at Agent Paris, following his line of sight to the front of King's Bakery. Being on the other side of the law, Clarion knew what was going on. They must be watching Gray Coat and the drug buy he was just involved in. Clarion wondered if Agent Paris had seen Gray Coat meet up with Roy Torrington, seen him hand over the money. Maybe even listening in on their phone calls. At a minimum, they must have Gray Coat's cell records and know he contracted Roy Torrington regarding the transaction. If things turned out bad and Roy Torrington was arrested, the question was: *Would Roy dime me out?*

Clarion stepped back onto the sidewalk and leaned inside an alleyway, out of sight. The secluded place gave him time to ponder his situation. Looking up and down the street, he knew there had to be more police around. They were like wolves. They usually traveled in packs. He pulled his cell phone from his pocket and took a chance on calling Torrington.

"Yeah?"

"Roy, it's me. Have you heard from your contact?"

"Christ, Robert, he just left. Give him time."

"You need to get out of the area."

"What the fuck?"

"I said get out of here. I think the cops are watching. You get in your car and get out of the area. When your guy calls you, you tell him that you're stuck in traffic, anything to stall him."

Torrington's voice elevated with a stammer. "Jesus H—H—How do you know there's cops?"

"Just listen to me, Roy. Get the hell out of here and don't do anything until I talk to you later. You call me as soon as you hear from him, understand? Whatever you do, do *not* take the delivery."

"But—"

Clarion didn't give Torrington a chance to continue their conversation. He ended the call and shoved his phone in his pocket.

Five minutes ticked by. Clarion watched the front door of King's Bakery then back over at Agent Paris. Several cars floated by that Clarion had seen drive by more than once. He kept mental notes of the cars' descriptions. Everything was now in a state of flux, and the only plan he was sure of: stay on Gray Coat. He hoped the man would take him to find Pete Kennedy, Finch's supplier. From there, Clarion would have to figure out what to do, which would require shaking the cops, now crawling out from every direction. In the end, he'd get Pete to admit he'd threatened his family or he'd tell him just who was.

As Clarion turned back toward King's Bakery, he spotted someone coming out. It wasn't his guy. This guy was older, thinner and balding wearing a navy jacket. Clarion stood, looked over to his right, and saw Agent Paris stand. The slender man in the blue jacket started walking up the street, and Agent Paris began following him, maintaining a safe distance. Clarion wondered if this guy could be the supplier?

He didn't have much time to think about it. A moment later, Clarion saw Gray Coat stepping out the front door, walking in the opposite direction. Gray Coat had the bag Torrington gave him, slung over his shoulder. From Clarion's vantage point, it still appeared to be weighted, meaning the money was probably still in the bag. Gray Coat took off up the street. Clarion reverted back to Agent Paris, now a considerable distance away, knew he needed to decide quickly on which person to stick with. Agent Paris probably knew what he was doing by pursuing the slender guy in the navy blue jacket, having information that Clarion didn't. Trailing behind Paris could get him spotted and that could put an end to him finding Peter Kennedy and, subsequently, the supplier. He had little time to decide.

Clarion gave Agent Paris one last look, then turned and made his move in the direction of Gray Coat. It made sense. He was the one who met with Roy Torrington, and most likely he would be the one coming back with the drugs. If he was lucky enough, maybe Clarion would be able to intercept him before that happened—and out of Agent Paris's surveillance.

Clarion quick-stepped across the street and fell in behind Gray Coat, who continued south along Grant Avenue, eventually ending up at a public parking garage off of Washington Street. Clarion, cautiously, counted to three, then followed after him. Less than twenty-five yards down, Gray Coat was standing in front of a bank of elevators, behind a nun and two young kids. The door opened and the group stepped inside. Clarion turned and ran back to the garage entry. He approached the exit booth and rapped on the glass window, startling a man inside reading a Chinese newspaper. The man nearly fell out of his chair. He slid back the window and scowled at Clarion.

"Is this the only way out of this building?"

The man responded in a heavy Chinese accent. "What?"

"Is this the only way out?"

Still scowling, the man barely nodded, returning to his paper.

Clarion bolted from the garage, flagging down a passing taxi.

"Where to?" the taxi driver asked.

Clarion peeled off a hundred dollar bill and slapped it down on the front seat. "Loop around to the other side of the street—and fast! Wait at the end near that garage exit."

The cabbie didn't move. "Hey, this don't sound right."

Clarion pulled out another hundred and held it up. "Look, there's another hundred if you just do as I say and not ask any questions."

The cabbie wasn't buying it.

"I'm a private investigator and I'm following a guy cheating on his wife, okay?"

The driver plucked the second hundred.

The cab accelerated through a U-Turn and into position, like Clarion requested. A couple minutes ticked by before a white Mercedes AMG sedan pulled out of the garage. Clarion could see the driver was Gray Coat.

"Follow him."

The cab driver shifted into drive and slowly crawled behind the Mercedes with another car sandwiched in between. Slowly at first, they wound through busy streets and intersections until coming onto the highway, where they picked up speed. Gray Coat breezed down the freeway, squeezing between traffic, zooming in and out without difficulty. A couple of miles down the road, Gray Coat signaled to the right, veering onto the off-ramp, which led toward Rincon Hill. Clarion followed. City traffic crawled to a snail-like pace. Clarion could feel his impatience growing. At the corner, the Mercedes turned toward a high-rise tower apartment, a luxury condo with a view of the bay. The driver whistled.

"Whoa. This guy's got some bucks, eh?"

Clarion didn't respond.

The Mercedes braked in front of a metal box, where he rolled down his window and waved a card in front of it. The metal garage door steadily crept open.

"Pull over to the side," Clarion ordered.

"How long are we going to stay with this guy?" the cab driver asked.

"Don't worry. You'll be compensated for your time."

Clarion looked up at the building and wondered which one belonged to Gray Coat—or maybe his boss. He stepped out of the cab and walked over to the building. At the entrance, there was an electronic calling board. He scrolled down the list of names, not really sure of what he was looking for. Then one name popped on the screen: *P. Kennedy.*

Clarion, stood static, letting the name sink in. How long would it take Gray Coat to get up to his apartment? Clarion waited as long as he could and then pushed the call button. A man answered.

"Yeah?"

Clarion responded. "Yeah, is this Mr. Kennedy?"

"Who's this?"

"Gas and Electric Company, sir. Sorry to bother you but we're trying to fix a circuit box failure and we think we traced the problem to your suite."

There was a pause. "What do you want me to do about it?"

"Just wanted to confirm the floor before we go ripping through cables."

There was silence on the other end. Clarion looked up and counted the number of floors. "I don't want to have to shut off your power. If I've got to pull cable, it could be out for at least until tomorrow. You're above ten, correct?"

"Yeah, twelve-oh-seven."

"Okay, thanks."

"What about the power?"

"I'll make sure it stays on."

As luck would have it, Clarion spotted a couple approaching the entry before waving a card over a keypad. There was a buzzing sound and the man pulled open the door. Clarion reached past him and grabbed the door handle, holding it wide for the woman who was struggling with three over-stuffed shopping bags from Saks. He followed them in and waited for an elevator. A second later, a door beeped and slid aside. The three entered.

The man looked over at Clarion. "What floor?"

"Twelve."

The young woman smiled. "You must have a nice view."

Clarion acted nonchalant. "Only what money can buy."

The man fabricated a smile and only pressed six. The woman kept her smile on Clarion while she gently reached over and touched the button for twelve.

CHAPTER 15

THE DOORS OPENED ON SIX and the two stepped off. The woman took a little more time than her male friend. Clarion waved goodbye. She gave Clarion another quiet smile before disappearing down the hallway arm-and-arm with her man. The man didn't bother giving Clarion a second look.

The lift jolted upward and Clarion needed to think fast, wondering what he was going to do next. He didn't have time to plan this through, running solely on instinct. Now he may be faced with something he hadn't planned or prepared to do. The elevator slowed and came to a stop. Clarion looked up and saw the number twelve glowing. He heard the chime and the doors yawned apart. Clarion stepped off and looked left, then right.

Empty.

Twelve-oh-seven was down the hall to the left. Passing cathedral doors with brightly polished brass handles, he moved with purpose toward the end of the hall on thick plush carpet. The entry was separated from the others, indicating that it was a larger condo, most likely taking an entire corner of the building for its panoramic view. Clarion approached cautiously, straining to hear any sounds coming from within. He stopped inches from the heavily lacquered door and leaned against the frame. He reached into his jacket pocket and wrapped his hand around the grip of his PPK, thumb resting over the safety. Clarion knew if Gray Coat were to step out, he would have to take him and his boss, P. Kennedy, at gunpoint.

Down the hall, a door opened. A woman with a small dog on a leash stepped out, giving Clarion a look before turning back to the yapping dog. The woman moved along and stood waiting in front of the elevator. Seconds later, the elevator dinged. As the woman got on, Clarion caught movement from the corner of his eye. Others were stepping out. Two men, talking in low voices appeared, now walking toward Clarion. At first, they didn't notice him standing next to the last suite. The man in front was shorter, his face thin but sinewy, all muscle with a sharp jaw line. He kept talking to the other guy over his shoulder.

Clarion wasn't going to wait for the two to see him loitering in front of Kennedy's apartment so he started moving back toward the elevator. That was when he got a look at the second guy.

It was Gray Coat. He had the bag slung over his shoulder. Clarion could only assume the second henchman was waiting for Gray Coat in the garage, maybe in the lobby. Bottom line: there were two of them and one of him. Clarion looked down, trying to shield his face from being seen as he walked past the two.

Suddenly, the two men stopped talking and the hallway feel silent again. Clarion kept moving until he felt a hand reach out and touch him on his arm.

"Can I help you?" The sinewy man stepped in front of Clarion, blocking his way out. Gray Coat flanked him, giving Clarion no easy way around the two.

"No," he said. "Just got turned around." Clarion pointed down the hallway. "I'm supposed to be down that side." Clarion smiled and tried to blade his way between them.

"Not so fast," Sinewy said. "Who you here to see?"

"An old friend and her dog."

Gray Coat stepped closer, his eyes narrowing into slits. "I've seen you somewhere before, haven't I?"

"Yeah, if you live here, you would've seen me visiting my friend."

"Okay then, who's that?" Gray Coat's tone was aggressive.

A bead of sweat dripped down Clarion's forehead and Gray Coat noticed it. Clarion had to make a decision. He took a step closer to Gray Coat, putting them inches apart as the other started to make a move. Clarion reached into his jacket, pulled out his pistol. He grabbed Gray Coat in a bear hug and then screwed the barrel into the side of Gray Coat's left ear.

"It's my friend, Walther."

Sinewy froze, fixating on the gun. Gray Coat didn't move a muscle, only his eyes bouncing slowly between the PPK and Clarion.

Clarion could feel the henchman ready to make a move. "Don't even think about it." He waved a hand for Sinewy to pull back his coat so that Clarion could see if he was armed. He wasn't.

"Look, pal," Gray Coat said. "I don't know what you want, but you're making a big mistake here."

Clarion rolled around the back of Gray Coat, keeping the gun trained at his head. He reached around his waist, found a Kimber .45 auto-pistol. "I hope you're wrong."

"What is it you want?" Sinewy asked.

"Just looking for some answers."

Sinewy raised his hands above his waist. "To what questions?"

"In just a minute," Clarion responded. He reached into Gray Coat's pocket and removed a key ring. There were a number of keys, including the Mercedes'. "Which one to the apartment?"

Gray Coat looked down and harrumphed.

Clarion pressed the pistol hard against his ear, making him flinch. "That kind of a response is going to get you killed."

Gray Coat hesitated, and then reluctantly answered, "The gold one."

Clarion shook out the key and held it up in his hand. "Anyone inside?"

"No."

"Then who answered the phone when I called a minute ago?"

Gray Coat cocked his head toward Clarion. "So, that was you?"

Clarion remained silent. Gray Coat slowly reached into his coat and pulled out a cell phone, held it up. "Call forwarding."

Clarion shoved Gray Coat toward the door, then hooked a finger with his free hand for sinewy to follow. "You better be right, because if you're not, you'll be the first one I shoot."

"Take it easy, pal." Gray Coat was cool, giving no signs of concern.

"I ain't your *pal.*" To drive home the message, Clarion gave Gray Coat a hard kidney punch, buckling the man's legs as they shuffled toward the door.

"Open it."

Gray Coat slid in the key in the lock and pushed. Grabbing Gray Coat by the collar, Clarion held him back, looked over at his partner, and waved the pistol at him to take the first step inside. The man slowly stepped through the entryway, followed by Clarion using Gray Coat as a shield.

The large room splayed open, a wall made entirely of glass offering a stunning, panoramic view of the shoreline and Pacific Ocean. The furniture, high-polished dark wood and leather, had been neatly arranged like a house professionally staged for a sale. With his gun, Clarion directed Sinewy over to the sofa. Gray Coat took his time, dragging himself into the living area, sliding the bag Torrington gave him on top of a mirrored coffee table. Still using Gray Coat as a shield, Clarion secured the corners, pushing doors open to make sure he hadn't been set up. Feeling satisfied, he returned to the living room, and shoved Gray Coat down on the opposite side of the couch. He reached into his coat, fishing out his cellphone. The two men's eyes remained locked on Clarion, a pair of hungry lions waiting for the opportunity to seize their prey.

Clarion pushed the bag onto an open space on the coffee table and pulled the zipper open.

"Either one of you guys got names?"

Neither one answered.

"Either one of you guys Peter?"

Again, no response.

"Maybe I'll have to check your wallets. When I take them off your dead bodies."

Gray Coat sneered. "No, neither of us is Peter."

"Where's Peter then?"

The two shrugged.

"Figures."

Inside the bag sat a pink pastry box, tied shut with thin red string, the name King's Bakery stenciled on top. Clarion lifted out the box, pulled on the string, and opened the lid.

A small, solid brick of white powder, shrink-wrapped tightly in plastic, rested inside.

"Kind of expensive pastries, don't you think?"

"Look," Gray Coat said. "If you're here to rip us off, you're making a big mistake."

"You said that already."

"I'm trying to save you from getting hurt."

"Tell you what," Clarion replied. "You tell me where this guy Peter is and *I'll* make sure *you* don't get hurt."

Gray Coat dipped his head down, shook it, and tsked.

There was a buzz coming from the coffee table. It was Gray Coat's cell phone. Neither one of the two showed any signs of concern. Clarion reached over and picked it up, pressed the middle button, and discovered a text message waiting.

"Oh, look," Clarion said as he looked up at Gray Coat. "You've got mail."

The header read, *El Jafe—*

The Boss.

He scrolled down the message, which was short but to the point. *Package ready for pick up.*

"You're making a mistake," Gray Coat said again.

Before Clarion could respond, a knock thumped on the door. The unexpected sound drew his attention away from his prisoners for just a second, long enough for Gray Coat to take advantage of the distraction. Springing from the couch, the man pile-drove Clarion across the room, both of them tumbling over a leather chair. The two wrestled for Clarion's gun. Pulling his arms in tight to his chest so that Gray Coat couldn't tear the gun free, Clarion felt the sting of a hard punch to the side of his head, causing his ears to ring.

Out of the corner of his eye, Clarion saw the other man make his move, and knew with two against one, this wasn't a fight he could win. With all his energy, Clarion twisted his body, coming face to face with Gray Coat, even though it left him exposed. As Gray Coat lifted a fist to strike Clarion in the face, Clarion shoved the pistol into Gray Coat's belly and pulled the trigger. There was a quiet pop, muffled by Gray Coat's massive frame. Clarion felt the heat of the gunfire, his hand feeling the flash burning his skin.

He tried to pull the trigger again but the gun jammed, unable to complete its cycle to spit out the casing, known as a stove-pipe. The dead man's body stiffened, then went limp. Clarion shoved him off, raked the spent casing from the ejection port and chambered a new round. He beaded on Sinewy, who froze facing the front end of the barrel, hands slowly lifting in surrender. Another knock at the door. Clarion knew if he answered the door sweating, cut, and covered in blood, he would have a hard time explaining. The police would be called. He waved his only live prisoner over to the door, gun aimed squarely at his back.

"Get rid of whoever it is," Clarion whispered, "or you'll end up like your buddy, got it?"

The man nodded, walked to the door, pulled it open a crack.

"Everything okay?" The voice was filled with concern. It was the dog woman from down the hall. "I heard loud noises."

"Everything is fine, thanks." The man tried to shut the door, but the woman continued talking.

"There was a man standing next to your apartment before I went out for my walk. He looked kind of suspicious. Thought you should know."

"Friend of mine. Everything's fine, thanks."

The dog poked his head inside, looked up at Clarion, and barked.

The woman pulled her dog back just before the door slammed on its head.

Clarion dragged the man back to the couch, pushed him down, hovering over him.

"How about a name," Clarion asked.

"Corbin Everett," the man said, wisely deciding that honesty was the only policy that might keep him alive.

"All right, Corbin. Want to tell me where we can find Peter?"

"Got no idea, don't work for the man."

"Who do you work for?"

Everett didn't respond. A bead of sweat slid down the side of his temple. It told Clarion one thing: Everett was more scared of a man not in the room than the one holding a gun to his head.

"Would I be safe in saying your boss works with Peter?"

"Hardly." Everett forced a half-grin. "Let's just say my boss has acquired Peter Kennedy's business interests."

Peter Kennedy. Besides seeing the name on the electronic calling board, this was the first time someone had confirmed his target's full name.

"Well, Corbin, we better get going. We got a package to pick up."

Everett pointed at the dead man, lying face down, blood now pooling below his chest where the bullet entered his heart. "Am I going to end up like him?"

"Him? That depends."

"On what?"

Clarion smiled. "On whether I get a chance to meet your boss and get my answers. Let's go." He motioned with his pistol toward the entrance and the two slowly crossed the room, Everett with less enthusiasm and a fading sense of aggravated surrender.

Before making it to the door, Clarion looked back at the dead man on the floor, and he felt his breath catch high in his throat. The killing made everything more real. It was only a flash in time, something that could have been measured in nanoseconds. But Clarion had been forced to take a life. At least, that was what he was trying to convince himself. The killing placed him on a path that he no longer was able to retreat from. Gray Coat was nothing more than the messenger but he worked for the man Clarion was after. His choice. And even though it was Gray Coat's decision to work in a world that included violence, forcing him to take a life angered Clarion, scraping at the lining of his stomach like a knife carving away at his conscience. He didn't know Gray Coat, had never seen him before in his life. He didn't even know his real name.

CHAPTER 16

THE SKINNY MAN PICKED UP HIS PACE. He stopped twice, once at a hotel where he walked into the lobby and used a public payphone, and then when he ducked in the corner bar, talking on his cell. After the man left, a surveillance agent placed a call from the same payphone to mark the time.

An agent at the field office called Paris. They were able to identify the subscriber who called Soto to set up the deal. The court order to have a pen register up and running by end of the day had already been prepared and filed.

There was a lull in the surveillance while the skinny man waited in front of a gas station, smoking a cigarette, pacing in front of an open bay door. Paris got on the phone with Agent Jim Harrington, who was running down leads being called in by the surveillance agents.

"I think I got your guy IDed."

Paris looked back over at the skinny man, who was lighting up his third smoke. "Talk to me. Who am I watching?"

"Name's Michael Shafter. Doesn't have a DL in California but I was able to locate one in Illinois. Got an address in Chicago as of last year. He fits your description. Six feet, one seventy-five. Face that resembles a block of granite."

"'Crim' history?"

"Did time for assault, armed robbery. Looks like he was arrested on state drug charges, but those charges were later dropped."

Paris grunted. "Why am I not surprised?"

He asked Harrington to keep digging. Maybe the arresting detectives would remember whom Shafter was working for. The dismissed charges could mean two things: a weak case or he cooperated. Paris was hoping for the latter. He called Dools, still driving around on surveillance with Agent Tim Langan, and told him what Harrington said. Dools was glad to put a name to the skinny man's face, made him feel like they were making progress.

"Shafter, eh?" Dools repeated.

Fifteen minutes passed when another agent noticed a black Cadillac pull into the gas station, idling next to Shafter. He leaned in the driver's side window, briefly, before making his way around the other side of the car and into the passenger seat. The Cadillac exited the gas station, heading north. Dools picked up Paris, while two other cars, backed up by a California Department of Justice fixed-wing airplane, kept close watch. Dools had taken over driving duties, complaining Agent Tim Langan drove like his mother.

"After they retrieved the dope," Dools announced, driving and jotting notes at the same time, "the team that debriefed Soto said it looked good, high quality."

"What about the other six thousand?"

Dools scoffed. "Soto gave it up to your man, Shafter, for the second half." Dools clicked his tongue against his cheek. "I guess we'll see if he delivers or rips us off."

There was more chatter on the radio. The Cadillac had been spotted entering the eastbound lane of highway 80. The front car pulled away, allowing the car behind him to take point. The rest of the team jumped onto the freeway where traffic was thick but moving. The Cadillac weaved between slower cars but it didn't appear he was trying to clean himself, unsuspecting of being followed. They continued north, onto the Bay Bridge, passing over Yerba Buena and Treasure Island onto the east side. They made their way up the 580, cutting past Emeryville and Albany, two of the nicer areas. The Cadillac stayed on 580, then glided over to the right lane, coming up on the Habour Way off-ramp.

"Richmond," Paris said as a one-word commentary. The city was known for its crime rate. There were some nice areas such as Marina Point but they were the exception.

"Copy," a surveillance agent called out. "We're off at Harbour, northbound."

They followed the Cadillac through a series of green lights for a couple more miles, busting through a red light or two. As they moved farther north, the scenery began to degrade. By the time they crossed MacDonald Avenue, Paris knew they were getting into the roughest area of Richmond known as the Iron Triangle, so named because the area was wedged between the Union Pacific Railroad on the east and the Burlington Northern on the west. The Rapid Transit system was now using the eastside track for daily commuters but a good portion of the tracks on the west had been abandoned, opening up opportunities for street gangs, armed robberies, drug trafficking, and murderers to flourish out in the open and unobstructed. Richmond had become the ninth most dangerous city in the country. Paris could see why.

Dools pointed forward, spotting the Cadillac five cars in front. "He's turning left."

He turned one block south from the SUV, running parallel, while the airplane kept point. The houses were old, some abandoned, most in need of major repairs. Three blocks to the west, the airplane called out the Cadillac had slowed, pulling to the curb.

"Passenger side door is open and your guy is on foot, car continuing north."

Keeping his tail, Dools spotted the Cadillac making a right, Shafter walking away toward the entrance of a three story on the north side of the street.

"Your call," Dools said to Paris.

"Keep three cars on the Cadillac. We'll stay here with the rest of the crew along with the bird."

Dools called out over the radio and gave the orders, confirmations flooding back in response. Eventually, the second team switched channels to keep order. Each agent reported they'd surrounded the building, and then the radio went quite.

"Stash house?" Dools asked.

Paris nodded. "Don't think Shafter lives here."

They all watched as Shafter entered the front entry using a key. Two men, one Hispanic and the other, an African-American, loitered out front, both dressed in thrift store clothes, their stares distant and oblivious of the time.

Paris doubted they were lookouts. More than likely the men were just unemployed, down and out. Dools did a slow drive-by, then took up a position two blocks down, far enough not to be noticed but close enough to catch anyone coming out.

Slumping down in the front seat, he got comfortable for a long wait, Agent Langan following suit.

"You think we're going to be able to catch Shafter dealing with Kennedy or any other boss," Dools asked, "by sittin' on this dump?"

"Maybe we'll get lucky, see him pass off the money to pick up the other half pound."

Dools wasn't as optimistic.

With the wind starting to whip off the nearby Pacific waters, the air chilled with each passing gust, even with the bright sun above. Little street activity rendered drive-bys tough for this location. Surveillance had noted an Econoline van driving through the area several times but hadn't been around since.

By late afternoon, everyone had grown antsy. The plane had to pull off to refuel, and two of the detectives were called back to their station. An old box truck pulled up in front of the building, and the team stirred. But it turned out to be a Hispanic family moving into one of the flats. A husband and wife with three young kids, two girls and a boy. They began removing belongings from the back of their truck, their furniture no better than what you would find on the side of the road. It was sparse but it was theirs. The youngest, a girl, stood idly and watched, clutching a stuffed animal while the rest of the family worked.

Paris's phone vibrated. It was Soto.

"What do you know?"

Soto sounded anxious. "Hey, man, he called."

"What did he say?"

Soto responded like it was obvious. "Said he's got it and to meet him in thirty minutes."

"Where, Enrique?"

"Same place."

Before the call ended, Shafter stepped from the front door of the building with a small black gym bag slung over his shoulder. He paused for a minute, watching the Hispanic man struggle with a well-worn over-stuffed chair. Shafter said something to the man, got a response and a nod. Afterward, Shafter pulled out his cell phone, placed it up to his ear as he walked to the corner. The other surveillance crew was already calling Paris. The Cadillac was heading back his way. A few moments later, the Cadillac pulled up to the curb, barely stopping as Shafter jumped into the passenger side. The big car took off, flipping a U-turn, backtracking the same route it had taken to get here. Paris wanted to leave a couple of agents behind to watch the stash house but he was already short-handed. They trailed the Cadillac back onto the freeway, and made their way toward Chinatown.

"This guy's bee-lining straight back to the meet spot," Paris said. "I guess we know where the dope's coming from. Question is which unit in the building is the stash pad and who is in control?"

"We can jam up Mr. Shafter," Dools replied, "and maybe he'll give up who his boss is."

Paris considered it. With his criminal history, Shafter could be looking at a lengthy prison stint. The easy way out would be to get search warrants, one on this stash pad, the other on Kennedy's condo, then arrest both and see what falls out. On the other hand, if they didn't cooperate right away, the person Paris really wanted would catch wind and run—be gone forever. Worse, if Rachel Clarion was kidnapped, she would never be found. Staying on Shafter was the best bet, see where it would take him. One block from where Soto first met Shafter on Washington, Dools pulled to the corner. Paris got out on foot and made his way back to the Muni bench, where he'd sat the last time he watched the two. Shafter rounded a corner a minute later, gym bag still slung over his shoulder.

Soto waited nervously, sucking hard on a cigarette that was now barely a stub. He spotted Shafter, stiffened, and tossed the cigarette in the street. The two stood next to each other for only a minute, a couple more words exchanged—Soto listening more than talking—before Shafter finally placed the gym bag down by Soto's feet, turned, and walked away.

"He's on the move toward Grant Avenue," came over the radio.

Paris walked then started to jog in Shafter's direction, flagging down Dools, who was coming from the south. Paris hopped into the car and Dools crushed the accelerator as the back door slammed shut.

"You think Rachel could be in that stash house?" Dools asked.

Highly unlikely but Paris didn't have an answer he could give with confidence.

Dools shrugged. "I guess we can just kick in the doors to see. If she's not in there, we round everyone up and squeeze them until they cooperate."

Paris shook his head. "We're still weak on Kennedy."

Dools glowered. "What are you talking about?"

"Soto never talked to Kennedy. He only spoke to this guy, Shafter. Unless he flips, we have nothing."

Dools slowed the car as Shafter came into view. "We got Soto calling his number."

"Still weak."

"You get Soto to testify."

Paris shook his head. "A drug dealer's testimony in exchange for leniency? Not good enough to support our entire case." Besides, it wasn't a *conviction* that Paris wanted. He wanted Rachel.

Shafter made his way up Grant Avenue, crossed the street through congested traffic. Dools kept his eye on Shafter as he spoke. "Like I said, we kick in the doors to the stash house and Kennedy's apartment and see what we find." His voice was lowered to a growl and cracked his knuckles. "And if we come up empty, I'll make him tell me where that girl is."

Paris knew Dools was just blowing off steam. He wasn't the kind to cross the legal line but that didn't mean he wouldn't dangle over it. And his point wasn't entirely invalid. They had two good buys with Shafter, enough to get them into the stash house. And even though the probable cause was weak on Kennedy's condo, it didn't matter. Weak or not, they were going in. Problem was, if Kennedy wasn't in there, he would soon learn of Shafter's arrest, and he'd be in the wind. Without Kennedy, the odds of finding Rachel Clarion dropped significantly. In the big picture, that was what this was all about.

"It's too risky," Paris said. "Let's stay on Shafter, find Kennedy. Our real target."

Dools wasn't totally convinced but acquiesced. Frustration seeped through his response. "Okay, Michael Shafter, let's see where you go and who you meet."

Suddenly, Shafter sprinted to a car approaching in the opposite direction.

"He's catching a ride," Dools shouted.

A dark gray Lexus LS Sedan slowed in front of Shafter. He swung around to the passenger side and pulled open the back door. Paris tried to see how many people were in the car but couldn't through the dark tinted glass. Dools grabbed up the microphone. "Anyone able to take this car away?"

There was a moment of silence before someone responded, saying they were caught at a red light, one block up.

The Lexus rocketed forward, weaving between a city garbage truck and a slow-moving four-door sedan. If Paris were to lay chase, he would most likely be spotted.

"That's not good," Paris grumbled.

"Where's the bird?" Dools asked.

"Lost it back at the residence for refueling," Langan responded.

Dools stalled for as long as he could before swinging the car around without looking too obvious but it was too late. Too many cars and too many slow drivers. All they could do was watch the dark gray Lexus blow through the intersection as the light turned red and a line of cars filled the gap between them and their mark.

CHAPTER 17

C LARION SAT WITH HIS BACK PRESSED against the passenger door while Everett drove. They took the Cadillac because, Clarion hoped, Agent Paris hadn't seen this one. Everett, sitting board straight, drove like a professional chauffeur, a tight grin frozen across his face.

"What are you so happy about?"

Everett's lips stretched into a broad smile. "You don't see the train coming, do you?"

"Tell me."

"You keep digging yourself a shit hole you can't get out of."

"You mean, even after killing your partner, there's still a chance that I could?"

Everett shook his head, didn't say a word.

"Just drive to the stash house," Clarion ordered.

Cutting through town, they jumped onto the freeway, and made their way into Richmond. They passed a three-story building, circled it twice, searching for surveillance, before deciding to park a block away. Everett was about to pull on the door handle when Clarion laid a strong hand on his shoulder.

"I don't know if you're setting me up, but if you are, whatever happens, you're the first person I shoot. You got that?"

Everett nodded and gave Clarion a look of indifference. "Yeah, so you've already told me."

The two got out and advanced toward the stucco building. A lone Ryder box-truck was parked in front. A heavy-set man, possibly Central

American, sat on the back ramp, taking a break, wiping sweat from his head with a brown handkerchief that used to be white. The man paid little attention to Clarion as he walked by. A young girl clutching a small stuffed animal . . . the man's daughter? . . . came out of the front door, holding it open.

Everett swept by her as if she didn't exist. Clarion followed close behind. He looked at the little girl as he passed and thought, *She's someone's daughter*. Like Rachel. He gave the young girl a kind smile.

The interior was as dilapidated as the outside. The hallway air smelled stale and the white paint, now yellow from age, was thick, looking like it was brushed on with a heavy hand. A stairway led to the upper levels.

Everett indicated upward with his chin. "Second floor," he muttered, climbing the stairs without waiting for a response, his shoes scratching across the worn wooden steps like sandpaper, echoing down the well.

Clarion kept close to Everett, hand wrapped around his Walther pistol still tucked inside his coat. They came to a stop at the top of the landing, staring down a corridor, two doors on each side with a window leading to the emergency fire escape. Clarion looked back downstairs, seeing the Hispanic man dragging a mattress through the entryway and into one of the lower level apartments.

"What are we doing, Chief?" Everett's tone verged on annoyance.

"Which one?"

Everett tapped twice on the first door, and then inserted a key into the lock. They entered an empty apartment. There was a small kitchen table of Formica and chrome, something out of the fifties, surrounded by three matching chairs and an out-of-place spindly wooden fourth. The refrigerator compressor started to whir, working overtime to keep whatever was inside, cool. An old couch, covered in a cheap fabric, was so worn you could barely tell the original color. The only other piece of furniture in the one-bedroom apartment was a sixteen-inch television atop a rickety wooden stand.

"Nice place," Clarion said. "Come here often?"

There were two pink boxes from King's Bakery perched on the kitchen table, just like the one he'd seen in Gray Coat's bag. A thin red string circled one box, tied into a knot. The other box was already opened. And empty. He tugged the string on the second and lifted the lid. Inside another clear plastic bag filled with white powder. Clarion pulled it out and judged the weight in his hand.

"Look, Corbin. More pastries."

Everett rolled his eyes and turned away.

Clarion held up the plastic brick. "Is there more?"

The skin along Everett's temples stretched tight as he continued staring out the living room window and shrugged.

"What's in the back room?"

"See for yourself." Everett said with impertinence

Clarion rammed the barrel of the pistol into Everett's back, causing his hands to rise about waist-level, like he was surrendering. The prisoner began shuffling toward the bedroom. With the exception of the mattress on the floor covered by cheap floral sheets and a stained green blanket, the small space was empty. Everett went first and then stepped aside, giving Clarion a full view of the room. That's when he saw the man pressed into the corner, sitting on the floor. At first glance, his clothes screamed expensive and designer but as if he'd been wearing them too long, now tattered and stained. The man's hands were cuffed behind his back and secured around a large water pipe that was exposed through a rough hole in the wall. A thick strip of silver duct tape covered his mouth. He had apparently taken a couple of blows to the head, his left eye swollen, purple, his cheek sporting scabbed wounds slow to heal.

Clarion probed Everett. "Friend of yours?"

"You might say he's the previous management."

Clarion motioned Everett over to the mattress with his pistol, indicating for him to kneel and look away. Clarion shoved his pistol into his waistband and grabbed the large role of duct tape lying next to the man. He wrenched Everett's hands behind him and bound them with half the roll.

Everett winced. "You're cutting off the circulation in my hands."

"Feel lucky you have any circulation at all." Clarion moved toward the man bound on the floor and pulled the tape off of his mouth. The man twitched, sucking air deep into his lungs like he'd been underwater too long. Still straining, he looked up toward Clarion, nodded a thanks.

Clarion took a knee. "Okay, pal, who the hell are you?"

"Pete Kennedy."

Clarion leaned back against the wall, sizing up the turn of events and the now two bound men before him. "Well, Peter Kennedy, I don't know if I'm supposed to rescue you or kill you."

"There's another thirty keys over there." Kennedy pointed with his chin over toward the mattress, where a bag jammed up against the wall. "Take it. It's all yours. I can get more."

Clarion remained quiet, thinking. He hadn't done business with Kennedy in years. The two had never met, every deal brokered via a common associate: Roy Torrington. Drug buys were always held in confidence, especially between conspirators. Doing so gave value to the supplier and deniability should police become involved. But Clarion finally made it to the first rung, face-to-face.

Everett chimed in. "I don't think that's a smart move."

"Shut up." Clarion looked back at Kennedy, taking his time. "I don't want your dope."

Kennedy's mouth fell open. He was visibly worried that the man standing above him was more interested in the second part of his original remark. "I was kidnapped by that man's boss—" he said, again pointing with his chin at Everett. "—and don't know why."

Everett let out a condescending chuckle.

"What's his boss' name?" Clarion asked Kennedy, knowing he wouldn't get an answer from Everett.

"Ramone Santiago."

"Is he your supplier?" Clarion hoped it was Santiago. That way, he would know who was the threat, who may have Rachel.

"Fuck no," Kennedy spat. "He's a nobody." He turned his attention back to Everett, concerned he just may tell Ramone Santiago about his remark—if he ever got the chance. He added in a conciliatory tone, "No offense."

"None taken," Everett calmly replied.

"Hey, if you two are done making nice, I suggest you—" Clarion aimed his gun at Everett. "—shut your mouth before I decide to tape it shut. And you," he added, swinging the muzzle toward Kennedy, "give me some straight answers."

Everett turned his head toward the wall. Kennedy just nodded like a child trying to please a parent. "Yeah, whatever you want, man."

"You know who I am?"

Kennedy shook his head.

"My name is Robert Clarion."

Kennedy's expression was flat, nothing registering.

"Kevin Finch was my supplier."

Kennedy closed his eyes for a moment, trying to put all the pieces together. Suddenly he got it. His eyes sagged as his head dangled. "Oh, shit."

"Before Finch was killed, did you demand money from him? From me?"

Kennedy looked up, his brow furrowed and eyes narrowed. "What? No. I had nothing to do with Finch when he was supplying you. The fucker kidnapped your daughter, right?"

"That's right, Pete."

Everett looked stunned. "Is that why you're here?"

Clarion stood, walked over to Everett. "You should have listened to me the first time." He grabbed up the silver duct tape, snapped off a long piece and placed it over his mouth, wrapping it around Everett's head. He returned to Kennedy who had turned another shade of white.

"As I was saying," Clarion continued, "Finch was my supplier and I know Finch was getting his drugs from you."

"Yeah, he was but I had nothing to do with your daughter's kidnapping. That was all Finch."

Clarion's eyes narrowed. "No, Finch wouldn't kidnap my daughter on his own. Someone told him to do it and I'm guessing it was Finch's supplier. For the money owed."

"I'm giving it to you straight," Kennedy said. "I had nothing to do with Finch kidnapping your daughter because of some owed money. You got it wrong. I don't kidnap. Hell, I wasn't involved in that deal."

Clarion exhaled, frustrated. He pushed himself up against the wall, trying to make sense of it all. "If you weren't his supplier at that time, who was?"

"Look, I didn't say he wasn't buying from me at the time. I'm saying he didn't buy from me on that transaction."

"Then who did it come from?"

Kennedy's head oscillated like a fan. "I got no idea. Could have been from a handful of guys."

"Then you better come up with the names or I'll leave you here for Mr. Santiago."

"No, man," Kennedy shot back. "I want to help."

"Good, then start helping."

Clarion felt in his pocket for the keys he took from Everett. Finding a handcuff key attached, he pulled Kennedy forward and unhooked him. Kennedy gingerly stretched out his arms like a cat awakening from a long sleep and rubbed his wrists. "Thanks."

Clarion hauled Kennedy up to a stand. "Don't thank me yet. I'm not done with you."

"What do you mean?"

"You're coming with me."

Kennedy's jaw fell slack.

"We're going to find Finch's suppliers and see who knows where my daughter is."

"What do you mean? She's kidnapped? Again?"

Clarion nodded. "Whoever made Finch do it the first time has decided to come back and finish it himself."

"But why?"

Clarion looked at Kennedy, unable to hide his fatherly rage and disdain. "I can only assume he doesn't let go of a grudge very easily. So, I'm going to find the guy and make him understand."

It took Kennedy a minute to figure out what Clarion was saying. "What are you going to do?" He stuttered a few words, searching for a response, then smirked. "What? You going to put a hurt on him?"

Clarion dug his fingertips deep into his forehead and let the reality of the question sink in. With all that had gone on, he knew he would eventually confront his enemy, but hadn't really accepted what would be his end game. He was there to protect his family, that was all that mattered. Right now, he was on an emotional rollercoaster, rushing forward without much consideration as to the *how* part. He had already killed a man, albeit, in self-defense. In that situation, there wasn't time to decide on what to do, he just did it. This was pre-mediated, calculated.

When he actually found the bastard responsible for his daughter's kidnapping—who had now returned—how far was he willing to go? Clarion was confident he knew the right choice. He weighed Kennedy's question again, ground his teeth, and then relaxed his shoulders. "Yeah, Pete," he said. "When I find him, I'm going to kill him."

CHAPTER 18

PARIS STEPPED OUT OF THE CAR next to the one he left behind, two blocks down from where Soto had set up the original deal earlier that morning. After losing Shafter, Paris had Dools circle back toward King's Bakery, the last visual they had following the first half pound delivery of coke. The rest of the surveillance team rushed to other known locations but couldn't find either Shafter or the green Lexus.

"What about the stash house?" Paris asked the men still in the car.

"Got two agents heading that way now. Traffic's bad. Should have an answer soon."

Cell phone up to his ear, Langan leaned over to Dools, looking out the car window at Paris. "We ran the plate on the Cadillac. Comes back to a Mario and Esther Neufeldt out of Oakland."

"Well?"

"Don't kill the messenger," Langan said. "The only Mario Neufeldt we found is listed as eighty-six years old.

"Yeah," Dools quipped. "Not our guy."

"Have someone check with the state and locals," Paris said. "Check with the DEA too. See if anyone has anything on the address."

"And what about Mario Neufeldt himself?" Dools added, ever the smartass.

"Why don't you find where he was when Lincoln was assassinated?"

Dools mocked writing on an imaginary pad. "Lincoln—assassinated—got it."

"Get over to Kennedy's condo," Paris said to Dools. "Maybe we'll get lucky and see Shafter show up with Kennedy."

Paris unlocked his car and slid behind the wheel, mentally sorting out what he had: the drug buys, the identity of Shafter, and the stash house. For a drug case, he had plenty. In finding a missing girl, he had squat. It was time to kick this up a notch. The pen registers were up but the tech agents monitoring the equipment told Paris the phones had been off. Paris's started to vibrate. He looked at the screen and saw it was Harrington.

"Talk to me."

"I got the photograph of Michael Shafter scanned and it's coming shortly on your Blackberry."

"Thanks." Paris hung up and waited a moment before seeing the e-mail from Harrington. He pulled up the photo and squinted at the small screen. A black and white taken five years ago, but it was clear enough for Paris to see it was his guy. His cell vibrated again. Detective Calloway this time. He considered not answering, still angry over her lack of accountability. He forced himself to exhale a deep breath, muster the energy to remain calm, have an open mind. Maybe there was a reason she hadn't called.

"Where the hell have you been?"

So much for an open mind.

There was a moment of silence before Calloway spoke. "I'm sorry. Got tied up with an informant."

"You couldn't call us to let us know you weren't going to help today with *our case*?" Paris felt the sting of his own words. He hated saying things like *you couldn't call* or *where have you been?* The chastising felt eerily close to conversations with his estranged wife, Emily, when he was out late on surveillance or executing warrants. He felt his neck tighten, sparks firing through his veins and he couldn't find a way to put it in reverse.

"Look, I said I was sorry."

The line went silent. Then he heard Calloway sigh on the other end. "I screwed up, okay?"

Paris forced himself to stay calm, choke back the ferocity in his tone. "Yeah, okay. We got it handled." He caught her up on the buy and locating the stash house. Calloway quietly listened. "Problem is no one can seem to find Kennedy and his cell has been inactive."

"Kennedy may not be the guy we're looking for," she said.

"What do you mean?"

"I think there's someone above Kennedy's pay grade who was pulling all the strings."

"Is this from your informant?"

"Yep." Her voice was elevated and clearly conciliatory. "How about we find a quiet spot to talk?"

THIRTY MINUTES LATER, CALLOWAY PULLED UP on a side street under a row of eucalyptus trees, about quarter mile down from Kennedy's condo. The street sloped up a steep hill, allowing an ocean breeze to pulse through the area sweeping away fallen leaves. The detective got out of her car and tugged down her ball cap, shielding her eyes from the bright sun.

Paris had already arrived a few minutes prior. He got out of his car thinking it would be better to talk outside, where both would have the ability to give each other some distance.

"Hey," was all she said as she approached.

Paris forced himself to feign a smile. "Hey back." As comebacks go, it wasn't his best and he felt stupid saying it.

"So, this guy Shafter. You know anything about him?"

"Not yet, but he has a past drug arrest. DEA did him several years back."

Calloway hesitated, looked around before her eyes drifted toward the ground as he spoke.

"What?" he asked.

"I know who he is."

"And this is from your source?"

She nodded. "Uh-huh."

Paris knew Calloway wanted to make up for being AWOL, but until now she hadn't been too forthcoming. He didn't anticipate she'd surrender the identity of her source. He leaned against the car, crossed his arms and let her talk.

"This guy Shafter works for Ramone Santiago, an up-and-coming trafficker. From what my source says, he's a big player."

"Is he Kennedy's supplier?"

Calloway shook her head. "No. Santiago hasn't been in the area for long. Supposedly, he's angling for a foothold in the bay area, using hired guns to shake down the competition. Shafter is one of his muscles."

"How does your source know this?"

"He knows Shafter, did some work for him in the past."

She said he. "Does your source have a name?"

"He does."

"Look, Valerie, I'm trying to work with you here. It's mutually beneficial. We catch your drug dealer, we find my missing girl." *That's if she's still alive.* "But you have to give me something."

She was now looking directly at him. "He's not comfortable with others knowing who he is quite yet."

In the cop-world, sources were the lifeblood to survival, and their value increased proportionately to their involvement with the other side of the law. On the flip-side, the more people who knew their identity, the greater the chance they could end up as a chalk outline. Reluctantly—very reluctantly—Paris opted on giving her some time to gain his trust. But the time had to be short.

"What does he have to say about Santiago?"

"For starters, says he's been talking to Kennedy."

"What's their relationship?"

Calloway stared at her shoes again, contemplating what to say next. "He thinks Santiago is pretending to collaborate with Kennedy but in reality, he's going to make a move on Kennedy's territory."

For such a powerful figure in the drug world, it was odd Paris had never heard the name Santiago ever mentioned before. Dools had been working close with most of the dope agents and Santiago's name had never come up.

"So you're saying if Shafter is currently working for Ramone Santiago —"

"You may not be buying from Kennedy. You may be buying from Santiago."

There was a pause. "Then why are we chasing him?"

"*We're* not," Calloway said. "You are."

Paris pressed his lips together, tight, couldn't believe how caustic her few words could be. He uncrossed his arms and let his hands rest on the car behind him. "Maybe we go kick in Shafter's door, arrest him, and find out what he can do to help us find Kennedy."

Calloway bit down hard on her lower lip. She pulled out a pack, shook loose a cigarette, and lit it before finally responding. "You could, but you'd be taking a big risk," she said, as if she was drawing a line in the sand.

Uncomfortable seconds ticked by, each holding back from saying a word, part anger, part frustration.

Calloway pulled back, spoke in a conciliatory tone. "Look, arresting Shafter may get you Santiago but it won't get you Kennedy. And according to my source, Kennedy isn't your kidnapper. Doesn't have the balls to pull off such a bold statement. If anything, the order came from above him. You need Kennedy to find our target."

"What do you suggest we do?"

"Let me put a surveillance team back on Kennedy's condo. If we see him, we grab him up and shake it out of him. If he's as spineless as my source says he is, he'll fold."

Paris hated to think all their hard work so far had taken them in the wrong direction. Dools's suggestion to kick in all the doors—Kennedy's condo, the stash house, King's Bakery—started to sound like a good idea. See what they would find and who would be willing to cooperate. They had the evidence to lock them all up for a very long time. But was that a risk he was willing to take, to roll it all with Rachel Clarion's life on the line? The truth was, Paris was frustrated, tired and, with that combination, it was never the best time to pull the trigger on *any* move. Up to this point, it was about Kennedy. Now, according to Calloway's source, Paris needed to move up one more level. Without him—or her—Clarion's daughter would never be out of danger, worse, may never be found. As much as he felt like kicking in every door, Paris knew Calloway was right.

"Set it up," he said.

"Good," Calloway said, exhaling with relief. She took a step toward Paris and leaned in, close. "Let me go talk to my source," she said. "Give him orders to stay close to Shafter. If Santiago is talking to Kennedy, Shafter may be their conduit." Then she added, "Whatever he finds out, you'll know first."

Paris felt a brick of distrust fall from the wall he'd built.

"It won't take more than half an hour." She touched him on the arm with a nervous look, almost awkward as she uttered, "After, you want to meet for dinner?"

The offer took him by surprise.

"I could use the company," she confessed before clarifying her last remark, adding, "I mean, 'I'd *like* the company."

Paris remained guarded, holding back long enough to make sure he understood he heard her correctly. It was an invitation out of left field, but it sounded genuine and, deep down inside, it was appealing.

Calloway let go of a smile. In that moment, he welcomed the warmth. After all the hitches between the two, maybe—he was hoping—she was reaching out.

Paris returned the smile. "I'd like that. Pick a spot."

CHAPTER 19

THE SUN HAD ALREADY GONE BEHIND the building when Alexei Mogilevich saw the two surveillance cars drive away. He took a spin around the block to see if there were any replacements coming. Nothing. He parked his Cadillac down the street from the stash house and made his way to the front door. It was supposed to be locked, only accessible by the tenants. Instead he found the deadbolt broken and intercom smashed, not entirely uncommon in this neighborhood. Still, it gave him cause for concern. He pushed against the gate and into the dark vestibule. Mogilevich scanned down the hall and up the stairs, searching for movement. Looking for cops. He reached into his coat pocket and withdrew a key, rolling it in his hands, confirming it was the one given to him by his boss. He'd started up the staircase when he heard a door open on the lobby level, shaft of harsh light splitting the vestibule as the door sneaked open.

A little girl in pajamas peered out, her head and small body crowded into the gap as she stood on the threshold. Their television was on, rapid Spanish voices emanating from inside. The girl quietly watched Mogilevich as he crept three steps up. He gave the child a counterfeit smile and placed a finger to his lips before motioning her to go back inside the apartment. Without a word, she slowly closed the door, the sounds blasting inside muffled into muted tones.

Mogilevich continued up the stairs and moved to the door on his right. He waited a beat, listening closely for any sounds within. Inserting the key into the lock, he entered. It was the first time in the apartment so he was unfamiliar with the layout. He spied two pink boxes on the table, both opened, and, more importantly, both empty. As he made his way around, the hardwood floor creaked under his boots. That's when he heard the faint cries coming from the other room. Mogilevich pulled his pistol as he approached the closed door. More stifled noise, like grunting and heavy breathing under a canvas sack. He quickly turned the handle, shoved open the door and jammed the pistol forward, scanning for a target. On the floor to his right, Mogilevich saw the man in a long gray coat, duct tape across his mouth, hands secured to a large pipe. The man's groaning grew louder upon seeing Mogilevich. The man flailed, trying to break free from his constraints. Mogilevich lowered his weapon and ripped the tape from his mouth.

Corbin Everett gasped a huge gulp of air, his chest heaving in relief. "Holy shit. Thanks," he said, spitting tape debris from his tongue and lips.

"Where is it?" Mogilevich asked.

Everett's relief turned to caution, knowing exactly why Mogilevich had come to the apartment.

"A guy came in and took it."

Mogilevich loomed large with a clear look of disappointment on his face while the clock in the kitchen unhurriedly went tick, tick, tick. "Who was he?"

"No idea. But he's with Kennedy."

Mogilevich lapsed back into silence, assessing the response.

"Hey, partner," Everett pleaded. "Mind cutting me loose? These bindings are killing me."

"Who's dope did he take?"

Everett gave his rescuer a hard look. "Who are you?"

"You work for Santiago, right?"

Everett's voice became heated, borderline threatening as he thrashed around in his attempt to get free. "Look, it would be in your best interest to cut me loose."

Mogilevich stood up and reached back into his jacket pocket, extracting a long cylindrical tube. He screwed it onto the barrel of his pistol then pointed it at the aggravated man's forehead.

Everett pushed back against the wall, eyes now wide open, staring down the length of the suppressor. "Hold on there, partner. Don't need to do anything drastic." He looked to his right and pointed with his chin. "He didn't get it all. There's thirty more over there, hidden under the floorboard. Take it, it's yours. Just let me go."

Mogilevich turned and walked over to the designated spot, a gap revealing itself between slats in the hardwood floor. Pulling out a knife, he dug into the crack, easily lifting several pieces of flooring, exposing a hidden compartment with a number of white bricks wrapped in plastic and silver duct tape.

Mogilevich slowly let the sections fall back into place before returning to the man. "Tell me whose dope this is?"

"Kennedy. Pete Kennedy."

"Yeah, and who does Peter Kennedy get his dope from?"

Everett shook his head, his frustration now skyrocketing. "How the hell do I know?"

"Okay then. Thanks for the help." With that, Mogilevich pressed the pistol into the man's chest and squeezed the trigger, twice for good measure.

CHAPTER 20

T HE WAITER BROUGHT PARIS A BEER and Calloway a glass of white wine. He had arrived first at Marlowe's, south of Market Street, grabbing a small table near a window, a rarity to score this time of day. He had to face the door. It was a cop thing, out of habit. Calloway did exactly what she promised: she took only thirty minutes to meet with her source and was back within the hour.

The daily menu was prominently posted on butcher paper and hung next to the bar. Paris was still inspecting the menu when he noticed Calloway was staring out the window.

"I've never been here before," Paris said.

She broke into a breezy smile and he couldn't help but smile back. Calloway had changed her clothes, now wearing a light-colored dress with a gray cashmere sweater—a look much different than what Paris was used to seeing her in. For the first time, her eyes projected calmness, a lack of distraction.

The hard edge of the woman detective was momentarily gone. No barriers or defensiveness. As if she was able to walk away from the job and be nothing more than a person, faults and all.

They continued to study the menu, giving them something to do.

"I come here a lot," Calloway said, opening the conversation. "The food's always good and the people leave you alone." She raised a finger off the table and waved it from side to side. "Not a pick-up joint."

"Good to know."

They kept the conversation light, conscious not to say something that would start an argument. As they spoke, Paris couldn't keep from smiling, finding comfort in hearing her voice, calm and warm, all the while, scratching at the corners of the beer's label, slowly tearing a length of it from the bottle. Another one of his habits, just something he did. Not thinking about it, he pushed the small fragments together, creating a tiny mountain. The more beer, the bigger the mountain. Calloway studied the growing pile but decided to ignore it.

As nice as it felt to have a relaxing conversation with Calloway, in the back of his mind, Paris was interested to hear about the meeting with her informant. There were a few times the opportunity opened up but he couldn't bring himself to broach the topic. At that moment, the room felt warm, comforting with Calloway in it and he didn't want to step out into the harsh world of reality. Right now, she just looked beautiful.

"You like coming to the city?"

Calloway nodded as she sampled the wine from her glass "My mom lives here . . ."

There was hesitation in her voice, a sudden look of vulnerability in her face as if she had second thoughts about what she revealed.

Paris decided to nudge the conversation forward anyway. "Did you live here in San Francisco with your mother before coming to Sacramento?"

Calloway lifted her glass again, sipping her wine, searching for a way to stall. She patted her lips with her napkin. "I did."

Paris kept quiet, hoping Calloway would continue. She was opening up but he could sense her apprehension. She was no different than any other cop. She had a past, a life before joining the PD. Old friends. From Paris's perspective, he could tell a part of her wanted—or needed—to talk about anything other than work. She just couldn't find a way. Calloway was a person imprisoned in an invisible coat of armor and Paris wanted to know what, or who, put it there. Far from just being an introvert, she never built close friendships, in or out of the department, at least as far as he could tell.

"I don't want to pry into your private life, Val. I just want to get to know you better. I wouldn't mind being a friend."

She forced a half-smile. "That would be nice."

The waiter appeared beside her. "Good to see you tonight, Ms. Calloway. The usual?"

Calloway's eyes softened as she smiled with a look of familiarity. Obviously she was well known to the staff. "Yes, thank you, Jess."

Jess, the waiter, glanced at Paris curiously then down at his mountainous shreds of label.

"Nervous habit?" Calloway asked.

"Sorry. I'll have whatever she's having," Paris said, taking the attention off his litter on the pristine white tablecloth. He had no idea what she ordered but gambled on her knowing what was best.

The waiter refilled their water glasses, scraped away the trash from the table, and brought their orders to the kitchen.

"My mother is in a home here," Calloway said. "She hasn't been doing well for some time and she needs constant care."

"That must be hard on you."

Calloway swallowed and turned away.

"How often do you get to see her?"

"As often as I can get up here . . ." She found her wine glass and this time managed a longer taste. "She gets good care and, honestly, half the time I visit, she doesn't even know who I am . . ."

Calloway's voice trailed off at the end of each sentence, sounding as if there was a great deal of guilt pent up inside her. Conversations regarding family problems are difficult for anyone, even during the best of times. From what Paris knew about Calloway, this must had been excruciating.

"Do you have any family members who can help?"

Calloway's expression turned more pensive before she managed a weak grin, which Paris interpreted as appreciation that he cared. "No, there's only me."

"If you ever need anything—" Paris lifted his hands off the table in a gesture of openness but not trying to sound intrusive. "Something I can do—"

Calloway's eyes relaxed. This time, she didn't have to force a smile.

A short while later, two waiters arrived with their meals along with a bottle of *Domaine Coillot,* a beautiful Pinot Noir.

"Poulet Vert with broccolini, roasted baby carrots, and marble potatoes," waiter Jess said, introducing the fare. Calloway nodded appreciatively to both waiters. Jess pulled the cork from the Pinot, gave it a moment to breathe, and poured each a generous glass, before departing. Calloway leaned forward and in a quiet voice, said, "It's chicken."

"Yeah, I got that," Paris said. "Semester of High School French."

"*Tres bien,*" she said, followed by a soft laugh.

Time passed with more light conversation and more laughs.

When their glasses were empty, he poured more wine. Each time, Calloway grinned appreciatively. And when she did, Paris couldn't help but see how striking she looked. Simple and open. Vulnerable. Dools was wrong about her. She wasn't cold and distant. She just needed someone worth sharing time with.

The crowd was starting to thin as it neared eleven p.m., closing time. Calloway didn't seem concerned, assuming she was probably given special privileges beyond the average patron.

"My source is out looking for Kennedy," she offered up.

Paris was guarded about taking the conversation back to work but was glad it was her who did it. His first inclination was to ask for her source's true identity but he caught himself, reconsidered. Instead, he just replied, "Good."

The waiter returned, cleared their plates, and poured the last of the wine into Calloway's glass. Another employee turned the *Closed* sign over the front door. Paris checked with Calloway, who was now sitting quietly, eyes distant, lost in thought. Though looking calm and relaxed, it was obvious the day's stress had left her tired.

"We've got a long drive back," Paris said. "You could use some rest. Let me drive you home."

Calloway shook her head, finishing off the rest of her wine. "I appreciate the offer but my mother still has a place here. I planned on spending the night."

She confessed her mother never wanted to let the place go, part of their agreement when she moved her into the assisted living facility. Her mother was adamant that, when she got better, she would move back into the home. Calloway admitted that was three years ago.

"It's still best to keep the place," Calloway said. "Just in case."

The apartment was in the Marina District. Calloway had taken a cab over from her mother's. Paris offered to drive her back, noticing with each passing minute, her eyes would remain closed for a tick longer. She accepted. There was a short-lived debate over who would pay for dinner, with Paris overruling any of Calloway's arguments. Afterward, the two walked down the street to his car. Within fifteen minutes, they were in front of her building.

"You look exhausted," Calloway remarked.

"I'll be fine," he replied.

Calloway paused and shook her head, knowing better. "Come on up and I'll make you coffee. It'll keep you awake for the drive home."

He glanced at his watch, feeling the fatigue getting the better of him, and agreed.

THE TWO-BEDROOM APARTMENT rested on the third floor of a renovated building. Like most flats in the Marina, the walls were white with fixtures dating back to the 'fifties, and the hardwood floors creaked under every step. Calloway flipped on the light switch, hooked her jacket on the rack in the hallway and walked into the kitchen. Paris watched as she slid off her service weapon and placed it on the countertop, then he stepped into the living room and looked around. The place was neatly decorated with framed photos and comfortable furniture. From where he stood, Paris could hear Calloway preparing the coffee.

"Be ready in a few minutes," she called out. "Blue Bottle. It's my favorite."

A moment later, Calloway appeared, clicking on music, adjusting the volume before sitting down on the couch. Across the way, a finely crafted wood cabinet with glass doors containing many artifacts, organic objects, and sentimental pieces, bathed in the low light emanating from within. The cabinet was familiar to Paris. His grandmother on his father's side had a similar one. An antique. Standing beside the exquisite piece, he gazed at the items displayed on each shelf: seashells of all shapes, brightly colored butterflies, the skeleton of a small animal, some red coral, old books and unique clocks. And insects. A whole assortment of them had found their final resting place inside chunks of resin. Paris lingered on the Praying Mantis trapped forever in his last pose. As interesting as they were to observe, they each had their own story.

"Cabinet of curiosities," Calloway explained. "The curio is my mother's. She loved finding interesting pieces to add. Porcelain figurines to ancient rock formations."

Paris gave the display a closer look. The showpieces were remarkable. His eyes fell on the tiny figures gazing back at him, each delicately crafted. Calloway watched Paris from across the room as he studied the mixture of natural and man-made objects before her attention drifted out the window.

Brilliant, honey-colored squares of light glowed from apartments across the street, warm, inviting. She pointed at the windows, not any one in particular. "Funny how they return each night to their safe homes, not knowing if a neighbor right next door could be in the throes of a crisis." After a brief moment of silence, she added, "I can only imagine what the Clarions are going through." Her last words sounding more like an open thought to herself, she continued, speaking without wanting to evoke a conversation. "We're asked to work around the clock to solve their problems and keep them safe. I guess it doesn't really matter. We're not supposed to have a life of our own."

"It doesn't have to be that way," he said.

She stood, took a few steps closer, and sat on the arm of the couch. "Where would you be," Calloway asked, "if you hadn't gotten into the FBI?"

He stifled a laugh. "Probably in jail."

Calloway held back a smirk and pointed at the items in the cabinet. "That's us. That's who we are. In that cabinet of curiosities." She shook a finger at Paris. "Eventually to be replaced when we're no longer interesting."

Paris looked back into the curio.

"You're wearing a wedding ring." Calloway interjected, her tone sounding apprehensive but curious.

The remark caught Paris off guard. He looked down at this hand, rolled the gold band around with his thumb and index finger a few times.

"Separated," he answered.

Tilting the conversation toward Paris's personal life brought on a feeling of uneasiness, an ache one feels when confronted with being vulnerable. But if he wanted Calloway to open up, he knew he'd have to do the same.

"What we do for a living isn't for everyone." The admission wasn't easy to make. "It wasn't her fault."

Calloway nodded like she understood.

"How about you?"

Arms folded, she rested a hand under her chin, fingers nervously touching her lips, like she was feeling them for the first time. Calloway looked back toward the window. "I made a promise long ago and it doesn't give me much time for a personal life."

"We all need balance in our lives." Paris said, knowing there was hypocrisy in his reply.

"Guys don't want to be with a woman cop. At least not forever." Her words sounded wistful as if to suggest her assertion was as predictably defined as the theory of gravity.

Paris knew what she meant. Man, woman, didn't matter. The lifestyle was taxing on anyone. In the end, no one wanted to be second. The late nights alone, darkness being their only companion, like an unwanted guest living in their house. Without you. Because the job always came first. He was bored with dating, even dreaded it. His dates liked the stories about cases. The intrigue. They grew excited, the voyeuristic thrill, and they had an undisguised urge to know.

But the reality of living in an agent's life, day in and day out, was much different. They were nothing more than conversations of curiosity. Calloway was right. *We are the curiosity pieces.* Like those in the curio.

Lost for a minute behind those panes of glass, Paris suddenly sensed Calloway's presence. She had crossed the room and made her way beside him. When he turned toward her, there was no hesitation. Her body filled the empty space between them and he felt her arms slowly encircle his waist. She kissed him softly on the neck, twice, and then remained there. Paris was caught in a moment of indecision, but without thought, drew her closer in his embrace.

His hands slid down, aware of every curve and finding a place at the small of her back. Pulling slightly away, she looked at him and paused. Was this what they wanted? Didn't they deserve this? The answer was there. She moved her hands until they were flat against his chest and she gently pressed him against the wall. Her beautiful mouth was on his. Paris responded, holding her tight and returning her kiss. Then, it was his desire, his choosing. He spun them both around, touching, pressing hard, this time bruising her lips with his, moving his kiss down her collarbone, something he so admired before.

"Few understand who we are," she said in a hushed voice, and then, "I know, you do."

Her head relaxed deep into his shoulder. Her words were careful, whispered, but sure in their intent. "It's just for tonight," she said unbuttoning his shirt. "That's all. Understand."

Paris heard himself repeat, "Just tonight."

Calloway's hand trailed down his arm and fell away as she walked to her bedroom, disappearing out of sight. A light came on, bathing walls in a golden hue. Then he heard her voice. "Are you coming?"

Paris closed his eyes, a debate raging in his mind.

Are you sure this the right thing to do?

There were a number of logical arguments why he should walk away but at that moment, every one of them came out jumbled, incoherent, as if spoken in a foreign language. Rational thought and reasoning went out the window, discarded and drifting away into the night, like tiny pieces of burning paper carried on the wind. Paris was tired and running on emotions. Tonight, he wanted her. He needed her. In the background, Paris heard the music coming from Calloway's stereo. Ella Fitzgerald singing,

"The Nearness of You." It was as if the volume had turned up on its own to get his attention.

"I need no soft lights to enchant me,
If you'll only grant me the right,
To hold you ever so tight,
And to feel in the night, the nearness of you."

He opened his eyes, tried unsuccessfully to hold back a grin. He walked over to the kitchen counter, slid off his holster and weapon and, placed them next to hers. He turned back toward the open bedroom door and relaxed against the counter. "What about the coffee?"

Paris saw Calloway appear into view, her naked body slipping under the bed sheets, the light dress and gray sweater now intertwined and looking lonely on the bedroom floor.

"You won't need it," she replied.

CHAPTER 21

Pete Kennedy nursed the contusion on his lower lip with a towel packed with ice. The cold stung each time he moved the icepack but anything felt better than being bound and smacked around by a bunch of thugs. He kept an eye on Robert Clarion, who was rocking on the back two legs of a chair, pistol in hand, remaining silent.

Kennedy was sitting on the corner of the hotel room bed, the curtains drawn shut and the TV turned on to the evening news.

"Thanks for rescuing me," Kennedy again said, obviously stoking the conversation to figure out what Clarion was planning next.

Clarion tapped the barrel of his pistol along the side of his thigh. "What makes you think I rescued you?"

Kennedy forced a nervous laugh. "What do you want from me?"

Without warning, the two front legs of the chair hit the floor and Clarion lurched forward, the barrel of his pistol gravitating in the direction of Kennedy's chest. Even though the carpeting suppressed the hard thump of the front legs, it startled Kennedy.

"The guy you're getting your drugs from is the guy who was supplying Finch and I want to know who he is."

Kennedy shook his head and dropped the ice-filled cloth. "Shit, Rob . . ." His voice trailed off. "Can I call you Rob?" He said it like they were becoming best friends.

Clarion's face tightened.

"I told you, I don't know the guy. He drops off the product, I give him the money. That's it."

"What's his name, *Pete?*" Clarion said, putting a heavy emphasis on his name, like a poke with a sharp knife, to underscore their relationship. Simply put: they were not friends. At best, they were involuntary conspirators drawn together by a common enemy.

Kennedy hesitated, unsure if he gave up what he knew, his new *friend* would let him see tomorrow's sunrise. "I only know him as Manoso."

Clarion had a slight grasp on the Spanish language, enough to know what the word meant: *Slick.*

"How do you get a hold of Manoso?"

"How else?" Kennedy shot back. "I call him."

"It's time to call him and put in another order."

Kennedy backed off. "No can do, boss—"

Before Kennedy could finish speaking, Clarion smacked him across the head with the butt of his pistol. Not hard but enough to get his attention. Kennedy dropped to the ground, clutching his head and curling his body into the fetal position.

"You must have misunderstood me," Clarion spat. "I wasn't asking."

"Fuck, you don't understand," Kennedy screamed. "I can't because he won't talk to me anymore. I owe him for the twenty Ramone Santiago stole. I guarantee you—Manoso probably thinks I ripped him off. If anything, he's looking to kill me."

Clarion jerked Kennedy up from the floor and sat him back on the bed. "Then make him understand you didn't, you're sorry for not calling sooner, and that you have his money."

Kennedy stopped rubbing his sore head and gave Clarion the look of a lost dog. "How the fuck do you think I'm going to be able to come up with three hundred large when his henchman comes to collect?"

Clarion lowered his voice, calm and methodical: "You're going to tell him if he wants his money, he's going to have to come get it himself."

"You're fucking crazy."

Clarion felt his anger well up, his free hand tightening into a fist. Kennedy sensed it and recoiled.

The two sat in a tense stare, not in a stalemate because Clarion was going to get his way, no matter what, but each wondering how they were going to make the best of this situation. For Clarion, it was luring his kidnapper—now known to him only as Manoso— out in the open and getting his daughter back. For Kennedy, he needed to rid himself of his debt—and keep his skin in the process. That was going to be a tough double-bill.

"So how do you want to play this out?" Clarion waved the gun again but the barrel stayed on Kennedy. "You want to take your chances with me or do you think you can convince Manoso to give you a second chance?"

"What are you going to do to me?" Kennedy had a suspicion he knew what he was about to hear—but had to ask.

Clarion thumbed back the hammer on the Walther PPK. "A threat to my family doesn't go without me accepting extreme options."

Kennedy forced himself to look up at Clarion. He knew exactly what the man was saying. He closed his eyes, took in a deep breath, and accepted his fate. "Let me see if I can get him to meet. I can't guarantee he's going to want to talk to me."

"Right now, it's your only option."

Kennedy stood in front of Clarion and held out his hand. "Give me your phone."

CHAPTER 22

PARIS WAS ON INTERSTATE 80, heading back to Sacramento, talking to Dools on his cellphone and trying to get an update on Shafter and his associates. Dools knew Paris had spent the night in San Francisco and he wasn't alone. Between questions about the case, Dools kept shifting the conversation back to *why* Paris had felt the need to stay overnight, and, possibly, with whom he'd spent it with.

"I was tired," Paris said.

"I'm sure you were," Dools said. "Did you get Frank's approval to charge off your hotel room?" It was a given fact: Paris would never ask Frank Porter, their supervisor, for approval. The unspoken Bureau motto: *charge first, find out how to pay later.* Dools was digging for dirt, and Paris wasn't going to give him the shovel.

"Yep."

"Where did you stay?"

"Christ's sake, Dools. Just tell me what you've learned about Shafter."

A deep raspy breath came over the line, followed by a sigh of resignation. The subject of his love life was far from over. Dools would bring it back up upon his arrival. The noise of papers shuffled over the phone droned on for a few seconds. Before the courts opened, Dools had prepared a pen register affidavit on Shafter's cellphones. The order also requested tracking. With this court authorization, Paris and his team would be able to monitor the movements of Shafter and Kennedy, with the hopes this would lead them straight to the supplier, the man that may have taken Rachel Clarion.

"Pole cam at Kennedy's condo hasn't kicked up much so we are placing one at the stash house. There's a power transformer next to the residence. Problem is, could be a couple of days."

Old cities offered great opportunities for law enforcement to mount cameras on power and telephone poles without being noticed. The Bureau's tech squad, under the cover of a utility truck or telephone repair company, would be dispatched to install the CCTV, with the signal being piped back to the field office in San Francisco. But like everything bureaucratic about the government, these things took time.

Paris interrupted Dools. "I've got one more request."

"What?"

"Get a pen and tracking order on Clarion's cellphone."

Dools chuckled. "Done that already."

Smart move on Dools's part. He told Paris that, for the past two days, he had been placing calls to Robert Clarion at the request of Barbara Clarion. She wanted to make sure the FBI was at the front of Clarion's mind. Each call rang for a while before going to voicemail. This told Dools that Clarion was screening his calls. Whether he answered the phone or not, it allowed Dools to triangulate Clarion's whereabouts.

"See who he's talking to," Paris said.

"You suspect something?"

Paris looked up in his review mirror and saw Calloway following close behind, his mind drifting to their night together. He thought about something she said, about the demands by those needing help. How a parent would react under the same circumstance, like Clarion. Paris knew the answer.

"Just let me know who he's been talking to and where he's been. More importantly, where he is now."

Dools said he would get right on it and would have an analysis by the time Paris got back to Sacramento.

"So, you gonna tell me where you spent your evening?"

Paris rocked his head forward, knowing Dools wasn't going to let go. "Not really."

"Suit yourself," Dools replied. "Just remember who your friends are."

"What's that supposed to mean?"

"Means we're the ones that pick you up and put you back together when things turn to shit."

"I appreciate your concern, Dools."

"Yeah, I hear what you're saying. You're telling me to fuck off."
Paris smiled then hung up the phone.

DOOLS HAD SPREAD OUT PAGES of phone records he had pulled from the pen registers for he and Paris to review. Standing over ream of printouts, Paris studied the call times, marrying them up to their location.

"Where's Calloway?" Dools asked.

Paris kept his concentration on the documents when he responded. "Had to meet with her source."

Dools sat there with a quizzical look, neck veins bulging out his starch white collar as if his tie was cinched too tight.

Paris refused to take the bait and give him an excuse for more interrogation. He continued to pore through the records. One thing stood out: Clarion's whereabouts. San Francisco. "Look at this, Dools," he said as he pulled a report from a second stack. It was the pen register information on Kennedy's phone.

"A common number between Clarion and Kennedy at the same time we were making our purchase."

Dools took the report from Paris and checked it against his list of the known cell numbers of drug dealers.

"We have a winner," Dools said. "Belongs to a guy by the name of Roy Torrington. That number started coming up on Clarion's two days ago."

"Right after Rachel Clarion came up missing."

Whoever this guy Roy Torrington was to Clarion, he must have been important for Clarion to make the connection with Kennedy. With Kennedy's phone off, Paris couldn't get the data to his whereabouts, but he didn't need it.

He had Clarion's number now. If Clarion were to meet with Kennedy, Paris would be one step closer to finding the supplier, finding Rachel. The question was: If Clarion got there first, what was he planning on doing once he found him? It was a question Paris already knew the answer to.

"What's the status on Clarion's phone?"

"Was on earlier but off now."

That meant, at this time, Clarion couldn't be found.

"The same with Kennedy's," Dools added.

"Give me the last place Clarion's phone was used. We'll start there."

"Got it." Dools sat in an open chair, rocking back and forth, finger tapping beneath his lip. "You think he's going after the same guy we are?"

Paris nodded. "I wouldn't put it past him. Why trust us when he could take care of the problem himself?"

"You mean kill him," Dools said, articulating what they both had been thinking.

A father himself, Paris looked straight at his partner. "If I were him, I would."

CHAPTER 23

S PEECHLESS, BARBARA CLARION STUDIED the black and white DL photo of Michael Shafter that had popped up on her cellphone. Paris had texted the picture, which was the fastest way for her to get it. After sending, Paris gave her a minute before calling back. She had a hard time looking at the screen, as if her cell was suddenly radioactive. But she studied the image, hard, making sure when Paris called back, she would be able to envision every detail. Paris kept quiet on the other end, waiting for her to say something. Anything.

"You recognize him?" he asked.

There was a long pause, as if Barbara wanted to say something positive, anything that might help Special Agent Paris move the case forward, find her daughter. She had studied the image from every angle, hoping she would have a revelation. But it didn't come. The face wasn't familiar.

"I'm sorry, Agent Paris."

Paris said he understood that it was a shot in the dark but had to ask. He reassured Barbara they were working on the case and making progress, but he didn't give specifics. He asked how she was holding up and if she had heard anything from her daughter. Barbara said she had not a word and with each passing day, her thoughts reaffirmed something horrible has happened.

"Where is your husband, Barbara?"

It was a question she was hoping to avoid. Barbara hesitated, then offered a flimsy excuse, something about Robert being on a job. She could tell Agent Paris knew she was lying.

"I'm trying to help you, Barbara, help you find Rachel. I can't do that if you're holding back."

"I know."

Paris's voice hardened when he asked, "Who is Roy Torrington?"

Barbara closed her eyes. Another question she feared would eventually come up. In her mind, it only meant one thing: Robert was going after the drug supplier, the one who ordered Finch to take Rachel. And Barbara knew, when he was found, what he was going to do to him. Staying on the phone, she hurried into Robert's office. On a shelf sat an antique cigar box. She lifted the lid, where he kept the spare key to his desk. She never told him she knew.

Opening the top left-hand drawer, she sifted through the same papers Robert had two days prior. But like her husband, it wasn't the papers she cared about. The gun was gone.

She feared Agent Paris could hear her heart pounding through the telephone.

"I know Robert's been talking with him," Paris said. "I know their history."

"What do you want to know?" she asked.

"I want to know where he is," he replied, this time, his voice resonating with the authority he commanded.

She held quiet, not knowing what to do. Who would she help, who would she betray?

"We both know what he is going to do," Paris said. "If he gets to him before I do, I can't guarantee he's going to survive. These men are dangerous."

Barbara's eyes started to well up and her hands began to shake. She promised Robert she would give him a couple of days, a gesture that said she trusted him to do the right thing. Now she was faced with a missing gun, fueling uncertainty of how far he was willing to go. She knew stopping him might mean they would never find their daughter. But allowing him to go forward could cost him his life. "Let me call him."

"We've tried. His phone has been off for some time."

"Please," she said. "Let me try. Let me find him and see what I can do. I will let you know where he is. I promise."

Paris acquiesced to Barbara's request. He had no other choice. "Find him, Barbara," he said. "Otherwise, I have a feeling things could turn out ugly."

Hanging up the phone, she felt alone and powerless. Although she'd gotten what she wanted, Barbara had no idea how to make it happen. Her impetuous promise was going to rely heavily on luck.

The doorbell rang, jolting Barbara from her daze, her cup of hot tea took a hop, splashing onto her freshly washed tablecloth. Before she could make her way to the front of the house, she heard something being shoved under the door, indistinct voices in the background, a clamoring and something banging against the wall. Barbara's heart picked up speed.

Running down the hallway and into the foyer, she caught sight of an envelope halfway under the door. Then there was the sound of a car door slam, an engine roar, and the screech of tires as it quickly vanished into the distance. She pulled on the envelope, held it tight in her hands. Slowly, she opened the door, looked out, hoping to see Rachel standing there, a possibility she knew only to be a fantasy. The front entry was void of anyone. But on the ground at the foot of the entry was a lone shoe. She recognized it as belonging to Rachel. Her breath stuck high in her chest, airless and suffocating. She picked up the shoe and squeezed it tight in her hands. Then she remembered she had the envelope. Barbara opened it, pulling out the one page note, written in block letters. The words spilled from her lips, spoken only to herself as if she needed to hear them aloud.

We have your daughter. The cost has doubled.

Her fear of something bad was confirmed. "Rachel," she whispered.

Barbara barely made it back in the doorway, finding the stair's railing as her only brace. She struggled to keep her balance, ending up sitting on the bottom step. After all this time, all these years, she'd believed their past lives were behind them.

Agent Dooley told them so. But now she knew it was only a cruel dream. The darkness of their reality was waiting for them just around the corner. It was given to Barbara in the form of a note. A confirmation no mother should ever receive. Trembling and lost in disbelief, she fell to her knees and howled a cry that could wake the dead.

CHAPTER 24

PARIS SPOTTED CALLOWAY STANDING next to her car with the driver's side door open. Earlier, he had changed out his surveillance car for his Crown Vic. He pulled the larger vehicle to the side of the street, across from a small park located in downtown Sacramento, an area known as the Fab Forties, so named because the homes were located along the Forties block of streets.

Mansion-sized homes, many built during the Great Depression, had been refurbished, the streets lined in hundred-year-old deodar cedar trees, established, thick and tall, like soldiers at address, shading the wide streets and expansive neighborhood.

The evening had started to cool, the air smelling of dark mulch and withering leaves. Calloway pulled off her sunglasses and watched as Paris moved closer. From a distance, her eyes appeared to be looking through him. Her mood was dark, sharing nothing. It made him worry. They'd spent a night together, which was the extent of their intimacy, and he was wondering if she might think it was a mistake. Worse, that maybe it meant nothing to her.

But that night meant something to him. It was more than he had felt with someone in a long time. Seeing her revert back to cold and removed made his chest tighten.

As he approached, a slight smile formed on her lips, and his uncomfortable feeling slowly began to dissipate. By the time he made it to her car, the two stood less than a foot apart. Dipping her head down, she nudged a chunk of asphalt with her shoe. He reached out and gently touched her on the shoulder. She didn't pull away but he felt her flinch. Paris didn't want to make this awkward so he took a step back and eased into the conversation.

"What's the latest from your informant?" he asked as he leaned against the side of her car waiting for her response.

She shoved her cellphone in her handbag. "He's having problems getting Shafter but he's got something better."

"Tell me."

"Thinks he might have a bead on Kennedy."

Paris stood straight, waiting for more.

"Thinks he'll be able to get us to Kennedy's supplier soon."

Paris contemplated this new information, feeling skeptical but wanting to be optimistic. So far, her source had not been all that productive and, with each passing day, their evidence from the drug-buy was going stale and losing its value. Either her source was stringing Calloway on, or Calloway was holding back. He didn't like either option.

He turned toward Calloway and suddenly realized she was only inches from him. Her shoulder brushed gently against his, her familiar fragrance reminding him of their night together. Unlike her initial reaction, he didn't flinch. And he didn't pull away.

He took a deep breath and forced himself to focus on the case. "Why not stick to the original options? Since we don't have either Shafter or Kennedy in pocket, we get an arrest warrant for Shafter, kick in all the doors—Kennedy's, the stash house, King's Bakery—shake it up and see what falls out of the interrogations."

Calloway folded her arms across her body and looked like she was considering the option but Paris could see, she didn't like the idea. "You're only strong on Shafter, a convicted felon. His last stint in prison didn't seem to deter him from getting back in the drug business. Warrants on the addresses may get us others, but what if they don't talk?" Calloway made a fist with one hand, tapping the palm of the other, her frustration coming through like the first shock of an earthquake. "If our primary target is as bad as we think, no one's going to dime him out. But now, he'll know we're after him. I lose my kingpin and you'll never find your girl."

The consequences were severe, and Paris couldn't argue with what she was saying.

Calloway stepped away from the car, turned, and faced Paris to get his full attention. She placed both hands on his arms and looked into his eyes. "Give my guy another day or two. He'll find Kennedy, I have no doubt, but if he can't, I'll go along with getting the warrants and kicking in the doors."

They were both quiet, uneasiness gone, feeling the comfort of each other's presence. Less than a week ago, Paris knew Calloway only as a cop, one who liked being alone, who didn't share. That was from Dools's perspective.

But Calloway was nothing like that. She was far more complex, someone that he hadn't even begun to understand. Except that she was just like him. Both with few allowed into their lives. Maybe now, things could be different.

"That works," he said, agreeing to her proposal.

Calloway took a step back.

"Dools is tracking Kennedy's and Clarion's phones," he said. "Let's see who gets to them first."

"Why Clarion?"

Paris told her what he had learned, what he suspected. "He's going after the supplier and get his daughter back—his way."

Calloway nodded. "I'll stay on top of the information with Dools. I've got historical information that may help understand who's talking to whom."

Paris scratched at the stubble along his jaw. "We can head over to the office and look over what we have. Maybe the pen registers will give us a few new leads." He looked up and saw the sun drifting below the roofline of the houses across the street, bright shafts of light bleeding through the thick branches of the surrounding oaks. It was getting late. Neither one of them had eaten all day. "We can get dinner after," he offered.

Calloway hesitated, hands nervously manipulating a ring of keys. "I can't, tonight."

Paris wondered if he had misinterpreted things so he pretended to act indifferent to her reply. "Okay, that's fine."

"I have to go see my mom."

"Is she okay?"

Calloway managed a slight smile but it was clear she was visibly upset. "She's fine," she said, an obvious lie. "The nurse who cares for her called. My mother's been asking for me, which is becoming more infrequent. I need to catch her when she remembers who I am, while she still can."

Paris listened. At first, it was hard to hear her speak of her mother's failing health. Previously, they had scratched the surface of their personal lives. But now, she was opening up, giving Paris an intimate view that he was drawn into. Like a cloudburst, her words poured out. Calloway sounded as if she had been holding back her emotions for a long time. She shared the pain of losing her mother to Alzheimer's, little by little, of lost memories and the inevitability of what was to come. It was only a matter of time. It wasn't all that different when Paris lost his mother.

"Let me take you," Paris said.

The offer caught Calloway off guard. Her response came out haltingly. "I can't ask you to do that."

He anticipated her reaction and put up a comforting hand. "You're not asking, I am. I want to."

"It's a long drive back to San Francisco."

His hands softly reached out to her. "It's fine."

She fell silent, calculating the significance and complications swirling around in her brain. At last, she agreed, although Paris couldn't tell if her acceptance was one of gratitude or surrender.

While she was locking up her car, Paris texted Dools to let him know he would be out of the area for a while. He didn't say why, adding a request to gather everything he had on Clarion and Kennedy for Calloway's review and added he would call later. Then he turned his phone off.

They took his car. Calloway gave directions as Paris weaved through patches of freeway congestion. The drive was quiet, a jazz station playing soft and low in the background. Paris knew how difficult this must be for Calloway, slowly losing her mother this way. There was no need to invade her space with small talk. Headlights illuminated the interior of the car offering vignettes of Calloway's restlessness. Paris studied Calloway in their moment of silence. He knew she could take care of herself, had always done so. Even with her frailties and insecurities, she possessed a strength and resilience that kept her afloat. She was a force onto herself. Until she wasn't. Independence was never free, and trouble would eventually find her. And when it did, Paris wanted to be the one to comfort her, make her feel safe. Everyone needed that in their darkest moments. He wanted her to trust him. He glanced over, seeing her leaning her head against the window. Her eyes were closed but tension pulsed through her temples. He reached over and placed a soothing hand on her leg, to reassure her that everything would be okay. Before he could draw it back, Calloway reached over and placed her hand over his, squeezing it tight, as if wanting to feel his presence. It felt good being there, that moment, with her. He felt Calloway's arm relax.

An hour and twenty minutes later, Paris turned into a small parking lot in South San Francisco. A squat brick building sat between two dark alleyways. Scattered squares of yellow fluorescents checkered different floors, the brightest light emanating from the ground-level sign marked "Entrance." The entire structure was a series of impersonal right angles, dull, prefab. For a place that cared for the dying, the facility felt cold and indifferent.

Faded interior light filtered out a side window on the lower floor, the weak glow slipping through thin slits between the blinds. Paris pulled into a space near the circular driveway, and parked. Other than a few employee vehicles positioned in a dark section away from the building, the rest of the lot was empty. He killed car and the two sat for a minute, the only sound coming from the tick of a hot engine starting to cool.

"Are you ready to do this?" he asked.

Calloway didn't move, seeming to gather her courage before hesitantly nodding. "Yeah."

When they entered the facility, the world became bright white from ceiling to floor. The telltale smell of hospital hit him: urine, bleach, the hint of life flitting away. A nurse stood at the entry desk, peering over a pair reading glasses, following data on a computer monitor. Another nurse appeared from a side door, holding a clipboard in one hand and a specimen cup filled with piss in the other. Calloway moved ahead of Paris. She knew where she was going, down a long hallway and to the right, to a bank of elevators and up to the third floor.

She closed her eyes and rubbed her temples with both hands. She didn't look over at Paris when she started to speak. "She may not recognize me and she won't know who you are. Even if I tell her."

"Understood."

"If she asks, say you're a friend. It's easier."

"Got it," Paris said, careful to sound understanding.

The elevator doors opened and Calloway led them down another hallway. Televisions cross-talking, the occasional cough, lonely eyes staring, and glimpses of a world devoid of privacy. They stopped at an open door marked three-oh-five.

The room was small. A single window overlooked the parking lot and distant bank of street lamps. Family pictures and trinkets were scattered around the room, the walls blank, nothing permanently affixed, nothing to make the place hers.

A Hispanic woman, or maybe Caribbean, sat in a chair beside

Calloway's mother, who was asleep. The nurse had a black and white nametag. Selma.

She glanced up at Calloway without a smile, clearly taking note of the time before returning an icy stare. Selma stood and closed the distance, stopping Calloway before she could get to the side of her mother's bed.

"She just fell asleep. Been asking for you for the past five hours."

Calloway's eyes met the nurse's admonishing scowl. Lines ostensibly etching deeper into her skin, judgment discernable, floating, penalizing. Selma huffed a deep breath and eventually her eyes softened.

"I'm sorry," Calloway said, her voice barely above a whisper. "Work."

Selma nodded, signaling forgiveness but not completely forgiving. "That's all right, Miss Valerie."

Calloway came to the bed and held her mother's hand. "How is she?"

Selma shrugged. "Each day, she's awake less, forgetting more."

Calloway cringed, squeezing her mother's hand a little tighter.

"I'll let you have some time alone with her." Selma gave Paris an inquisitive stare before exiting the room. Following her lead, Paris trailed behind. The nurse was a few feet ahead of him, down the hallway, when Paris called after her.

"How long has she been here?"

Selma stopped and spun around to face Paris, conviction being her axis. She looked him over, considering whether she should answer his question.

"I'm a friend," he said.

His words were suspended for a second. She was being cautious, protective of her patient's privacy. "Going on three years."

Paris ran a hand through his hair. "What can we do to help?"

Selma shook her head, like a mother to a child. "We can do nothing. Miss Valerie can make herself more available to Miss Ruth." Selma bowed her head. "Pretty soon, she won't know her own daughter, and that's when Miss Valerie is going to regret not spending enough time with her."

Calloway's predicament was no different than the one Paris faced when his mother died nearly two decades ago. Her battle with cancer pushed her in and out of hospitals, his father dealing with the pain and stress of the fight, the unknown, trying to make every day feel normal. Paris had just gotten into the FBI, assigned to the Seattle Field Office, a long distance from home in Sacramento. Trips to see her became difficult. The ones he didn't make, walling up the guilt. During those few, final months, the only comfort he could offer was a phone call filled with silent moments, punctuated with the sense of failure.

"I'll get her here," Paris said. "I promise." His voice broke from a tinge of onus the moment he said, *I promise*, one he wasn't sure he could keep. Feeling uncomfortable, he shoved his hands in his pants pockets and looked down the corridor at nothing.

Selma shrugged with indifference.

"Is this the extent of her visits?"

Selma drifted back against the wall. "Early on, they would talk about the past. Miss Valerie would bring in pictures to remind her of who she was, where they came from. Things like that. At first, she would look at the pictures, remembering the scene, captured, celebrated, cherished, and laugh with Miss Valerie. Now, she just has that distant look in her eyes."

"For what it's worth," Paris said, "this isn't easy for Valerie either. We all deal with pain in different ways."

Selma gazed up, a slight smile on her face, as if she understood and, more importantly, agreed. Paris could see Selma was only looking after her patient, everyday watching death slowly reaching out. He was right. Everyone dealt with pain differently. That included Selma.

"She still likes all the little figurines Miss Valerie brings in," Selma offered. "She may not remember her past but she seems to always remember them."

The nurse quietly walked away—as if the conversation had a natural end—stood by her desk, and started sifting through stacks of paper. Paris pictured Calloway with her mother, alone and without help from others. There was no one. He thought about his mother's passing, about Calloway, and how the two tragic circumstances shared a common guilt and compromise. He couldn't help but feel suddenness of being overwhelmed. Abruptly claustrophobic, he desperately needed air and open space. He doubled his steps and pushed out the front door, walking deep into the parking lot, and didn't stop until he felt his lungs fill with the cold night air. It permeated deep in his skin. He felt it. The coldness of night.

CHAPTER 25

CLARION FELT AS IF HE'D BEEN PUNCHED in the stomach, his wobbly knees making it hard to stand up straight. Outside his hotel room, he answered his cell, hearing Barbara's hysterical voice. Through the uncontrollable screams and tears, Barbara tried to explain her finding the note confirming the worst had happened, Rachel's lone shoe as evidence. Then about her call from Agent Paris, the suspect photo she received, and the urgency for Robert to speak with Paris.

It was no longer going to be a compromise. They took Rachel. Now, she was demanding Robert get the FBI involved.

"I can call back Agent Paris," Barbara said.

"No."

"Our daughter's life, Robert—"

"I know," he replied, trying to sound in control of his emotions. "I know."

"Why?"

"Let me handle this my way," he said.

Barbara was stunned. He could hear her stammer, shocked at what she was hearing, couldn't find the right words to say.

"I have something in motion," he said.

He tried to placate her, swearing he had a plan, people who could help—she needed to trust him—but none of this gave Barbara any comfort.

"If it doesn't work by tonight, I'll call the FBI. I promise."

She eventually capitulated, demanding he be held to his word. Or she would do it herself. The father—not the drug dealer—reached for the lie, and it was there. "Of course," he said, as he hung up, buying time.

His head buzzed, confused, agitated, growing desperate. He didn't know if what he was about to do was his best option to get his daughter back. But he felt calling in the FBI would only make matters worse. He knew these people better than most, knew the type. He was once one of them.

But what if he was wrong?

For the second time in his life, Robert felt lost, out of control, mind jammed with things he must now do, unable to prioritize for fear of missing a critical step in the rescue of his daughter. *Which one was right, which one first?* His world was no longer his to control. Lost to a kidnapper. Their fate seemed like dying embers that he kept trying to breathe life into. Kennedy's call to Manoso to pay off the debt—now doubled— was his bait to bring him out and end this nightmare. Clarion no longer had the advantage. Manoso had his daughter, and Clarion's plan to trap him in this subterfuge now took on a greater risk. Rachel could easily become collateral damage.

Clarion forced himself to stand. His head went dizzy, as if a fogbank blinded his view. It took him a second to find his balance. He turned back toward the hotel door and saw Kennedy.

"You okay?" Kennedy's voice was more like a worried friend than a prisoner.

Clarion shook his head. "Change of plans."

He brushed past Kennedy and into the room, grabbed a duffle bag next to the nightstand, and pulled out a second cellphone. It was a throw-away, untraceable, one he knew he needed, now more than ever, to complete his task.

Kennedy ran back into the room, reached down and grasped Clarion by the arm in an effort to get his attention. "Slow down a sec," he said. "What's going on?"

Clarion ripped at the phone's plastic packaging. "He has my daughter. The fucker left a ransom note."

He felt Kennedy's hand fall away and saw him slump to the floor. Kennedy interlaced his fingers on top of his head, rolled his eyes upward and let out a groan.

Clarion paused, trying to get his jaw to relax, his teeth intensely clamped together like a vice. This train had flown off its rails but he needed to stay focused. "There's no negotiation now, Pete. We're going to meet him and then I'm going to kill him."

Kennedy put his face in his hands, his desperation evident. "Maybe we call the cops in on this one, Robert."

Clarion closed his eyes, Barbara's desperate plea to call the FBI echoing in his head. Trusting the police was not his way but he knew this might be way above his head. He was out-gunned, out-maneuvered and, more importantly, he held no bargaining chip.

But the police couldn't offer Clarion a permanent solution. Only he could.

Kill Manoso.

Captured and imprisoned, Manoso would still be able to communicate to the outside world, give orders to hunt down Clarion and his family. They'd be looking over their shoulders for the rest of their lives.

No, this was going to end tonight.

"Tell me everything you know about Manoso."

Kennedy sat back against the bed, resting his arms over his knees. "What's more to tell? He's my primary drug contact. He's got people all over the country."

"What's that mean?"

"People, you know, close associates in 'the business.'" He made quotation marks in the air. "The man's got a network of really bad people he has built over a long period of time."

"How about enemies?"

Kennedy laughed. "Who doesn't? A guy that powerful has just as many enemies as he does allies."

Clarion moved toward Kennedy, forcing eye contact. Suddenly the distance between the two was cut in half and Clarion could see sweat beading on Kennedy's upper lip.

"You know any of his enemies? Anyone who might be able to help us?"

Kennedy hesitated and Clarion knew he was hiding something. Clarion took a threatening step forward.

"W—What?" Kennedy stuttered.

"Who do you know?"

Clarion didn't have the time or the patience for games. He reached into his pocket and pulled out the PPK.

Kennedy held his hands out. "Whoa," he pleaded. "No need for that." He stretched out his neck, feeling a phantom hand squeezing it airtight. "I'm not the enemy."

"What's that supposed to mean?"

"I guess this may surprise you but we have a mutual friend who not only knows Manoso, but may be closer to him than me."

Clarion stood up, towering above Kennedy who remained sitting on the floor. He waved the gun in Kennedy's direction. "Talk."

Kennedy wouldn't look up. He just spoke to the shag carpeting under his feet. "Your buddy, Roy Torrington. He knows Manoso. Who do you think introduced me?"

The words made Clarion's head begin to spin again. He didn't know whom to trust. He sat on the bed, shoulders bent like a heavy coat draped on a wire hanger.

"You know, Robert, it's just business. Through and through." Kennedy tried to sound consoling.

The muscles in Clarion's face tightened.

"Give him the money and he'll give you back your daughter. Cut your losses."

"You said Roy knows Manoso. How well?"

Kennedy shrugged. "Pretty damn well. He'd be your best intermediary."

"You mean to get my daughter back."

Kennedy nodded.

"I'll need money," he said, the words more like a demand than a statement of fact. Before Kennedy could respond, truthfully or not, Clarion dropped down to Kennedy's level and poked the barrel of his pistol several times on his chest. "Don't tell me you don't have money squirreled away somewhere."

"I don't know what you're talking about," Kennedy said, looking in every direction except at Clarion, his voice cracking.

"No one walks away until I get my daughter back." Clarion again tapped Kennedy on the chest with the barrel of the pistol, this time with more prominence. "And that includes you."

Kennedy's body deflated. "Okay," he conceded. "So, I have some set aside. For a rainy day."

"It's raining, Pete. How much?"

Kennedy shook his head from side to side. "Enough."

Clarion suddenly found a better plan taking shape, one that required timing and a great deal of luck. He stood, grabbed the throw-down phone, and pressed the power button. Within seconds, it grabbed a cell signal, ready for use. He punched in Roy Torrington's number.

"Hello?" a hesitant voice responded.

"It's me, Roy. I need your help."

"Robert? Where are you?"

Clarion ignored the question, instead spouting the directions to a Marin County hotel in Larkspur Landing. "Meet me there in two hours."

"It's fucking rush hour, Robert!"

"Then you better hurry." Hanging up the phone, he looked back at Kennedy. "Now, about that money."

CHAPTER 26

I T WAS CLOSE TO SIX P.M. when Clarion cruised past the Richmond stash house where, earlier in the day, he'd left Everett bound in the back room. He glanced at every vehicle in the vicinity, looking for someone—anyone—sitting and watching. Like cops. After two passes, he edged to the corner and parked. He shot a look at Kennedy whose attention was focused on the front door. "You sure the money is still in there?"

He shook his head. "I'm not sure of anything anymore."

Both exited the car, making for entrance of the building. The door was ajar. A little girl stood on the porch, as if waiting for someone. Clarion recognized her from his last visit and remembered she lived on first floor. He smiled at her but she did not smile back. Clarion and Kennedy advanced up the dimly lit stairwell, stopping short of opening the door. He pulled out his pistol, held it tight to his waist. Reaching for the knob, he found it unlocked. They entered, flicked on an overhead light, headed for the dark room where he'd left Everett, who was still there, slumped against the wall, eyes closed.

Clarion called out in a low, hushed voice, "Hey, sleepyhead, time to wake up."

He nudged Everett with his foot. That's when he noticed the dark splotches of red seeping from a hole in Everett's chest. Clarion checked his neck for a pulse, knowing what he'd find. Nothing but coldness.

"Shit," Kennedy said.

Clarion saw Kennedy searching the floorboards on the other side of the room, leaning over a hole in the floor, sweeping an arm deep below.

"It's fucking empty!"

"Are you telling me there's no money?"

Kennedy spun around and swiped a sleeve across the sweat on his chin. "No, not the money. They got the rest of my stash."

Clarion walked over and lifted Kennedy by the scruff. "Fuck the drugs. Where's the cash?"

The corner of Kennedy's mouth curled, like he wanted to spit. He pointed out the door. "Over there. I kept them separate. Just in case."

Kennedy broke free from Clarion's grip, found his balance, and angled toward the kitchen, unsure what he'd find. He leaned hard onto the stove, grabbing it on both sides, then pulled. Metal feet gouged the linoleum floor. Kennedy threaded himself behind the stove where he dislocated a small piece of particleboard, uncovering a small cubbyhole stuffed with cash.

"This is all I got left," Kennedy confessed. "They got everything else."

As he extracted each bundle, Clarion shoved them into a duffle bag until it was full.

"That's almost a hundred and fifty grand," Clarion estimated.

"If they hadn't had taken my stash, we could have made up the difference. And then some."

"This will have to do," Clarion replied.

Kennedy leaned back, bumped the oven, and a rack fell inside causing a loud *clank*. Clarion jumped, drew his pistol, swinging it across the room searching for a target.

"Jesus."

Dead bodies and dark rooms made him jumpy. "Who else knows about this place?"

Kennedy looked away and rubbed his neck, tense and stiff. "Your dead man's boss, guy by the name of Ramone Santiago."

"No one else?"

"Not that I know of."

It didn't make sense to Clarion. Why would Santiago kill his own henchman?

"Someone else knows about your stash house, Pete."

Kennedy took a step back and motioned to the room. "The place is not in my name. Far as I'm concerned, I was never here."

With a body in the bedroom and the apartment void of drugs and cash, Clarion and Kennedy quickly wiped down everything they'd touched before stepping outside and hustling down the stairs. By this time, the little girl was standing in front of her apartment door. Her father stepped out and saw the two leaving the building as he pulled his daughter inside.

Clarion tossed the bag of cash in the back seat and looked down at his watch. By his calculation, Roy Torrington should be at the hotel in another thirty minutes, enough time for Clarion and Kennedy to make it back to get things set. He glanced down at his phone, the one Kennedy used to call Manoso.

Kennedy had left him a message. *I have your money. Call me back.*

Clarion didn't want to leave the phone on, unsure of who else might be listening. The phone cycled on but there were no messages.

Kennedy noticed the tiny beads of sweat on Clarion's face, jaw tightening, as if on cue. "You want me to call him again?"

Clarion shook his head. "Nope. This time, it's Roy's turn."

CHAPTER 27

AFTER AN HOUR AT THE ASSISTED LIVING FACILITY, the two drove to a local restaurant. No one spoke. Strangely enough, the time never felt uncomfortable or awkward, both feeling, maybe knowing, that just being together offered solace. When Calloway excused herself to use the restroom, she paused beside Paris and rested a hand on his shoulder. A smile stole across his face, and she knew the small gesture reassured him. When she returned, Calloway slid her wine glass to one side and concentrated all her attention on Paris.

Although she was quiet, he could sense words filling her head. Calloway wanted to have a conversation.

She spoke first, explaining that, as visits go, this one wasn't the worse. But, overall, they certainly weren't getting any better. From his short time there, Paris had seen that Ruth Calloway's memory was slipping into a dark void, and that it was only a matter of time before she wouldn't recognize her daughter again.

This was one reason why others perceived Valerie Calloway as a loner, consumed only in her work. They failed to see this distance was her only way to escape a figurative knife to the gut, the excruciating pain of permanent loss. It was horribly obvious. She had no one to turn to, whether by intent or circumstance, and that made it worse.

"You going to be all right?"

Her smile was contrived. "I'm fine."

The talk shifted between work and personal life, each side letting their guard down, learning more about each other in the process. Calloway occasionally laughed, and, when she did, her beautiful smile flashed to life. It was addictive. Paris eventually paid the bill and the two walked to his car.

On their drive back to Sacramento, Calloway closed her eyes and dozed and Paris got back to work. He was thinking about his past conversation with Calloway, about her informant and his new mission in locating Kennedy.

Dools was still at the field office, reviewing the pen register information. From the past data, Dools believed he had Clarion triangulated in a three-mile area in Marin County. "You want me to call San Francisco FBI?" Dools asked when Paris phoned him. "See if we can get an SOG crew out to canvass the area?"

Paris considered it. SOG was the FBI's Special Operations Group, whose sole mission was to provide surveillance and reconnaissance support for other agents' investigations. As much as Calloway felt her informant would find Kennedy, Paris knew the more boots on the ground looking, the better their chances. "Yeah," he responded. "Do it."

He never heard back from Dools. At least not during the rest of the drive. SOG teams were in high demand and their resource stretched thin. Last minute requests typically took a backseat, a long shot. Pairs was hopeful, just not optimistic. He would have stayed in the city to do the search himself but he looked over at Calloway, saw she was drained of all energy, and knew he needed to get her home. Tomorrow, he thought, would be a better option for him to pick it back up.

Back in Sacramento, Paris gave Calloway a gentle nudge, letting her know they had arrived. She slowly sat up, stretched, and looked out the window, seeing her car land-locked between two bumpers nearly touching. Residents returning home from work filled the streets with Calloway's car being the interloper in the neighborhood. She gave her predicament a moment of concentration before shrugging, plucking a set of keys from her purse, and climbing out. Paris, playing the gentleman, walked her to her car. As she slid behind the wheel, he leaned in and rested an arm over the top of the hood.

"Go home and get some rest," he said.

She reached out and ran her hand down his right arm. "I'll call you in the morning."

It took a few turns of the wheel and a couple of taps with her bumper for Calloway to pull away. Paris watched her disappear from view as her car crested the top of the street, blending into the dark purple skyline.

As tired as he was, he felt anxious, and knew the feeling wasn't leaving until he checked something out. He got back into his car, reached into his coat pocket, and took out a notebook. He flipped to a marked page containing the information where Clarion's phone was last tracked. Paris studied the entries. It wasn't that large of an area and, with a little effort, he believed he would be able to find Clarion. He decided to call Dools, who answered after the first ring.

"Want to take a drive to the Bay Area?"

"When?"

"Tonight."

Dools's voice dropped an octave. "How did I know you were going to say that?"

Paris shifted his cell to his other ear as he put the Crown Vic into gear. "Tonight, we're going to find Clarion and see just what he's up to. I'm heading to the office. Be ready to go." He accelerated down the road and onto the freeway onramp.

Paris checked his watch and calculated it would be another two hours before they reached the city. Nearly eleven o'clock. He was already feeling fatigued. He lowered the window and let the wind blow on his face. The cool evening air gave him a slight jolt. He sucked in a deep breath, prepping for the long night.

WHILE WAITING AT THE STOPLIGHT before turning onto the freeway, Calloway checked her rearview mirror, making sure no one was following her. Making sure she didn't see Paris. Feeling satisfied, Calloway picked up her phone and called her informant. Three rings and he answered.

"Yeah," the man said.

"Where are you?"

Answering in a flat tone, he responded, "San Francisco."

Calloway bit a fingernail. "How close are you finding Kennedy?"

"Very close."

"I have information that may help."

"I'm listening."

Calloway explained what she'd heard during the phone conversation between Paris and Dools on their drive back—when Paris thought she was asleep. The triangulation information gave her informant a better opportunity by narrowing his focus.

"That should help a lot," he replied.

"I'll see you shortly," Calloway said.

"Do you want me to wait?"

"No. Just find him. I'll be there in a couple hours. Maybe less."

She ended the call, and exhaled a breath as if expelling the betrayal that was in her body. She hated what she was doing but hated more that she didn't care.

Her phone immediately vibrated. Glancing between her rearview mirror and the glow of the screen, Calloway took the call.

The voice on the other end was all too familiar, and the second she heard it, it made her heart race.

"Miss Valerie," Selma said pensively. "I thought you should know, she's awake and remembering again."

Calloway, still holding onto her phone, gripped the steering wheel and squeezed as if she could rid the never-ending, always-at-the-wrong-time tension building up in her body.

"You hear me?"

"Yes, I hear you."

Calloway had to remind herself that spells when her mother was aware and coherent were few and far between. It didn't matter if Calloway had just been there. This time, her mother would know her. Recognize her.

This was when Calloway could provide her mother comfort, be her daughter. These moments always seemed to come when she was hours away, distracted with her obsession. Her head hurt. She pushed the palm of her free hand against her forehead, hoping the pressure would relieve the ache.

"I know you were just here," Selma said. "Didn't know if you were still in the area."

"Yeah, I am," she lied. "I'm coming."

"Promise?"

"Yeah, promise."

Calloway ended the call, fighting off the feeling of nausea and the tears welling in her eyes. She pushed them away with the back of her hand. Reaching into her coat pocket, she felt the smooth surface of porcelain, a figurine she'd started carrying these past few days, since the last time she saw her mother—a glass rabbit taken from her mother's curio. It was the next piece she wanted to take to her for comfort, to help her remember.

The feel of the small treasured object calmed Calloway enough for her to gain her composure, settle her mind, and set her priorities.

Again she looked into her rearview mirror as the signal light finally changed to green. She cleared the fog from her thoughts, hitting I-80 West, returning to the Bay area to see her mother. But first she needed a brief moment to meet her source. Enough time to help him track down, locate, and capture Peter Kennedy.

CHAPTER 28

ROY TORRINGTON ACCIDENTLY DROPPED HIS KEYS on the floor of his car. He was tired and frustrated, having just driven from one place to another, ending up somewhere in the Bay Area, disoriented and agitated. Earlier that evening, Torrington had received a call from Robert Clarion, telling him to get off his phone, find a payphone, call him at a number he'd never seen before. The cloak and dagger scenario gave Torrington a reason to worry, especially after the last drug transaction debacle.

It was inconceivable—this recent change of heart. *Robert Clarion, the man who swore he was out of the game, calling out of the blue, pushing for significant weight. Stranger, yet, agreeing to a deal with someone he's never met. Then the frantic, paranoid call that the cops are watching. And, after all that? He demands to meet—now!*

As much as Torrington wanted nothing more to do with Clarion and his daughter's situation, he knew from the gravity in the man's voice, this was beyond serious, more like desperate. So, how could he say no?

After scouring gas stations for the next thirty minutes, Torrington found what appeared to be the last working payphone in Sacramento. Graffiti, gum, and numbers to call for a good time covered every inch of glass and metal on the booth. He placed the call and listened carefully as Clarion gave him directions to the Marriot in Larkspur Landing, told him not to tell a soul where he was going, to turn off his cell until he arrived, and to make sure he wasn't being followed. Clarion refused to give any more specifics about the meeting, telling Torrington it required an in-person conversation, which made the hair on the back of Torrington's neck bristle. By the time Torrington fought his way through late-night traffic to the hotel, it was already nine-thirty p.m.

Wiping the sweat from his hands onto his pants, Torrington reached down into the dark, and, with an open hand, swept the floor mat until he felt the ring of keys catch between his fingers. He got out, locked the car, and maneuvered down a walking path between two buildings.

CLARION STOOD, PACING AROUND A BENCH, smoking a cigarette. As he blew out a long tunnel of smoke, he acknowledged Torrington and took a step forward.

"Thought you gave up smoking," Torrington said as he closed the gap.

"Thought you gave up dealing," Clarion countered.

Torrington stopped dead in his tracks, hooked his thumbs in his jean pockets. "What's that supposed to mean?"

Clarion took one last drag on his cigarette before tossing it to the ground. He stepped closer to Torrington, who'd started to sweat again.

Torrington took a step back. "Look, whatever is going on here, I had nothing to do with it."

Clarion shoved a finger in Torrington's face. "Tell me who Manoso is."

He watched as Torrington's eyes widened briefly before turning languid again. Torrington slipped past Clarion to the bench, dropped to the seat, and hooked an arm over the backrest. He glanced up at Clarion with an expression that signaled submission. "You got one of those smokes for me?"

Clarion pulled the pack from his shirt pocket, shook one loose, and pushed it toward Torrington.

"Thanks."

"You knew that's who was supplying Kennedy, didn't you?"

Torrington hesitated but knew he had to come clean. He nodded reluctantly.

"Why didn't you tell me?"

Torrington looked directly into Clarion's eyes. "It's complicated."

Clarion slammed a fist on the backrest. "Who is Manoso?"

Torrington gestured for Clarion to stay calm. "He's a huge dealer, got lots of people working for him, lots of contacts all over the country. I got introduced to him on a trip down south in '03. Picked up a couple of loads for a friend. He took a liking to me, gave me credit."

"Did you know he had taken Rachel?"

Torrington's eyes went wide. "Hell no, I swear."

It took Clarion a minute to think his response through, whether he was being honest. In the end, he did. "Since you two are such good friends, here's what you're going to do. You're going to ask for a favor. Tonight."

Torrington tensed. "Don't fuck with him. He's dangerous."

"It's past that stage," Clarion said. "He's got Rachel."

Torrington blanched, reeling from the news.

"You're going to help me get him here," Clarion continued.

Torrington kept silent, like an obedient dog.

"And you're going to make sure he brings my daughter."

Torrington closed his eyes and nodded. Kennedy stepped out of the hotel room and, mid-stride, caught sight of Torrington. Torrington's attention shot toward the door, then he whipped around to face Clarion. "Christ, what's he doing here?"

Clarion waved over Kennedy. "He's helping."

"Really?"

"He put in a call to Manoso. No answer. Left a message but we haven't heard back." Clarion leaned in close and spoke in an assertive tone. "That's where you come in, Roy." He reached down, lifted a black duffle bag lying next to the bench, and set the bag between the two of them. It landed heavy like a sack of wheat. He unzipped the top and reached in, pulling out a .40 caliber Glock. Delving deeper, he found a sixteen-round magazine, seating it into the butt of the pistol, then chambered a round. Kennedy hung back and watched.

Clarion swung the pistol around, grip first, in Torrington's direction. "What you want me to do with that?"

Clarion shoved the pistol into Torrington's hand. "You're going to tell him to bring my daughter back in exchange for his money."

"You really going to give him his money?"

Clarion let the inquiry hang in the air between them. "You just get them both here."

"I suppose you want me to shoot him if he doesn't go for it?"

"No, Roy, you won't have to." Clarion's eyes hardened. "I plan on doing that myself."

CHAPTER 29

Lorenzo "Zo" Guzman pulled the Cadillac SUV up in front of the stash house and threw it into park. His boss, Ramone Santiago sat in the passenger seat, giving him directions. Zo killed the engine, seconds ticking by as he scanned the area like a gun on a turret. Seeing the area was clear of danger, Zo exited the car, two more strongmen joining him from the backseat. Zo straightened his leather coat and patted just under his left arm where he concealed a holstered nine-millimeter Browning High Power pistol. In the cold air, Zo watched his breath cloud in front of his face, then opened the passenger door for his boss. Santiago glanced up at the second-floor windows. No lights or activity. He motioned for his muscle to lead the way. Santiago followed, Zo taking up the rear.

The entry door to the building was supposed to be locked, tenants buzzing visitors in via the intercom, he thought. Santiago saw the door latch and the intercom were busted. A real shithole.

The four strolled into the lobby. The two big men made their way up the stairs, rubber-soled shoes doing nothing to conceal their size, each step echoing like massive redwoods being felled. An apartment door cracked at the bottom of the stairwell and a man's face appeared. Santiago stopped. The man nodded, redirecting his gaze, and disappeared behind the door. The soft clank of a metal lock being turned was heard.

Santiago knew the man. It hadn't been more than a day after taking over Kennedy's business that Santiago and his men had come to the stash house to check on his drugs. The apartment building wasn't remotely secure enough. But that's the way most stash houses were set up—low profile and inconspicuous, drawing no attention from would-be robbers.

But they did need some monitoring and, with Kennedy out of the picture, Santiago needed someone to be his eyes and ears. Santiago had introduced himself to the man and his family who were moving in. Oscar Orozco had no job, recently emigrating from Central America, most likely illegally. Everything they owned had been packed into the beat-up truck they'd arrived in, spewing oil and smoke, clearly on its last legs.

Santiago knew the type. Farm workers, gardeners, ditch diggers, housekeepers, and day laborers. They babysat the rich kids and bathed the elderly, washed dishes, polished your car. They took on any job to make enough money to feed their family. Anything to survive. And that would include watching over stash houses. Recognizing this, he had peeled away two one-hundred-dollar bills, passing them to Orozco, conveying how important the apartment upstairs was. If anyone were to come to the location, Orozco was to let Santiago know. He wrote down his cellphone number on a piece of paper and gave it to the man. Since that day, Santiago had not heard a word from Orozco. Not even today.

The four men stood at the entryway of the apartment, finding it unlocked. As soon as the door was flung wide, Santiago knew something was wrong. The coolness of the evening air wasn't enough to ward off the blowflies swarming inside, buzzing like a dying florescent bulb.

Zo pulled his pistol and moved toward the back room where they kept their stash. Santiago lingered on the threshold, scanning the surrounding area, searching for answers, while the other two started checking behind doors and furniture, both ending up in the kitchen. Drapes pulled back, the window overlooked the street below.

Zo rushed out of the bedroom room—pistol in one hand, his other hand over his mouth and nose.

"Better get a look at this," Zo croaked, motioning for Santiago to follow.

Everyone followed Zo to the back, slowly crowding through the door, giving the body slumped in the corner a quick look before turning their attention to the open floorboards.

Santiago walked to the other side of the room, took a knee, and carefully moved a cockeyed plank that had once concealed twenty kilos. He swiped the bottom of the compartment, rubbing a thin layer of powder and dust between two fingers, the strong medicinal smell still prevalent.

"He took two to the chest," one man said from behind. "Executed."

Santiago paused before turning his head back toward the body. From his vantage point, he could see the remnants of rope and duct tape still attached to the pipe on the wall, could see scuff marks on the floor, hard shoes crisscrossing in all directions. A fight.

He'd had Kennedy here, not more than a day ago. Now he, along with the dope, was gone. Santiago wondered if Kennedy had the wherewithal to overtake his captor, the nerve to kill. Santiago doubted it. Kennedy was a businessman, only in it for the money. He wasn't a killer. Someone else had been here, and it wasn't the cops. Whoever did this *was* a killer, a cold-blooded killer. And not seeing Kennedy's body alongside his dead associate, Santiago concluded whoever did this had to be a friend of Kennedy's.

Santiago remained crouched as the man standing guard by the front window entered the room.

"We found other stash compartments," his man said, before adding, "all empty."

Santiago felt his face begin to heat up. "Whoever was here, got it all."

With all the chaos that happened in the apartment, there was no way Orozco hadn't heard or seen something. Unless he was in on it. It wouldn't have been the first time a person had turned allegiance for a dollar. Santiago felt the bones in his back and hips pop like bubble wrap as he straightened to a stand.

Hooking a finger, he gestured toward the front door and said to his men, "Let's go pay our friend downstairs a visit."

THERE WAS A GENTLE TAP AT THE DOOR. Orozco turned the handle and pulled it open. He knew who it was, hearing all the commotion upstairs, the shuffling of heavy boots, and then a low murmur just outside his apartment. It would have done no good for him to ignore the knock.

Mr. Santiago had seen him look out the door when they'd come into the building and that misstep, Orozco realized, was the mistake of his life.

He stood facing a wall of three men directly behind Mr. Santiago, clones of each other.

Santiago forced a tight smile, dipping his chin, his way of a polite greeting. His expression indicated he was waiting for an invitation. Orozco stepped aside, knowing he had no choice in the matter.

Inside the small one-bedroom apartment, Orozco's wife, Amelia, stood over the kitchen stove, boiling a pot of turnips. His two daughters sat on the couch, originally watching TV but now focused on the room crowded with large men.

"Do you have something to tell me, Oscar?"

Santiago's words were controlled but Orozco could tell he was holding back a wave of anger. Before he could answer, the three men worked their way around him—one standing directly behind him, another by the TV, the last in the kitchen.

"I see nothing," Orozco replied.

Santiago reacted with a look of distrust. "It appears the apartment is missing all my valuables." He took a step toward Orozco and quietly spoke, as if holding their conversation in confidence. "And there's a dead man up there." He then took a step back. "And you're telling me you saw nothing?"

Sweat bloomed above Orozco's upper lip. He reached deep into his pants pocket and pulled out a wadded $100 bill. He had spent the other hundred on food. He pushed it forward. "You can have your money back, I don't want it anymore."

Santiago blew out a long even breath. "Tell me what you know."

There was a hesitant moment. "I saw two men go upstairs."

"When?"

"Earlier today." Orozco twitched and looked down at his shoes. "Then again tonight."

Santiago folded his arms across his chest. "The same two?"

"Yes." Again a pause. "No . . . maybe."

"You didn't call me."

"I think they with you."

"You—think—they with me?" Santiago repeated slowly.

Suddenly Orozco felt his legs start to shake, barely able to support the weight of his body.

Amelia dropped the large wooden spoon and pressed her hands hard against the sides of her face. The small woman made a move toward her children, only to be blocked by Santiago's henchman.

Santiago signaled to Zo standing next to the TV to turn up the volume. "I'm going to ask you a question, Mr. Orozco, and I'm hoping you're going to answer truthfully. Otherwise, we are going to have some problems."

Orozco's arms were down by his side, his hands flexing nervously open and shut. "I tell you the truth."

The man in the kitchen reached into a drawer and pulled out a metal spatula.

Santiago gave him the go-ahead and his henchman moved the boiling pot of turnips off to the side. The flame from the gas stove flared up with the twist of the knob.

"What happened to my drugs?" Santiago demanded.

Orozco's eyes bounced between Santiago and Amelia. His breathing became labored, fueled by anxiety and fear.

"I won't ask again."

"I swear," Orozco said. "I don't know nothing about your drugs."

The TV volume was turned up again, laughter from a Mexican audience roared. Zo slid into the kitchen and grabbed the wife by the arm. She sucked in a startled breath and stiffened.

The man in the kitchen placed the metal spatula over the stove burner, and the edges began to blacken from the fire. Once the metal began to glow red and bow from the heat, the man lifted the spatula close to Amelia's cheek. She fought to push away but Zo held her in too strong of a grip, pressing her face inches from the hot metal.

"Please don't," Orozco pleaded.

He looked into Santiago's eyes, hoping for some compassion, and saw nothing but coldness—something he had seen before in his homeland where fear and corruption controlled the people, the government.

"Tell me," Santiago ordered.

Orozco fell to his knees as he begged. "I only saw the men come in. I don't know who they were. I swear."

There was silence as Santiago studied Orozco, his children, and his wife. Then he nodded. "I believe you, Oscar."

He returned his attention back to his henchman in the kitchen and motioned with his chin. The man turned back to the wife. He lowered the hot spatula, and Orozco let out a sigh. But instead, the man pressed the hot metal against her arm.

She screamed in agony as her skin seared, every muscle seizing from the pain. Paralyzed on the couch, the kids screamed too.

Orozco cried out but Santiago held him back, refusing to let him go to his wife. Orozco struggled to be by her side until all the strength in his body was exhausted. He fell back on his haunches, his arms folded over his head, and wailed like a wounded animal, covering his face from the guilt and regret churning inside him.

Santiago bent down and placed a hand on Orozco's shoulder, giving him a light consoling pat. "That's for not calling me," he whispered.

THE NIGHT AIR WAS EVEN COOLER than when they first arrived. Santiago pulled his collar up to stave off the chill outside as he left the building.

His henchmen formed a circle around him until he got in the car. Zo appeared to his right, pulling out a cigarette and lighting it up. He sucked deeply, making the tip burn bright orange. A trail of gray smoke followed the evening breeze, as if guiding their next move.

Zo exhaled into the cold. "You believe him?"

Santiago concentrated on the windows across the street, giving some thought before frowning. "Maybe," he said with a shrug.

"If he wasn't involved, who was it?"

Santiago cleared his throat, trying hard to put the pieces together in his mind. He waved two fingers at Zo, indicating he wanted a cigarette. Zo shook one out, passed it to Santiago along with his lighter.

Santiago lit the cigarette, finding comfort in the tobacco. *Someone who knew the dope was here, someone who knew of the hidden compartments, someone who would kill, and someone who might be on the side of Kennedy.*

He looked over at Zo, thinking about their history. Zo was his closest confidant, his most trusted worker. The two had come up the ranks in the drug business together, dealing with many others who had come and gone—jail or death—prevailing as a key force throughout the states. The two knew most of the same heavy-hitters in the business, like a Rolodex safely held in their minds. Filtering through them, it didn't take long for Santiago to come up with a name.

Zo held still, patiently waiting for Santiago to speak.

Santiago's eyes sharpened into slits, like a fighter pilot honing in on a target. He threw his cigarette into the gutter, then he said the name of the person he suspected, someone Santiago could not believe was back in the area. Back in his life.

Through clenched teeth, he whispered, "Manoso."

CHAPTER 30

No one else was in the Sacramento FBI office, besides the night desk operator. And Dools. Paris arrived fifteen minutes after calling him, going straight to the pen register room to review the telephone records for each of his targets. Knowing who was talking to whom—and where—was going to be the key.

He walked in, seeing Dools hunched over a stack of printouts. Pencil in hand, Dools had filled an entire page of his notepad with a spider web of lines connecting a dozen boxes. His other hand massaged his neck—the offending spot, angry and red at this point—a clear sign of fatigue and frustration. His shirt was rumpled more than usual, and he had pulled off his tie, an uncommon move for him. His weary eyes were yet another sign that he had been at it for a while.

Dools put down his pencil and rubbed his temples, stifling a yawn at the same time. When he caught sight of Paris, he motioned him over. Paris sat and started to pull folders for each target number but paid particular interest to Clarion's.

"Not a lot of activity," Dools said.

"He's up to something."

Dools scooped up a file folder, containing Roy Torrington's phone records, from the desk. It was smaller than the rest, indicating very little activity. But what was there drew Paris's interest. With a meaty finger, Dools tapped at the last entry, made a little over an hour ago.

The printouts displayed a pattern that Paris recognized from his years of investigations. It showed Torrington receiving a call from Clarion.

Cell tower triangulation revealed Clarion's phone was somewhere in San Francisco, Torrington's in Sacramento. Paris turned to the next page.

Dools jumped in. "An hour and half later, Torrington calls another number we conclude is to a throw-down phone. Suddenly, he's in San Francisco too." Dools leaned forward in his chair. "You think they're setting up another buy?"

Paris shrugged. "Maybe." He pushed the printouts forward, formed a steeple with both hands, and placed it against his mouth. "As much as it may look like another transaction, I think there's something else going on."

Clarion making a second buy meant he was trying to bring himself one step closer to his main target, the same as Paris.

The silence in the room was interrupted as the pen register machines began to flash and beep. Numbers lit up on the LED screen, indicating phone activity. Paris and Dools stood at the same time, moving to the one tracking Torrington's phone. An outgoing call was being placed. As the numbers appeared on the screen, Paris recognized it. He stepped back to the table and grabbed Clarion's records. Scanning the pages, he saw the number had been called two hours earlier. Then it hit him. He had seen it elsewhere.

"Dools, where are Calloway's charts?"

Confused, Dools turned his head and pointed toward the table.

Paris walked over and reached under the desk, pulling out the banded roll of documents. He unsnapped the rubber band, and the pages flared open, the large sheets still curled at the edges. He swiped them flat and peeled away sheets, one-by-one, until he found the hand-drawn flowchart. Calloway's latest rendition of associations and calls between suspects in her investigation. Like Dools's drawing, lines and boxes filled the sheet, all interconnected, like a schematic of a complex circuit board. They all funneled to one box. In it, Calloway wrote, *M*. Under it, she scribbled several telephone numbers with lines drawn through each one, indicating a number tossed in exchange for a new one. The last one, however, was not lined out. It was the last known number to her primary subject. The number that popped up on the pen register. They were also on Clarion and Torrington's cellphone records.

"Holy shit," Dools mumbled, before placing a finger on the paper, next to the box that grabbed their attention. "I remember asking her what 'M' stood for. She said 'Main,' as in 'Main Target.'"

"Did you put up a pen register on Mr. M?"

Dools shook his head, slightly embarrassed that he forgot the conversation he had with Calloway. "Didn't have to. Calloway said she had one up already at her office."

Paris pulled his cellphone from his back pocket and called Calloway. As much as he wanted to give her a respite from the case, what he had just learned was too important to wait. A current call to their primary target. He also knew Calloway would be livid if Paris held back something as critical as this.

The phone rang three times before going to voicemail. *Probably asleep.* He left a message to call but didn't include any details.

Something was going down tonight. Paris could feel it. Clarion calling Torrington, Torrington calling the main drug kingpin—it all pointed to one thing. Everyone was getting together for a meet.

But everyone, Paris suspected, had their own agenda, a recipe for disaster.

"Call over to the PD," he said. "Get the last location on M's cellphone."

Five minutes clicked past before the two hopped into Paris's Crown Vic on their way to the Bay Area. Dools was able to narrow in on Clarion's phone to a few blocks in Marin County, a location called Larkspur Landing. The PD hadn't gotten back to Dools on the location of M's phone but from what Paris had learned from the pen register data, he already knew. It was going to be in Larkspur.

On the way, he tried calling Calloway two more times but the calls went to voicemail. Aside from keeping her abreast to the new developments, Paris kept feeling their conversation was still very one-sided. He was becoming more curious about what her informant may know and mostly where he was at this moment. If he was in the middle of this meeting, not knowing who he was could cause Paris to follow the wrong person, waste time, or worse, get somebody hurt. He wanted to build Calloway's trust and, to do that, he hadn't pushed her to reveal the CI's identity.

But things were different now. If Calloway's CI was close, Paris needed to know who he was. Trust went both ways and, at this hour, Paris needed her to have faith in him. He glanced to the back of the car. In the dark, he caught sight of the roll of papers. Calloway's. He told Dools to bring them to the front and start going through the phone records but, this time, look for another number being called. The one calling Calloway. That would be her informant.

"You got to be kidding—" Dools said, his voice with a twinge of apprehension.

Paris cut him off. "You got a better idea?"

After a long pause and a deep sigh, Dools separated the phone records from the roll of papers and started searching. "I hope you know what you're doing."

Silently, Paris confessed that he didn't. Given a choice, the case always came first. His decision was predictable, addictive. But he couldn't help himself. He was self-destructive. He bowed his head for a second, as if he seeking forgiveness. It had been forever since he'd felt this drawn to someone. Calloway understood what it was like being with a cop, so she had to understand what he had to do. He could only hope. His mouth went dry. He tried to swallow down the feeling of guilt, but mostly betrayal.

THE REST OF THE DRIVE WAS QUIET as Paris dodged late-night drivers on Interstate 580. Crossing the San Rafael Bridge, San Quentin State Prison to their left, Paris took the 101 South and pulled over at Marin Joe's, a local restaurant, mostly because it was still open. He swung the sedan into the parking lot, cut the engine, and looked over at Dools, whose nose hadn't come up for air since he started digging through Calloway's investigative reports.

Dools glanced at Paris, an expression of discovery on his face.

Paris' heart skipped, his eyes filled with visions of Calloway jabbing an accusatory finger into his face. He felt the length of his spine shiver.

"I found him," Dools confessed. "I got the number to Calloway's informant."

With great reluctance, Paris made his decision. "Track him."

CHAPTER 31

E XCEPT FOR THE SPOT WHERE CLARION WAS STANDING, the rest of
the Marriott parking lot was pitch black. The overhead sodium lamp
cast a spotlight that lit Clarion up like an actor on stage. In the shadows
behind Clarion, Kennedy stood, the duffle bag stuffed with cash by his
feet. Clarion's order: if things turned to shit, grab the bag, run. Kennedy
didn't have any problem with that.

Clarion glanced sidelong at his watch, kicking ruptured tar loose
with the toe of his boot. It was nearly midnight, the time Manoso agreed
to meet. The tense call with Torrington did little to convince Manoso
Clarion was on the up and up. Originally Manoso hung up, believing the
whole thing was a set up. Manoso wasn't a fool. But Torrington called
him back, leaving messages, assuring him this was strictly "business."
All Clarion wanted was his daughter back. He wouldn't risk anything
to jeopardize her safe return. The caveat: Manoso had to guarantee the
threats would end tonight. In person. Then the two would be square.
Apparently his messages were convincing because Manoso called back
and agreed to the meeting.

As the minutes passed, Clarion's phone kept vibrating from incoming calls. He knew they were from Barbara, who wanted an update,
reassurance they would get their daughter back. He wanted to pick up,
promise everything was okay, that he had it all under control, but he
couldn't. It would be a lie. Clarion didn't know how the night would
end, but whatever happened he wasn't going to stop until Rachel was
safely in his arms.

Kennedy's phone beeped. Clarion turned and watched Kennedy study the incoming number.

"It's your friend Roy."

Clarion pivoted as Kennedy took the call. He didn't say much, nodding every so often, blurting short replies, like, "Yeah, we're in place," and "yes, he's got the money," before he clicked off the call. Kennedy stowed the phone back in his pocket. "Manoso just called. He'll be here momentarily."

Clarion had turned around to face the darkened parking lot when he saw two headlights coming from behind a row of maple trees. A second later, an SUV appeared, followed by another, slowly making their way toward the waiting men. The vehicles crawled to a halt twenty-five yards in front of them. Clarion had assessed the lot before their arrival. The scattering of cars offered enough protection from flying bullets but wouldn't hinder a quick escape.

Through the glare of the headlights, Clarion spotted two large figures immediately exiting the back of the vehicle, looking around. A few seconds later, the front passenger door was flung opened and a well-dressed man emerged.

"That's him," Kennedy said, pointing a cautious finger. "Manoso."

Clarion watched as the man stepped into the headlight beams, illuminating the outline of his body. An orange dot flared, and a billow of smoke drifted across the hood of the SUV, as Manoso casually enjoyed a cigarette on this cool, carefree evening. He saw the dark figure tilt his head forward. "That you, Peter?"

Using his hand for a visor, Kennedy shaded his eyes from the bright stream of light. He waved, nervous and unsure.

"Where's my daughter?" Clarion called out.

Manoso took a final drag from his smoke before flicking it to the ground. He turned and nodded at the men in the other SUV. The rear driver's door opened and a large man stepped out. Clarion's heart pounded so hard he'd swear Manoso and his thugs could hear it from where they stood. The man reached into the back seat and pulled out a small woman. Clarion could tell it was Rachel.

Clarion heard her yell, "Dad!"

Her scream made him choke. Instinctively, he advanced toward the sound of his daughter's voice and reached out but came to a stop as Manoso extended a hand forward.

Manoso's voice was calm. "Where's my money?"

Clarion strained to see if his daughter was all right. Manoso looked over at his henchman who then gave Rachel a hard push. Her legs buckled as she fell back into the vehicle. He slammed the car door shut and stood guard. Clarion wanted to call out but knew it would do no good.

"You want your money?" Clarion looked over at the SUV Rachel was in. "Bring her here."

Manoso shook his head and started to turn away.

Clarion picked up the bag and began walking toward Manoso. As he reached the halfway point, Clarion stopped. "This is as far as I go." He pointed at the SUV where his daughter was held captive, then down at the spot where he stood. "I said bring her here."

Manoso faced Clarion, flashed a grin, before gesturing for his man to bring her back out. The big thug jerked open the door, yanked her into the parking lot. He gave her a push, his grip still tight on her, and Rachel stumbled forward. They slowly made their way to the point of no return, ten feet from Clarion. The henchman tugged on Rachel's arm, keeping her slightly off balance, a move meant to illustrate he could snap her in half in a heartbeat if Clarion tried anything.

Wide, broad shouldered, with a square jaw and hands that could be mistaken as baseball mitts, the man didn't speak, just grunted at the package at Clarion's feet.

Clarion hooked two fingers in the man's direction. "Let her come to me and I'll hand you this," he said, calmly, pointing at the money.

The man bared his teeth, digging stiff fingers into Rachel's arm, causing her to flinch in discomfort.

"I'm warning you," Clarion said. "Don't do that."

The man pulled Rachel back a few inches and, again, pointed at the bag.

Clarion let a deep breath seep out as he reached down and hoisted the large duffle. "Last chance," he warned.

The henchman held his smile.

Clarion looked around the big man, toward Manoso. "You got him?"

The henchman's expression shifted—inquisitive, confused—before he obviously caught sight of the ear bud in Clarion's right ear, the microphone hanging just below his chin. Clarion nodded and spoke into the mic. "Take him."

The sharp crack of a gunshot rang out, then another. Clarion saw Manoso drop to the ground and was unsure if he was hit or diving from the bullets coming at him from Roy Torrington's gun. The other man had spun toward the sound of the gunshots before returning his attention to Clarion.

In the momentary confusion, Clarion had reached into the side pocket of the duffle bag to retrieve his Walther PPK. He let the bag fall to the pavement, raising the weapon, pointing it at the face of his adversary. The man's free hand went to the back of his waistband, obviously going for a gun, but it was too late.

Clarion squeezed the trigger twice, both bullets striking the thug in the head. His neck snapped back and he immediately crumpled to the ground. Rachel froze, eyes locked on her father.

Clarion leapt forward, stepping on the dead man as he grabbed his daughter, dragging her back into the darkness where he handed her off to Kennedy, who threw an arm around her and quickly guided her across the parking lot and into the open hotel room.

Clarion turned and started running to the left, thinking he could out-flank Manoso and whoever else was in the SUVs. As he sprinted forward, Clarion heard rapid fire coming from the back SUV. Submachine-gun fire. More gunshots being returned, striking the sides of the SUVs, windows shattering and side-view mirrors exploding into fragments. The second SUV screeched in reverse before slamming into another car, accelerating forward and speeding down the hill. The remaining SUV's front door was wide open, a man slumped out, head bloodied against the pavement.

Clarion screamed into his mic for Torrington to stop shooting. It was hard to hear over the loud concussion of gunfire and the ringing in his head, but he was able to make out Torrington screaming back.

"I'm not shooting, Robert. It's not coming from me!"

THERE WAS A POOL OF BLOOD next to the spot where Manoso stood not more than three minutes prior. Clarion carefully approached the mark, following the streak of dark red smeared on the pavement, away toward the open road. The SUV was riddled with bullet holes. Shards of glass glistened, reflecting the light coming from the overhead lamps. Clarion pushed his pistol forward as he scanned the inside of the vehicle for any signs of Manoso. Stepping over the dead driver, blood pooling under his body, he saw a figure to his right slowly approaching. He swung his pistol around and aimed it at the black mass, starting to apply pressure until he saw hands being raised.

"Hold up, it's me!"

Torrington came out from the shadows and into the parking lot lights, hands raised above his shoulders, gun still in his right hand. "Did you get him?"

Clarion turned back around, seeing only the body of the driver, no Manoso to be found.

"What do you mean, 'Did I get him?' You shot first."

Torrington approached the vehicle and studied it, counting the bullet holes. He spun around and gave Clarion a stunned look. "I only fired two rounds before I heard all hell break loose."

Completely confused, Clarion flashed a glance at the bullet-riddled SUV then back at Torrington. He heard footsteps coming from the hotel. It was Rachel, walking out the front door apprehensively. Her eyes went wide, filled with fear and confusion. They darted in every direction, looking for bad men and gunfire. Clarion called her name, as if to prove to himself it wasn't a dream, that he really had her back.

Rachel's entire body shook as she sobbed, running into her father's arms. She grabbed him tightly around his waist, refusing to let go. Clarity swirled around him as he realized what he'd once thought was important was nothing but smoke and mirrors. The sum of his past actions put that unforgettable fear into his daughter's eyes, and it overwhelmed him. He could only hope that, someday, Rachel would forgive him. His quiet solace was interrupted by a gentle tap on his shoulder.

"We've got company," Torrington said.

Clarion looked up to see two men approaching, one with a pistol drawn, the other with a shotgun at the ready position.

"Holy shit," Torrington said as he started to reach for his weapon. "They're back to finish us off."

Clarion placed a hand on Torrington's arm, stopping him from making a grave mistake. He recognized the men, and they weren't Manoso's. They were federal agents. Clarion turned and gently guided Rachel behind him as the two men approached. "Agent Paris, Agent Dooley," he said with a nod.

FBI Special Agent Paris holstered his weapon as Special Agent Dooley sidestepped away to clear the area of any danger. Paris looked around, studied the SUV, the bullet holes, the dead bodies. He peered behind Clarion and saw Rachel.

"Mr. Clarion," he said. "You've got some explaining to do."

CHAPTER 32

HAD IT NOT BEEN FOR THE SOUND OF THE GUNSHOTS, Paris would've missed the location. It was Paris's call to the Marin County Sheriff's Department Watch Commander that alerted him to the dozen nine-one-one calls. Nothing rattled a neighborhood like automatic gunfire. Paris and Dools sped up the hill, eventually hearing the rapid pops echoing off the hotel building walls.

By the time they made it to the top, Dools pointed to the blown-out SUV with a dead man slumped out the driver's side, body lying on the pavement with a bloody hole in his head. Paris recognized Rachel Clarion standing next to her father, and another man he knew was Roy Torrington. Not taking any chances, Dools decided to grab the Remington 870 shotgun from the backseat. The two bailed from the car, Dools heading straight to the bullet-ridden SUV while Paris went to Clarion.

There was no need for introductions. Everyone knew each other.

Paris wanted answers. The first thing he saw was Rachel standing behind her dad, a death grip around his waist. In a way, Paris felt relief that Rachel was back, safe. Seeing the expression on her face, he had a good idea what had occurred. Clarion was tentative at first but then decided to give up the entire story.

"I had no choice. I had to protect my daughter."

Paris raised a hand, cut to the chase. He pointed at the weapon in Clarion's waistband. "You know you can't possess a firearm. You're a convicted felon."

The statement made Clarion flinch. From the original kidnapping case five years earlier, he had confessed to his drug dealing, in exchange for getting back his daughter. After it was over, he pled guilty to one count of drug possession and was placed on probation. It was a break from the heavens. He could have been looking at significant time in a federal pen. But with the felony conviction, he wasn't allowed to possess a firearm. Under federal law, he was facing a five-year hit.

He stared up at the sky, as if he could call upon the gods for help. The veins in his temples bulged.

Paris saw that Rachel had made her way to the bench, coaxed away by Torrington, who was trying to console her. Her eyes were still locked on her father with a look of concern.

"What are we going to do now, Agent Paris?" Clarion asked.

Paris leaned a hand against the lamppost. "Let's go over your story." But he didn't let him speak, instead interjecting his own version of what happened. "So your daughter gets kidnapped for ransom. You meet this guy Manoso in the parking lot—"

Frustration warped Clarion's face, as he had clearly already gone over it more times than he cared.

"—then Manoso's muscle pulls a weapon to shoot you but your good friend, Roy Torrington—who is not a convicted felon—gets him first."

Clarion's eyes honed in on Paris.

Torrington heard Paris's version of the story, jumped up from the bench, and walked over to where they were standing.

"Yeah, that's right," Torrington said. "I shot him. I shot the asshole." He made a gesture with his hand in the form of a gun and snapped his thumb twice in the direction of the man on the ground. "Dead, bitch!"

Paris put out a hand and, again, pointed at Clarion. "Your weapon?"

Clarion reached in his back waistband, pulled out the Walther, and handed it to him.

Paris dropped the mag, unchambered the seated round, and handed the gun to Torrington. "Hold this."

Torrington smiled, took the weapon, and gave it a tight grip before handing it back. Paris needed Torrington's prints to make the story accurate.

Our secret.

No more than a minute had passed when siren-blaring police cars screamed up the road and into the bloody crime scene. Paris turned, held up his badge to identify himself as law enforcement. The officers squinted from a distance at the gold shield Paris held high before cautiously approaching. Dools had just cleared the shot-up vehicle and found Kennedy, shaken and bleary eyed, in the hotel room. He cuffed him and stuck him in the back of their Crown Vic.

"Manoso's still out there," Clarion said. "And to make matters worse, someone else was here."

Paris had already surmised this, seeing all the bullet holes. "Any idea?"

Clarion shook his head. "No one else knew we were meeting."

He had been so close. Paris was happy for Rachel's safe return, but this was far from over. At least he knew who his primary target was.

With a kidnapping and Clarion reluctantly convinced to testify, Paris had a name: Manoso. Clarion confirmed Manoso's cell number, and Paris instructed Dools to get someone over to the PD to monitor the cellphone activity on the pen register. If Manoso used the phone, hopefully they would be able to make some headway on his location.

Without saying it, both Clarion and Paris knew the situation had escalated beyond critical. Manoso's kidnapping of Rachel failed to secure his reward, his money. But, most importantly, the matter of disrespect was taken up another level. And Manoso was going to find a way to make Clarion pay.

Reaching for his phone, Paris placed a call to the Sacramento office and had two agents go retrieve Barbara Clarion. Robert had already called the house, told her what had happened, and that their daughter was safe. Moreover, he told her of his conversation with Paris. Interestingly enough, Paris thought, Clarion looked more relieved when he ended the call. He passed on a message from his wife to Paris: a simple, *Thank you.*

Paris poked an accusing finger into Clarion's chest. "From this moment on, you're out of this."

Clarion didn't hesitate. "Done."

He held his hand out and Paris and took it. As Clarion turned and started to walk away, Paris asked, "Forget something?"

Clarion looked back, seeing Paris pointing at the duffle bag where it had touched down, alone, almost forgotten, in the middle of the lot. Clarion shook his head and smiled. "Never seen that before in my life."

Drug proceeds, payoff funds, whatever the origin of the money, Paris thought, *it doesn't matter.*

The truth was, the cash represented every misguided endeavor Clarion had thought was so important in his life—decisions that nearly got his daughter killed. Paris took a step toward the bag, grabbing it up by the strap and holding it out as Dools approached. He handed it over.

Dools hefted it to assess the weight then gave a judgmental grin. "Someone is going to be really unhappy," he said as he slung the bag over his shoulder.

He didn't wait for a response, just walked to the back of the Crown Vic, popped the trunk, and tossed the heavy sack into the back, as if it were nothing more than dirty laundry.

It took another thirty minutes for the police to collect the evidence and listen to witness statements, another hour for the coroner's office to come collect the bodies. It was just past three a.m. before Paris was able to get a report back from the Sacramento PD: Manoso's phone went active. By Paris's calculations, it was minutes after the shooting, meaning Manoso was alive and on the run. Paris had ordered Dools to alert all hospitals, trauma centers, and Doc-in-the-Box facilities in the area, make them aware of the shooting. So far, nothing.

Paris held still, keeping his eyes on the remaining crew cleaning up the crime scene, now looking more like scattered trash after an outdoor concert. In the course of events, he had placed three calls to Valerie Calloway, each one going right to voicemail. He could only conclude her phone was either off or she was deep asleep. Finally, his cell buzzed.

Calloway.

Her voice was soft but not as if she had just woken up. She appeared distracted even after he explained to her what happened this past hour.

It took a break in their conversation for Paris to finally ask, "Where are you?"

Calloway stammered, sounding somewhat reticent. "I—I'm here in the Bay Area. I'm with my s—source."

Paris took a moment to absorb her words. He reflected back on his attempts to let her know what was going on—without a response. She had headed to San Francisco without a word. He was thrown off guard and wasn't sure how he felt. Deceived came to mind.

"Why didn't you call me back?" He waited, able to visualize her look on the other end.

"It's complicated."

Paris bit down hard enough for his jaw to pop. "I'm listening."

Calloway tried to explain but her excuse sounded thin. "I didn't want to disturb you," she said. "I wanted to find out for myself if the information was good."

Still, silence.

"The information my source gathered proved unreliable," she confessed. "When you left the message of the shootout, I tried to call you right back."

Paris looked at his phone. There were no incoming calls from Calloway. She was lying. She had to know Paris could hear it in her voice, but why? What was her reason from not coming clean with what she was doing? He didn't have the energy to fight. It was just easier to let it go, give up on the fantasy he could ever trust her. Then Paris heard her voice soften, confessional.

"That's not the only reason why I've been out of touch."

Paris held still, curious.

Selma called me," she added. "From the nursing home." Calloway's tone took on weight, like dragging iron shackles. "I need to get to her."

The only option was to surrender and forgive.

What else could I do?

He was tired. At that moment, he didn't care about the case, about hiding her informant's identity, about where she had been, about keeping secrets. That was a lie. The last one.

He wanted her to tell him the truth, the secrets that she held. It was all about trust, about being needed.

"I'll come get you," Paris said.

"No," she replied. "Not this time. I need to handle this myself." A slight hesitation before she added, "alone."

Her words hurt. He wasn't sure if she needed to deal with her dilemma alone or if he'd lost her behind the wall of distrust. Either way, she was pulling away.

"I'll call you after," she said, her words a compromise. "I Promise."

He replied with the only thing he could say to the person he cared for. A person who might never be able to care for him back—or anyone for that matter. "Okay."

CHAPTER 33

A HARD SHOVE FROM BEHIND sent Manoso tumbling from the back of the car. Blood dripped from his right arm as it came to rest on the hard concrete.

"Get up, asshole," Alexi Mogilevich said as he reached under Manoso's armpits, heaving him up with little sensitivity. Mogilevich watched the one-time powerhouse in the drug world stagger and sway, in an attempt to find his balance. He brushed the dirt from his coat as if it was just another ordinary day.

Timing was everything. With the cell tower data he had obtained from his phone company contacts, Mogilevich had searched the area, grid by grid, looking for any signs of Manoso and his crew. Then a lucky break. He came across faces he recognized, like Peter Kennedy. He had been watching him for months. Robert Clarion, too—the man his boss had spoken about and provided photos. Mogilevich felt like he knew the men personally. As he watched people gather outside the Larkspur hotel, he'd spotted Manoso.

But before he could report to his boss, shots were fired, people started shooting back, and then bodies began to fall. That's when the opportunity presented itself. Manoso started making a move to escape, running in Mogilevich's direction. Mogilevich opened fire, ensuring only Manoso was left alive. By the time the henchmen were dead or scattered, Mogilevich only had to screw his pistol into Manoso's ear when they crossed paths and toss him into the passenger seat of his car.

Now, Manoso glared at Mogilevich, waiting for direction.

"Move," Mogilevich commanded, indicating the stairs to an apartment that Manoso recognized as the middle of the Tenderloin District.

The hundred-year-old renovated apartment building, like most in the city, smelled of dust and old paint. They walked the narrow stairs, up three levels, to a flat where Mogilevich placed Manoso on a hard chair, his back to the windows, hands duct-taped from behind. The room was dark, with the exception of the floor lamp between the two men, mostly trained into Manoso's eyes causing him to squint every time he looked up.

The red marks across his face, soon to turn to purple, were from the blows he received via Mogilevich's fist, punishment for causing a series of problems that slowed his capture and could, potentially, bring heat to his ordered mission.

"Do you know who I am?" Manoso asked, trying to sound calm but unable to conceal his anger.

Mogilevich cracked a smile.

"What is it you want?" Manoso demanded.

"I want nothing," Mogilevich said. "It's my boss that wants something."

Manoso's eyes converged into thin lines, as he studied his captor.

"I will ask you a few simple questions, and I want simple answers, understood?"

Manoso reluctantly nodded.

"Good."

Mogilevich walked over to Manoso, leaned in close, made a fist, and punched him hard across the bridge of his nose.

Manoso grunted from the blow but resisted reacting or showing any indication of weakness. Blood spurted from his nose, spraying onto the floor. His head fell limp for a second before he forced himself to stare up in defiance.

"That's to give you an appreciation for what will happen if you fail to answer correctly." Mogilevich rubbed his knuckles as he took a seat square in front of Manoso. He folded his arms and scratched at his lips, contemplating his next move, strategically giving Manoso time to soak in the severity of his predicament. "Tell me, Manoso. How many years have you been in the business?"

"A lot."

"And how many people have worked for you?"

"Even more."

Mogilevich nodded and pondered the answers, wondering if he

should work him over for his arrogance but decided to hold off. "And how many people have you killed?"

This time, Manoso beamed with a sense of pride. "Not enough."

Mogilevich stood and walked to a dark area of the room. Manoso tried to follow his movement, but the glare of the lamp prevented it. Quietness filled the room, making Manoso squirm in his chair. The chair protested.

"Did I hurt someone you know?" he asked.

"Who was your most loyal and trusted associate?"

"Sergey," Manoso said through clenched teeth. "You killed him tonight in the parking lot." His tone rose toward indignation.

"I killed no one. You were set up by your trusted associate, Mr. Kennedy."

Manoso forced himself to stare through the bright light. "If you don't work with Kennedy, why have you taken me?"

"We need a favor."

"We?"

"I'll ask you again, Manoso. Who was your most trusted associate? Besides the late Sergey."

Manoso dipped his head and pondered the question in silence.

"A person that you trusted," Mogilevich repeated and then added, "but he betrayed you for money and power."

Manoso's head lifted high, his eyes sharp and focused, this time seemingly unimpeded by the blazing lamp, as if he could clearly see Mogilevich cloaked in the dark corner of the room. It was a revelation, the answer materializing in his mind the instant Mogilevich said the word, *betrayed*.

"Ramone Santiago," he seethed.

"Yes," Mogilevich responded. "Ramone Santiago. And do you know how to find of him?"

"If I could, he would be dead."

"But if I were to give you some help, could you? Would you be able to convince him to meet?"

He let the question sink in. It had been a while since parting ways. The separation was a collapse, a cataclysm in the natural order of all things in the drug world. Almost ten years ago, Santiago tried to muscle in on Manoso's territory. When Manoso noticed what was happening, it was Santiago who tried to make amends but it was too late. Manoso took swift action, killing off most of Santiago's associates, leaving him with only a small swath of territory he could call his.

A call today would be suspect but, then again, it might well be viewed as nothing more than a business deal. An opportunity to equalize. If anyone could make this happen, it would be him. Besides, he also knew that, unless he could stall for time, his value to Mogilevich would be worthless. "Of course," he said with full confidence. "I can make it happen."

"Good," Mogilevich responded. "I have a number. You can say you got it from your friend, Peter Kennedy."

With tonight's news coverage of the shooting, the world would know Kennedy was in police custody. Mogilevich knew Santiago wouldn't take a chance on calling Kennedy to check, at least not for a few days. That's all Mogilevich needed. By then, it would too late.

"Why so interested in Santiago?"

"Just make the call and get him here."

Manoso pursed his lips, a thought running through his head. "Who's to say you won't kill me after?"

"Do you have a choice?"

Manoso remained still.

"I promise you this: Do what I ask and I won't kill you. Fair enough?"

Manoso gave it a moment then half-heartedly nodded.

"Good call."

"Like you said, I don't have a choice, do I?"

From out of the dark, Mogilevich came into the light, a cloth bag and a rag in his hand. "Gotta step out."

Manoso leaned back but only as far as the chair would allow. "Is this necessary?"

"Unfortunately, yes," Mogilevich replied. He shoved the rag in Manoso's mouth, securing it with a long piece of duct tape. He took the bag and threw it over Manoso's head. "This shouldn't take long."

Manoso silently complied as if he had been in this type of situation before. Gagged from calling out and hooded to prevent him from seeing, he sat quietly alone in a darkened room, lit by a harsh shaft he could no longer see.

Mogilevich—satisfied he could leave to update his boss and get the approval needed to move forward on their plan—stepped out of the apartment, locking the door behind him. Not even the sound of breathing could be heard coming from his prisoner. Mogilevich wondered briefly if the rag would cause Manoso to suffocate. He needed him alive to complete their plan. His boss would not be happy if Manoso died now. Nevertheless, Mogilevich wouldn't be long.

Crossing the hall to the apartment on the other side, he reached into his pocket, pulled out a key, slipped it into the lock, gave it a twist, and entered. The apartment was no different than the one he was just in. It too was dark, with nothing but a few metal chairs, a small table and a floor lamp. But in this room, his boss sat, and, unlike Manoso, was free, smoking a cigarette. Legs crossed, one foot nervously tapping the floor like a drug addict coming off a high, the boss had been finishing up on a call when Mogilevich entered. Closing the phone and placing it on the chair, his handler dropped the cigarette onto the hardwood floor and ground it out with the toe of a shoe, looking directly at Mogilevich.

"Is he able to do it?"

Mogilevich nodded. "Yes, and he will."

The boss smirked, looking pleased with their progress or maybe anxious to finally get this over with.

The handler approached Mogilevich and gently placed a hand on his right arm. "Thank you, Alexi. You've done well."

CHAPTER 34

THE BENEFIT OF A CRIME SCENE was the opportunity to gather evidence that might identify the culprits. The bad part was that it was a crime scene—a spot, once unassuming, now a tragic blight on history.

Diluted blood flowed down the sides of parking lot drainage as the cleanup crew hosed the area clear. Paper towels, plastic IV bags, used gloves and masks were haplessly scattered around the stains where two thugs once lay, where paramedics desperately attempted to push blood and air into their lungs and brains, trying to keep them alive. Their attempt fell useless.

Paris had already spent an hour grilling Torrington. It didn't take much for him to give up information on the recent drug buys and Rachel Clarion's original kidnapping, especially after tonight's shootout. Torrington admitted being introduced to Manoso several years back when he was muling drugs for a local distributor by the name of Kevin Finch.

Torrington and Clarion went way back, having gone to the same high school together. The two hadn't been in touch but, about ten years ago, through a mutual drug associate, Torrington learned Clarion was in the business and doing extremely well. They rekindled a past friendship, Clarion bringing Torrington under his wing as his main distribution manager. That was when Torrington brought Clarion to Finch. It didn't take long for Clarion's drug operation to triple in size. Life was good. Until that day when Clarion thumbed his nose over what some would refer to as "an accounting difference." That was when Rachel Clarion was taken. With the FBI now involved in a drug-related kidnapping and Finch dead, Torrington believed he'd used up all his luck, deciding it was time to get out of the business. He had done his best to stay clear of trouble.

Sort of.

"How do you know Ramone Santiago?" Paris asked.

Torrington winced, caught by a question he'd been hoping to avoid.

Paris could hear Torrington whisper "Shit!" under his breath.

"I looked over past telephone records," Paris continued. "I connected calls between you, Kennedy, and Santiago."

Torrington rubbed his eyes with his palms, reluctant to admit his past criminal involvement to a federal agent. "I helped Kennedy transport—when he was in his weed business."

"And Santiago?"

"I freelanced for Santiago long before I worked with Robert."

"What happened?"

"Back then, Ramone Santiago was small-time but had a reliable network of buyers," Torrington replied, sounding as if he was regretting every word. "Kennedy had the smarts—and the money—to expand." He paused before exhaling. "So I introduced Kennedy to my good friend and coke supplier, Manoso."

It all fit. Clarion moving coke in Sacramento and Kennedy in San Francisco. Both being supplied by Manoso.

"Something else you should know, Agent Paris." Torrington leaned against the hotel room wall as he pulled a smoke from his back pocket and lit it, as if cigarettes were an integral part of revealing interesting news. "Santiago and Manoso, they hate each other."

"Why?"

Torrington shook his head slowly. "Back when I introduced Kennedy to Santiago, I had no idea Santiago knew Manoso. I later heard Santiago was once Manoso's right hand man. Then he disrespected him. Might have tried to take over part of his operation."

"Did Ramone Santiago know Kennedy was getting his drugs from Manoso?"

Torrington shrugged. "I think that's why Santiago strong-armed Kennedy for his business."

"And how do you think Ramone Santiago found out?"

Torrington looked down, hesitating. "I may have mentioned it."

Paris pointed a finger in Torrington's face. "So this is all your doing?"

"Look, if they really hated each other, as I was told, I'll guarantee you the two have been tracking each other's whereabouts for years. With Ramone knowing Manoso was moving weight in his territory, I knew he'd do something to secure his position."

"Something?"

"Like kill him."

Paris walked over to Torrington, crossing deep into his personal space. Torrington pressed his back against the wall, uneasy and apprehensive.

"You know how I can find Manoso?"

Torrington nodded, sucked the last bit of nicotine out of his cigarette before tossing the butt to the ground. "After what happened tonight, that's a tough one. But yeah, I think there's still a few options."

Paris stepped closer. "I think you better tell me."

"Like I said, they probably keep tabs on each other. If anyone could find Manoso, it's Ramone Santiago.

PARIS WALKED PAST THE CRIME SCENE TAPE, which drooped and swayed the length of the parking lot, thinking about what Torrington said. Even if Torrington was correct about Santiago knowing Manoso's whereabouts, surveilling him would be useless. Santiago had to be smart to survive in this business. He would have his muscle gathering the intelligence about Manoso and reporting back. Paris knew he had to get the information straight from Santiago himself, and for that to happen, he would need a pretty good hammer to trade for his cooperation. He might have it with Kennedy's, Torrington's, and Clarion's testimonies.

The problem was, once their cooperation was made known, until Manoso could be found and apprehended, their lives—as well as that of their families—would be in jeopardy.

After their conversation, Torrington appeared dejected. Paris didn't give him any option other than to help. Otherwise, Torrington was on his own, which meant watching his back for the rest of his life, hoping Manoso had better things to do other than to hunt him down and kill him. Torrington understood. He had set up the meet that was meant for Manoso to be killed. As far as Torrington was concerned, he was already on Manoso's hit list.

Kennedy was next. He, too, had given up his relationship with Manoso, revealing how Santiago double-crossed him by taking over his operation. When Paris told Kennedy of the past relationship between Manoso and Santiago, Kennedy dropped his head into both hands, realizing he had brought two enemies together, practically delivering them to his front door. Paris had the same talk he had with Torrington: cooperation was his best bet.

Kennedy, however, was resistant. "Look," he said, his hands animated. "The hell with Santiago. Lock him up, for all I care." His shoulders went slack, worry lines creasing his face. "Manoso on the other hand, he's big. He's got people all over the country. One word from his lips, and they'll hunt me down like a hungry pack of wolves."

"You don't think he's got his sights on you already?"

Kennedy gave Paris the courtesy of considering his question, but his mind was already made up. "You find Manoso first. Then we'll talk."

CHAPTER 35

*I*T'S ALL ABOUT THE CELLPHONES.

That was what Paris believed. With Manoso knowing he was being hunted, more than likely, his phone had been dropped and replaced with a private one, known only to his most trusted associates. Santiago was different. Paris was betting Santiago had not been made aware of the evening's shootout and, with that, didn't know Kennedy was cooperating with the FBI.

Grilled and threatened with mandatory prison time for drug trafficking, Kennedy finally gave up—at least partially—what he knew about the relationship between Manoso and Ramone Santiago. And it would be Santiago's cellphone that would be the key in finding Manoso.

"You get them and I'll testify," Kennedy said, trying to deflect any further involvement. "They may hate each other but Roy's right. Most likely, they share the same network of friends."

Paris pulled Dools over and had him focus on pinpointing Santiago's cellphone. If they found him, Paris hoped, Santiago or an associate would give up Manoso. That was, if Torrington's assumption was correct. The threat of prison made for strange bedfellows.

Paris took advantage of a lull in the investigation. Standing on the side of the building for privacy, he called Calloway. His fifth attempt since their last conversation, each one going to voicemail. Not a single call returned. Not even a text. This last time, the phone didn't even ring, going straight to her recording.

"I just want to know if you're okay," Paris said, trying not to sound demanding. "Call me, please."

He hung up, finding himself squeezing the phone, frustrated at her lack of responsiveness. Was what they shared nothing but a passing fling? It wasn't as if they had much of a relationship. Hell, he wasn't sure what they had. Against better instincts, Paris had found himself caring for her. Like him, she walked in and out of dark corners. Privately, he thought Calloway could be the one to help him find balance, just as much as he could help her. He shoved the phone back in his pocket and turned up the ring volume.

Paris made his way back toward the hotel room where Clarion and his daughter now sat while the police continued their interviews. A medic was checking over Rachel's vitals as she communicated her answers in unembellished, tempered tones to the investigators. Her father sat next to her, rubbing her shoulder. Paris walked in and Clarion looked up, the two exchanging a glance. Paris waved two fingers in his directions, indicating he wanted Clarion to join him outside. Clarion gently touched Rachel on the chin, guiding her to look at him.

"Give me a minute. You'll be okay."

Rachel quietly assured her dad she'd be fine.

Clarion stood and followed Paris out the door. They walked under the parking lot light, far enough away for Rachel not to hear their conversation. Moths circled the bright vapor lights like a ribbon in the wind and the lamppost's electricity droned on in a low key as Paris sized up Clarion. He wanted answers.

"Tell me what you know about Manoso."

"Besides him ordering Kevin Finch to kidnap my daughter five years ago? I can't tell you anything."

"Peter Kennedy thinks if I find Ramone Santiago, I'll find Manoso." Paris studied Clarion's face but saw no reaction, Clarion staring at empty cars and watching hotel guests detour past crime scene tape.

Paris saw Clarion's reluctance to give any more information than he had to. "Until I find him and take him into custody, Robert, your family is still in danger."

Clarion lit a smoke and Paris saw his hand tremble. "I know."

"Let me put your family up in a hotel, at least until we can figure out where we are with this whole thing."

Clarion's face twisted into an obligatory smile. "Thanks, but no. I'll take my chances."

"You're risking your family's lives."

"I caused this mess," Clarion said, voice clearly agitated. "If it comes to it, I'll finish it."

Paris didn't like the sound of that threat.

Clarion looked away but Paris could see the muscle in his jaw contract.

"Stay low, Robert. If not for you, for your family."

Clarion muttered "Sure" or something like it, an attempt to placate Paris. He gave Clarion one last chance to put his family up at a safe location but he again refused. If he changed his mind, he was to call. Paris hoped Barbara Clarion would be able to convince her husband to reconsider. Until then, Paris had to make it his priority to find Ramone Santiago and get him to cooperate in finding Manoso. Only then, would Rachel Clarion be free from danger. In his mind, that was a tall order.

Clarion walked back to the hotel room where the detectives were wrapping up things with Rachel.

Paris watched Clarion put his arms around his daughter, her head falling onto his shoulder. Dools came over to Paris, both now watching Clarion escort Rachel to his car. The Evidence Response Team had already finished processing the crime scene, the bodies removed as if nothing had ever happened. Except it had. Rachel witnessed the horror firsthand, something she would never forget.

Paris clenched his fist, releasing and clenching again, his anger rising. Most of it was directed at Manoso, but some at Robert Clarion. Had it not been for his bad decisions made years ago, none of this would have happened.

"Pen registers show activity on Santiago's phone," Dools said. "Don't have a specific location but we're close."

"Then we better get on it."

Dools pulled his cellphone and called the Sacramento office, ordering the tech squad to start tracking the phone. Agents with hand-held directional finders would roam the area in covert cars and vans, playing a cat-and-mouse game to pinpoint Santiago's whereabouts.

The technique was more finesse than science, and the hunt might require agents to ping the phone to give the cell towers a chance to reveal the phone's coordinates. But doing so could raise suspicion on Santiago's part.

He could easily toss the phone into a nearby dumpster if he got spooked. If that happened, Santiago would disappear back into the shadows. That was the risk Paris had to take.

"What now?" Dools asked as they made their way to the car.

Paris grasped the door handle, retrieving keys from his coat pocket.

The situation had changed, and it was time to take overt action. "We get search warrants for everyone's home, stash house, and last known addresses."

Dools smiled as he slid into the front passenger seat.

"Get prepared. We're going to kick in every door," Paris said. "And then we're going to stomp on the back of every cockroach that runs out."

CHAPTER 36

W HEN CALLOWAY ENTERED HER MOTHER'S ROOM for the second time that day, her heart felt like an anchor on her chest. She tried to steady her nerves but found it hard to control her emotions. The monitor's beeping punctuated the air, a constant reminder her mother was dying. It was late, most of the staff in the middle of a shift change, giving Calloway the opportunity to have this moment uninhibited.

Her mother was lying on her back, the cotton sheet still neatly tucked up to her chest, bed cover folded down by her feet. She was slightly canted to her right, giving Calloway a profile of her face, her eyes closed.

Calloway stood next to the bed, listening to her breathing, lingering and absorbing every detail. Only three hours had passed since she'd seen her last, and yet, she looked thinner.

It was as if her mother were simply evaporating, into the heavens, the atoms of her physical being disbursing into the atmosphere like stars at morning's first light. Calloway reflected on the past, about how perfectly smooth and glowing her mother's skin once was. Now it looked paper-thin and pale.

Witnessing this downward spiral was difficult for Calloway, even if it had been coming for some time. When she was a child, she remembered how full of life her mother was, self-assured. Her voice breathed confidence. After her father's death, Calloway's mother became even more focused, keeping them together, to survive. She was brave, a force of nature. No matter how prepared Calloway thought she was, seeing her mother like this made her feel helpless.

Her greatest fear: someday soon her mother would be gone and Calloway would be alone.

It had only been a couple of hours since Selma had called. She said her mother was awake and asking for her. What had happened? Did she slide back into a lost state? Was Calloway too late?

She pulled a chair to her mother's bedside, sitting close, and slid a gentle hand over her mother's hair, smoothing it neatly behind an ear. Just touching her made Calloway smile.

She reached into her jacket pocket and felt the glazed porcelain figurine she had taken from the curio. Running her fingers effortlessly over the contours, she withdrew the figurine from her pocket and carefully placed it on the small portable table beside a pitcher of water and a half-filled plastic cup.

"I brought this one for you."

She kept her eyes on her mother—the room silent, save for the erratic beeping from the monitor. Calloway sank back into her chair, looked around the room, and then turned her attention to the door. Seeing no one, she sighed.

"I'm almost there," she confessed. "All these years and it's almost over."

She leaned close to her mother's face, trying to feel her presence. Her mother wasn't awake to hear her speak, but Calloway didn't care. She needed to say it, aloud. A tear fell, landing on her mother's hand, which she held dearly.

As if she felt the pain from that fallen drop, her mother's eyes opened. Her head rocked slowly from side-to-side, eyes clouded, trying to bring the world into focus.

"Valerie," her mother said, her voice warm, tender.

Calloway smiled.

Her mother's expression changed, as if suddenly her memory came back to reality, her eyes widening with concern. "No, Valerie."

"It's okay, really," Calloway replied, trying to calm her.

"Please," her mother begged. "Stay with me. Stay here."

Suddenly Calloway's body tensed as more tears started falling. She tried to wipe them with her shoulder, not wanting to let go of her mother's hand. If she did, she feared her mother's mind would slip back into a fog, her last thought being without the touch and comfort of her only daughter, the only person left in her life. "I'm right here," she replied. "I'm not going anywhere."

She looked away and closed her eyes, trying to find the strength to regain her composure. She felt her mother's hand on her back and it made her flinch, then the undemanding words in a tone of surrender: "Don't go. You don't need to go."

Calloway turned back with a false smile. "Look, I brought you a new figurine. The one I promised."

Her mother gazed at the porcelain piece sitting up on its hind legs, the smooth shiny surface interrupted by a small chip on its long right ear.

"I told you someday I would bring it to you."

In a swift stroke, her mother forced an arm across the table. Weak as she was, it was enough to rake the small table of its items, including the newly placed rabbit. The figurine tumbled to the linoleum floor and bounced under the bed. Calloway jumped up in surprise, cursing. Her mother fell silent, eyes fixed on a distant spot outside the window. Then slowly, her eyelids fell shut.

There was a strong voice from behind. "What's going on?"

Calloway turned to see Selma standing at the doorway and put up her hands to say everything was okay. "Mom's just upset."

Selma bee-lined to her patient's side, pushing aside the rolling table, pushing aside Calloway. She checked Ruth Calloway's vitals and made sure she was secure in her bed.

"This is not good," Selma chastised, "getting her all worked up."

Calloway took a step back, giving Selma room to do her job. She wanted to help, be the daughter she was supposed to be, but too much time had passed. She'd left the hard work of caring to others, like Selma. Calloway had become a stranger, whose face was only familiar on the weekends.

"She knew me," she said.

Selma never looked over at Calloway as she continued to straighten the bed sheets and the cords from the machines that monitored Ruth's every move. "Then be good to her when she has her senses. You won't get many more occasions like that, if ever."

A deep feeling of depression smothered Calloway—failure and embarrassment. Not knowing what else to do, she studied the black and white patterned floor before spotting the chipped rabbit. She quickly retrieved it and placed it in her pocket. The figurine had suffered another chip, a new rough white textured spot exposed along the base.

She made sure the rabbit was safe, knowing the importance of the piece to her mother, broken or not, and then turned and walked out.

"Goodbye," she said, barely above a whisper, and headed out the front door and into the empty parking lot.

SELMA HADN'T NOTICED CALLOWAY HAD LEFT the room until she was done getting her patient situated back in the bed, sopping up the spilled water with towels from the bathroom. By the time she finished, she noticed Ruth's eyes were now partially opened. Selma placed her head close to hers, offering a reassuring smile.

"How you doing, Miss Ruth?" She placed a consoling hand on her arm. "Can I get you anything?"

Ruth's mouth was opened but she had a hard time forming words. "Valerie?"

Selma strained to keep a smile. "She stepped out to make a phone call," she lied. "You just rest."

Ruth struggled to lift her head and look around, but it was too difficult, and she gave up. She looked into Selma's eyes, lifted a hand to express her thoughts. "She's making a mistake. Help her."

Selma pulled back but kept her gaze on Ruth. "What kind of mistake?"

Ruth fell back onto the pillow, exhausted. "A big mistake," she gasped. "And it will get her killed."

CHAPTER 37

ALEXI MOGILEVICH GRABBED MANOSO by his shirt collar and pushed him back over to the chair next to the window. Manoso fell heavily, causing the cheap wooden legs to squeal under the strain. He rubbed his sore wrists— partly to bring back the circulation from being bound, and partly out of a nervous habit.

Mogilevich turned and reached into a duffle bag on the floor, retrieving a new roll of tape.

"You don't need to do that," Manoso said.

Mogilevich didn't bother replying. He tore off the clear plastic wrap and shoved it back into the bag, peeling away a long length of silver tape from the roll. The loud zip from the tear made Manoso squirm.

"Why don't you wait a few minutes first?" Manoso said. "He may call back."

Mogilevich shifted toward Manoso, paused. Manoso managed a weak smile, hoping logic would prevail.

"You have tried three times already without success," Mogilevich said. "What makes you think Santiago will call you back?"

Manoso gestured as if to say, *It's obvious.* "I know Ramone. His curiosity will get the better of him."

Mogilevich considered his response before shaking his head. "No," he said, motioning Manoso to hold out his hands.

"Wait," Manoso begged. "I have an idea."

Mogilevich groaned, eyes rolling upward.

"I have an idea," Manoso repeated. "I do know a person who can get a hold of Ramone. A trusted friend."

Mogilevich held steady, suspicious.

"If anyone can get Ramone to meet, he can." Manoso put out a hand and snapped his fingers, indicating the cellphone. "His name is Nicolai. We go way back. Both of us used him as our middleman. Still do."

"Why should I trust you?"

Manoso's mouth twisted into a grin, his eyes giving the impression of self-resignation. "Because if I'm not telling the truth, you will kill me."

There was what seemed like an eternal minute of silence. Manoso felt the sweat sliding down from his hairline.

Under the circumstances, this was his last chance. Even if he could pull this off, the odds of Mogilevich letting him live were less than slim. With both hands extended, Manoso wasn't sure if he'd get the phone or duct tape. It took another minute of contemplation before Mogilevich placed the cellphone in Manoso's hand.

Then Mogilevich pulled a Glock nine millimeter pistol from behind his back and cradled it in his lap. "I hear one thing out of place and the next thing your friend Nicolai will hear is the sound of your brains blowing out the other side of your head."

Manoso put the phone on speaker for Mogilevich to hear. The phone rang twice before a male voice answered.

"Nicolai, it's me, Manoso."

Four . . . five . . . six seconds ticked by before Nicolai responded. "Why are you calling?"

Manoso smiled nervously, relieved the two were able to connect. "Nicolai, I need your help. Find Ramone Santiago and have him come to me now. It is imperative you do me this one favor." The conversation went quiet as Manoso waited, more seconds ticking off like a metronome in his head. Mogilevich looked concerned. "Did you hear me?" Manoso demanded.

"I'll try but no guarantee," Nicolai responded.

"Thank you."

"If I can find him," Nicolai responded, "where do you want him to meet you?"

Mogilevich had had already given him an address to use for his call. It was an apartment building a few blocks down, so as not to give away their exact location. Manoso passed the information to Nicolai.

"Get him here tomorrow evening." Manoso wanted it to be sooner but Mogilevich set the day and time. There would be no compromise. "Five o'clock. Tell him I have a proposition for him that will make him rich."

There was a grunt on the other end of the line, which Manoso took as an acknowledgement.

"If I can make this happen," Nicolai said, "what's in it for me?"

"My unconditional dedication and loyalty," Manoso replied.

"I would rather have a ten percent partnership in the business."

"I can only see two percent."

There was a muffled laugh. "Deal."

Manoso mouthed an inaudible "Yes" and grinned. *Done*. "And, Nicolai, please bring him here yourself. It is imperative. No one else. Can you do that?"

"I will do my best."

Manoso forced himself to sound confident. "I know you will."

He told Nicolai to call him back as soon as he received confirmation that Santiago would meet, getting nothing more than another grunt for a response. The phone went dead as Manoso handed it back to Mogilevich.

"Does that work for you?"

Mogilevich didn't appear convinced. "We'll see."

He slipped the pistol behind his back, grabbing the tape and again motioned for Manoso's wrists. Manoso protested, pulling his arms closed to his chest.

"You're going to kill Santiago, aren't you?"

Mogilevich didn't answer the question, this time reaching out and yanking Manoso's wrists forward.

"Then you're going to kill me as well."

Mogilevich didn't answer one way or another but Manoso wasn't stupid. His fate had been sealed the minute he was taken. What other option could there be? They had strong-armed him at gunpoint, tied him into a chair, and forced him to call a past associate-turned-competitor, to set up a deadly meet. It was obvious Mogilevich's intention was to kill Ramone Santiago. Then what? With Santiago dead, Manoso was their only witness. And witnesses had to be dealt with. If their positions were reversed, Manoso would have been forced to do the same.

As Mogilevich tightly wrapped his wrists in tape, Manoso held steady, hoping he had just bought some more time to figure his way out of this situation—alive.

RAFAEL BRAVO ENDED THE CALL WITH MANOSO, his boss, while his security team of four waited for their instructions. Asking to speak with

"Nikolai" was an alert code set by Manoso to notify his security team when he was in danger.

Rafael played along, gathering the clues provided, trying to determine the severity of his situation. Manoso saying, "It is imperative," had given it away. It was all Rafael needed for him to know the circumstances were grave. A rescue was in order. With the address and time, Rafael would make sure his team would be in place well in advance to have the upper hand. The thing he was unsure of was the size of the abductor's security force. Manoso said "two percent," meaning there were only two abductors, a seemingly small number. And why did he mention Ramone Santiago? Could it have meant Santiago was responsible for his abduction?

"Are you sure he said 'two'?" one of Rafael's men asked.

"I'm not deaf," Rafael snapped back.

Suddenly everyone looked as if they had something else they'd rather be doing. It didn't pay to cross Rafael.

Rafael continued to ponder Manoso's reply, considering each angle, each statement, before making his way to the gun locker. He twisted the heavy metal handle, exposing a cache of automatic rifle: MP-5s and M-4s purchased from the Mexican Army, a well-known source for the drug cartels. He removed a key from his pocket to unlock a heavy chain that tethered the weapons to the rack. "If it's two, then there will be no problem," he emphasized as he pulled the chain clear of the entire row, releasing enough rifles for each of his men. "But I'm not taking any chances."

The men stood at attention, making a line in front of Rafael. One by one, each retrieved a rifle from the rack and grabbed a handful of fully loaded magazines. They were preparing to get Manoso back. And that included killing the men who took him.

CHAPTER 38

"THERE'S A DEAD BODY IN KENNEDY'S APARTMENT."

That was the first thing Dools said when he walked into the Sacramento Field Office's squad bay, before handing Paris a tall cup of Peet's Coffee.

Paris kept silent, waiting for the rest of the story.

Dools apparently decided to take his time. He leaned over and tapped the thermostat, as if thinking that would make the air conditioner kick on.

Morning had come quickly. By the time he made it home, Paris had a tough time falling asleep, his brain running over what his next move would be. And more importantly: what would his adversary do next?

"Looks like there was an argument," Dools said, his tone flat. He dropped a picture of the dead man onto the table. "He lost."

Paris picked up the photo, gave it a good look—obviously a henchman, belonging to one of the drug groups, his death being part of the ebb and flow of power and control.

He shrugged, dropping the photo back on the table. "Kennedy know anything about this?"

"Nah," Dools answered. "More pissed off about having to pay for his carpet to be replaced."

Paris heard the disgust in Dools's tone.

"Rich people," Dools said. "He's lucky he's not sitting in a ten-by-ten holding cell."

Before the morning sun rose above the bay, the Evidence Response Team was already dispatched to Kennedy's apartment, having collected

THE COLDNESS OF NIGHT 181

every fiber, hair, and fingerprint they could from the victim, but it was superfluous. Kennedy and Clarion didn't have to come clean for Paris and Dools to know what happened. Besides, Paris was far more focused on getting his warrants.

Dools slid a chair next to Paris, opened his notebook, and pointed a single finger in the air. "I've got a surveillance team at Shafter's last known residence, thanks to Valerie's reports." Two fingers in the air. "Another at King's Bakery." A third. "Got a lead on a residence in the city of Davis."

Paris leaned forward in his chair, tried to look calm but there was too much at stake, knowing he had to act fast before the other side had the chance to settle the score.

"Cellphone triangulations, car registration, and Intel I pulled from case files," Dools said. "I think the Davis residence could be Santiago's crib."

The two unrolled a large map of the area and laid it over the documents and reports that were strewn across the table. Paris smoothed the map best he could, the city of Davis displayed in their line of sight.

Dools smacked a finger off Interstate 80, a half mile inside of town. "There," he said. "Cell tower analysis gets me somewhere here." He lifted his hands from the map, shoved them behind his head, and stretched, letting out a big yawn. "I've got the tech guys out with their million dollar gadgets. They'll find the house."

Paris turned and considered the white board. The squares continued to be updated, names of the subjects identified in the investigation with lines connecting new relationships. New lines spider-webbed between boxes, the relationships coming from undercover drug buys, phone records, and source information, but mostly from Calloway's extensive investigation. The document was more than a chart. It was a road map to the one person everyone wanted.

The shot caller.

On the top of the chart sat Manoso. Paris kept his concentration on the box at the top. Everything that had happened, from the exchange of drugs and money, to Rachel Clarion's kidnapping, to a dead body in Kennedy's apartment, nothing would have been done without Manoso being in the middle of it all. Manoso was the end of the road.

By early evening, they had gathered enough fresh information and analysis for Dools to draft out his probable cause statements for the warrants. Alison Davis, a new assistant US attorney, took more time than Dools felt necessary to look over the affidavit, did some minor word-smithing to make her feel like she contributed, but eventually she pushed it forward to the magistrate's office. *Lawyers.*

Paris and Dools soon found themselves back in the office, sitting opposite one another. Dools played spin the bottle with his pen on his desk. Paris checked his watch. "How much longer for the warrants?" Paris asked.

Dools continued spinning the pen. "You know the drill. Can't push the magistrate. I was told to head over—" He sharpened one eye at the clock above his head "—in an hour."

Paris massaged both eyes with the heels of his palms. Everything was a process, and time was something he could not freely expend. With warrants in hands, Paris could focus on his targets like a chess game, sit on locations, watch who was coming, going, decide which door to kick in first, find out who was going to talk. A weak link, that was all he needed. As much as he wanted to be methodical, his thoughts kept flashing on Rachel Clarion, the ongoing threat still out there, the unknown.

His head was whirling. He was exhausted. Paris had been moving non-stop since last night. He hadn't even had time to change his clothes. He picked up his briefcase and started shoving maps and reports into it. "I'm going to the house," he said. "Give me an hour."

Dools stretched his arms above his head and yawned again. "Take your time. We've done everything we could. Besides, we won't be able to get everyone back until morning."

A door opened, the sound of someone walking in his direction. Paris hadn't had time to turn toward the footsteps before hearing the voice.

"Sorry I'm late."

It was Calloway.

CHAPTER 39

SHE WALKED INTO THE ROOM, hands shoved deep in lightweight jacket pockets, unable to hide the apprehension and uncertainty. She swayed toward the men like she was expected. But nothing in her physical appearance gave the impression everything was all right.

Neither Paris nor Dools said a word. Instead, they gave her space to settle in, everyone feeling awkward.

Scratch that. Drama. That was what it was. Too much drama. One step forward in their relationship followed by a sinkhole. *Everyone claims they hate the drama*, Paris thought. *But the truth is we really don't. We are drawn to it, like smoke to an open window.* Calloway was like that with pain, something she couldn't help feeling. The pain added a touch of real life, which was better than soul-sucking emptiness. Or maybe it was Paris who needed the drama, a substitute for feeling needed, having to be truly invested.

She walked up to Paris, bodies close enough to touch, laid a hand on his forearm, holding it there long enough for Dools to notice. "Sorry for not calling you back," she said. "I can explain."

Paris put his hands in his pockets, trying to remain calm, emotions rumbling under his skin.

Part of him wanted to reach out and touch her, make sure she was all right. The other part wanted to tell her to leave. At that moment, he was indifferent to either choice.

Paris moved to the side just so he didn't have to look in her eyes and pushed a nearby chair away with his foot. Dools pretended not to notice.

"Look, I got your messages." Her voice sounded strained and tired. "Like I said on the phone, Selma called right after you dropped me off."

There it was. Drama mixed with guilt.

"My mother."

Paris felt guilt winning.

"I had to go back. Last night." She stepped back. "It's hard dealing with my mother and work at the same time."

He instinctively reached out, wanting to take the pain away then, reconsidered.

"She recognized me, Jack." Tears started to fill her eyes, a tight smile flexed between dimples. "I'm here now." She turned and thumbed away her tears, smoothed out her clothes. "Tell me what I missed."

Papers rustled in the background. Dools was rolling up his reports and shoving them under his armpit. "I'll leave you two alone," he called out as he made a dash toward the exit.

"I don't have time right now," Paris lied. "I'm heading home to change." He turned and grabbed up his bag, tossing it over his shoulder.

Calloway stepped in front of Paris, words bouncing off her tongue, settling on, "Can I come with you?"

Paris hesitated, felt his heart sink in his chest. He wanted to continue being angry but it was easier to give in. To accept. To care.

"I promise, I won't let you down." She picked up her bag, looked over at the pen registers, then toward the door. She seemed nervous, waiting for Paris to make a move.

What else could he do? He walked over and placed a hand on the small of her back. "Let's go," he said as he gently guided her out of the room.

They made their way down the hall and past the command center. The dispatcher was lost in his own world of radio traffic from the local PDs, alert notices coming in from the California Law Enforcement Telecommunication System known as CLETS. A number of televisions hung high on the wall to monitor breaking news throughout the world. Someone had changed one of the TVs to a Giants ballgame on ESPN. As Paris pulled open the side door, the two stepped out into the warm evening air with Calloway taking any opportunity to maneuver close to Paris, their shoulders finding any excuse to touch. Before the door closed, a loud cheer came from the command center. Someone hit a home run.

CHAPTER 40

CALLOWAY REMAINED RELATIVELY QUIET during the drive, listening to Paris update her on all the details of the shooting, the abduction, the dead bodies. He told her that they had enough evidence, based on the testimony of Kennedy, Clarion, and Torrington, to charge Manoso for kidnapping and drug trafficking. Even racketeering. With Rachel back safe, moving forward on the charges was appropriate.

Calloway asked few questions, absorbing the evidence. He could see she was anxious, feeling the energy of closing in on the person she had been chasing all these years.

Turning off the freeway, he cut through the heart of downtown Sacramento before pulling onto the driveway of his home in Midtown. He rented the small house because it was close to the home he'd had with Emily. Where the kids came to visit. It gave him the opportunity to see them, however limited.

At nightfall, porch lights shined in single file, the sidewalk and neatly manicured landscapes were canopied in darkness by well-established oak, cottonwood and sycamore trees. Paris stepped out of his car and waited for Calloway to make her way around to his side. Together, they wandered to the front entrance with Calloway staring up as the evening stars emerged. He shook out the key from his pocket and slid it into the door. With the exception of a wedge of golden light streaming in from the porch lamps, the entry was dark. Two glowing dots emanated by their feet. It purred. Paris pointed down.

"That's Leroy."

Calloway watched the tuxedo cat stroll out of the darkness, making a figure eight between Paris's legs. After two turns, the cat did a Captain Kirk shoulder roll, exposing his seventeen-pound, black-and-white fur belly.

"Really?" Calloway remarked, although not necessarily looking for a response.

Paris shrugged. "Daughter's cat. Turns out, she can't have it at college." Leroy took a perturbed swipe at his leg. "Voila! He's all mine."

Calloway bent down and scratched Leroy under his chin. He purred loudly, like a fan on low speed.

Paris walked into the kitchen and flicked on the lights. Case files towered in the center of a small glass table surrounded by four black lacquered chairs. A report was splayed open, pen stabbed halfway down to mark its importance.

Just past the table, French doors led out to a small backyard. Paris pushed them open and cool air filtered in. Switching on the backyard lights, he exposed a more welcoming sight. Unlike the sparseness of the interior, the landscaping was a mixture of planters and hardscape with red brick and stone. The walkways complimented with foliage and colorful flowers. Well-manicured. Two fruit trees stood on each side of the yard, sturdy branches supporting a thick umbrella of lush green leaves, dotted with tiny white buds.

An outdoor couch, flanked by two wing chairs with footrests, gave the impression the area was designed for those late-night gatherings and cocktails with close friends. Nothing was further from the truth. He stood in the middle of the patio and absorbed the calmness, a feeling he rarely felt outside the confines of this space. He enjoyed his garden.

Calloway wandered out from the kitchen, stopping a few feet from the French doors. "Beautiful," she remarked.

Paris sat down on one of the footrests and relaxed, stretching his legs straight, one ankle crossed over the other. "I like it out here."

She walked over and sat down on the adjacent wing chair. Leroy sprinted past, taking ownership of the couch. Calloway rubbed the armrest. "So you never told me your plan to find Manoso."

Paris explained the key evidence and the testimony from all the players he had secured. He felt that would be enough to get someone to cooperate and give up something to help find their subject. "We'll have the warrants by morning."

Calloway looked unconvinced. "You really think someone's going to roll on a guy like Manoso?"

He knew there were no guarantees. "I'm hoping."

Leroy stiffened and leapt off the couch, attacking a spot on the ground.

Calloway bit down on her cheek, still not buying it. "I'm still not convinced this is a good idea."

"I don't think we have any other option."

"If you do this and don't get any cooperation, Manoso is going to know you're on to him."

Paris stood and took, three, four, five steps over to a rose covered archway—why in that direction, he did not know. He tried not to look upset. He had been the one working the case, to identify their target, to find a way to locate him. They had already agreed on this plan. Calloway had been a no-show this entire time, and now she was second-guessing his decisions? His judgment? There were risks in every investigative call, but it was something she refused to entertain.

He had to wonder: would she ever take a chance? Did she ever want this case to end? It was as if the investigation had become her entire life, to track Manoso, forever.

The more he thought, the more irritated he became. He chose his words carefully, not wanting to show his frustration. "We've got a dangerous man still hell-bent on hurting the Clarion family. We've got a lot of dead bodies, Val. I can't let this go on much longer."

"You're going to fuck it up, Jack." Calloway's voice was raised.

Paris snapped back. "For who, Val?"

Calloway caught herself before replying, swallowing hard. "For me," she said in a confessing tone. Then softer, "My work."

Paris shouldn't have but pressed the issue. "And what about your source?"

"What about him?"

"That's right. 'Him' is about all I know of the guy."

Calloway waved a dismissive arm. "Trust me."

He couldn't help but feel the irony in her last remark. "I do. Why don't you trust me?"

She took a long time to answer, "I do."

His anger cooled, being replaced with a feeling of sadness. As much as Calloway's response was self-serving, Paris understood. She feared if the plan failed, everyone—Paris included—would lose enthusiasm and slowly fade away, leaving Calloway with nothing but a stack of cardboard boxes full of worthless charts and old photographs.

"We have a chance to get this guy," Paris said. "We can stop him from ever hurting anyone again."

Calloway looked away, refusing to accept his explanation.

I'm not leaving, Valerie." Paris went back to Calloway and knelt down, coaxing her to look into his eyes. "No matter what happens, I'm here with you."

Calloway leaned forward, settling onto his chest. She felt warm. Paris slid his arms around her and all her muscles uncoiled.

With a slight nod, she whispered, "Okay."

They remained together, quiet, not speaking about the case, not about Santiago, or Manoso. In that moment, work was second to their need for normality. Times like this were rare and it had been too long for Paris. He had forgotten how it felt. He could tell it had been forever for Calloway, too.

Calloway lifted her head but kept her hands holding his. "What do we do now?"

"I told Dools we would be back tonight."

Calloway's body withered at the thought. "Really?"

Paris shrugged.

Leroy slammed a furry paw and flattened a lone grasshopper. Calloway's face scrunched.

"We're not going to be able to get everyone together until tomorrow," he said, adding, "Why don't you stay tonight? Keep Leroy company? If you want."

Work with me.

Calloway displayed a waning grin. She looked over at Leroy and the grasshopper. Leroy bit down and snapped off a leg.

Paris raised an eyebrow. "He's just playing with his toys."

The paw came down again. This time, green fluid oozed from the body.

Calloway gave it one last look. "Looks like he just pulled the batteries out."

Leroy got bored and left. Calloway turned her attention back to Paris. "How about we keep each other company?"

Winner.

They stood and headed back in the house. Paris closed and locked the French doors, walked into the kitchen and opened a bottle of wine. He let it breathe and took the opportunity to pick up the phone and call Dools. He tried telling him there was a slight change in plans and that they would connect early tomorrow. His excuse was transparent. So was Dools's response. As Paris poured two glasses, Calloway went out to the car and retrieved her bag. She had a change of clothes. For the morning.

CHAPTER 41

PARIS HURRIED BACK TO THE OFFICE to prepare the surveillance teams for their assignments. Calloway went to her car, still in the Bureau parking lot, and drove to the PD to update her management staff and arrange for officer back-up. Dools had retrieved the signed warrants, giving the FBI up to ten days to execute. They were under seal, meaning the supporting evidence in the affidavit would not be disclosed until after arrests were made. It was to protect Clarion, Torrington, and Kennedy. Sealed or not, Paris knew once the warrants were executed, word would get out. Everyone involved would need to be extra careful.

By mid-morning, Calloway returned to the FBI office. She tossed her gear onto Paris's desk, like she was claiming territory. Dools's days of riding shotgun with his partner were gone. Dools offered to take point at one of the other locations and gave Paris one of those looks.

By eleven a.m., the surveillance teams were in place. Dools had the eye on the Davis house, the Sacramento PD narcotics unit was on King's Bakery, and Paris and Calloway sat on the Shafter residence. In a flurry of radio chatter, everyone called in, confirming their locations and positions. A command post was set up at the FBI office, monitoring the radio traffic and coordinating any support needed by agents in the field. After check-in, the radio went silent. Now they waited to see who showed up.

Paris pulled his vehicle far down the street from Shafter's home. He barely had a view of the house located on the corner of an intersection, the driveway being the only part observable. The Cessna Skyhawk flying overhead gave them breathing room to keep a safe distance. The plane made wide, sweeping loops, the pilot calling out vehicle and pedestrian traffic.

A couple of hours passed, with little activity. Even King's Bakery had few customers, let alone anyone who fit the descriptions of the men they had followed earlier in the week.

Calloway spent most of her time on her cell phone, texting and emailing, while Paris kept his eye on the street. Every so often, Calloway would look up and out the window before returning to her phone. Paris had no idea if it were personal or case-related. She didn't seem to want to share. As much as he wanted to remind her of their latest conversation, he thought best not to push it.

Trust.

A surveillance agent called over the radio. A green sedan was heading down the street, coming toward Paris.

"Is it a Lexus?" Paris remembered Shafter vehicle when they lost him during the drug buy.

"Confirmed. It's a Lexus," the agent replied.

Paris sat up and Calloway shoved her phone into her pocket. They waited a few seconds before the car appeared down the street, coming toward them. Paris pulled out his binocular.

"Is it Shafter?" Calloway asked.

From a distance, the car looked like the one Paris recalled. It slowed before turning into the driveway, giving him a profile view of the passenger side.

"I got it." Paris called out over the radio. The bird confirmed the sighting and then reported the driver and another person in the front right seat had exited the vehicle. A few seconds later, Paris saw the two meet up at the back of the car, trunk popping open.

"Who is it?" Calloway asked, sounding anxious.

Both men were standing. The passenger hauled out a large bag. Their distance made the view hazy but when the men turned, Paris was able to get a better look at their faces.

"Well?"

Paris keyed his mic. "Yep, that's Shafter."

"Who's the other guy?"

With the mic still broadcasting, Paris said, "The other is Ramone Santiago."

CHAPTER 42

THERE WAS NOT MUCH TIME when opportunity knocked. When your primary subject walked up to the door and said "I'm here," you go for it.

This was Paris's opportunity to get Santiago and, hopefully, find Manoso. Paris reached behind his seat, pulling his ballistic vest from the bag, sliding it on. Calloway was already wearing hers. The bird fixed a point on their targets, watching them enter the house.

It looked as if Santiago had a key, suggesting no one else was inside, but that was only a guess, and not knowing how many suspects were in the house worried him. His targets had already proven they were heavily armed and didn't have a problem killing. As much as Paris wanted to storm the front door, he opted for caution.

He picked up his phone and called Dools. "Hold everyone off on making entry," he ordered. "Let's get a better handle on how many are in the residence."

Dools didn't want to wait, repeating Paris's own words about "kicking in the door" and something else about "cockroaches."

"Better to be certain," Paris told Dools. "Let's watch it for a few minutes."

They gave the surveillance another half hour. A neighbor's kid came out and practiced jumping the curb with his skateboard. Air conditioners kicked on and off in a dull whir as the afternoon temperature spiked. The house they were watching showed little sign of life. The minutes steadily marched forward, like soldiers in rhythmic cadence.

Paris looked at his watch then at Calloway, "Okay, time to go in."

She nodded approval, got on the radio, and instructed the team to meet down the street. Paris slowly drove past the house, glancing casually, before making their way to the MacDonald's parking lot a quarter mile down the road.

Seven agents stood together in a tight circle. Patrons walked past giving uneasy looks, knowing something was going down. After briefing the team, the tactical lead agent handed out assignments for the entry. They had already studied the layout of the home. The front door was wood with a glass pane, no metal security gate, the back emptied into a small fenced yard with one exit gate, no lock.

Two black and white units were called in to block the road as a safety precaution. Everyone suited up in their ballistic vests and helmets, checked their weapons, and tested their radios. Piling into the back of two vans, the agents conveyed to the target location where they bailed out, forming a stacked line along the garage. A couple of agents were readied to enter the back gate as soon as the front door was breached. Paris and Calloway waited in the rear of the stack.

With everyone in position, the lead agent gave the signal to advance. The front agent, carrying a heavy metal ram, led the five-man team to the front door. Swinging it hard, the handle fractured and gave way. The door banged open and the team poured in. Commands were given: "*Freeze, FBI!*" and "*Show me your hands!*" It took less than five minutes before the team cleared all the rooms and announced the house was secured. Paris had followed the last agent. In the living room, his subjects were flex-cuffed from behind, both faced down on the carpet. It only took Paris a second to recognize Santiago and Shafter and he went straight to them. Calloway followed close behind. He grabbed Santiago by his upper arm, rolled him to the side and pulled him up. Shafter remained still, eyes focused on the ground as if knowing his turn was coming soon enough.

"Come with me."

Paris led Santiago out the back door and sat him down at a patio table. Calloway sat to his left, Paris directly in front of him. Santiago squirmed. The flex-cuff made sitting uncomfortable. Paris didn't care.

"I'm giving you one opportunity to make a deal, Ramone."

Santiago sat expressionless.

It was explained to him. He was being arrested for drug trafficking and looking at a mandatory minimum of twenty years. "With what else I know about you," Paris added, "it could be life."

"What is it you want from me?"

Paris pressed both hands flat on the glass table and leaned close to Santiago. The table legs creaked. "Where's Manoso?"

Santiago's eyes went wide. He muffled a laugh deep in his throat. "Why do you think I would tell you?"

Calloway pushed her way forward. "Because you hate him and want him dead."

"And telling you would guarantee his death?"

"Day's not over."

Santiago brushed off her response and extended his arms forward, displaying his cuffed wrists. "Even if I would like to see him dead, how would helping you, help me?"

"You cooperate, and I'll talk to the US Attorney for consideration," Paris said. That was true.

"You could get me a significant reduction in time?"

"I will," Paris said. That was a lie.

Santiago leaned back, looking almost relaxed. "He is a very dangerous man, you know."

"We know," Paris said.

"My relationship with Manoso goes a long way back," Santiago continued. "I know his strengths as well as his weaknesses."

"What's his weakness?" Calloway asked.

"That's easy. His ego."

"And his strength?"

Santiago's smile disappeared. "The same." He sat up and spoke with clarity. "Manoso will stop at nothing to settle a score, no matter what it takes. He is driven by his enormous ego." He fell back into the chair, his expression that of a man giving up the fight. "Me helping you would only inflame his desire to hunt me down and kill me. Wherever I am."

"I'll hide you," Paris replied. "Put you in Witness Protection."

Ramone Santiago nodded slowly, a frown forming as if considering the proposition. Then he shrugged. "No fucking way."

A BLACK AND WHITE UNIT PULLED UP to the house, and Calloway decided to park Santiago in the back seat until they had a chance to speak with Shafter.

Without Santiago's cooperation, their last chance was with him. She listened to Paris telling Dools that, if this didn't work, he should be ready to kick in the other doors.

They regrouped, went over their strategy—not much different than what they did with Santiago—hoping, this time, it would be enough. Shafter was different. He was a worker-bee, a gun-for-hire. He had no loyalties. Shafter did what was best for Shafter. They played on that, staying clear of the possibility that Manoso would make him a target for the rest of his life. As far as Paris was concerned, it was the cost of doing business in the drug trade.

They sat Shafter up in the living room, which had already been cleared. The other agents had gone, except for a few still wrapping up paperwork. For a man Paris knew had killed—most likely more than once—Shafter appeared passive, almost friendly. As a gesture of goodwill, they moved his handcuffs from back to front. He was appreciative. Before Paris could speak, Shafter preempted the conversation with a quiet inviting grin and said, "I can help you," before politely requesting water.

The killer was thirsty.

Paris motioned for an agent to go to the kitchen.

"You'll talk to the prosecutor and cut me a deal?"

"Absolutely."

"My dealings with Manoso and Ramone are complicated," Shafter started out. "They hate each other." He looked over his shoulder, as if seeing if Santiago was still around. "He'd kill Manoso if given the chance."

"Why hasn't he?"

Shafter shrugged. "They have common associates. It would upset the balance of power."

Paris scanned one of Calloway's investigative reports. "You worked with Manoso, recently?"

Shafter nodded.

"Where can I find him?"

"I haven't a clue," he replied.

Calloway grabbed Shafter by the arm, yanking him to his feet. His legs wobbled then buckled. "I knew you wouldn't cooperate." She looked over at Paris. "We'll get the help from someone else."

"Wait," Shafter said. "You asked the wrong question." He found his balance. "It's not *where* can you find him, but *how.*"

"Quit screwing with me," Calloway said.

Mocking forgiveness and holding onto a tight smile, he repeated, "It's not *where* but *how.* I can tell you how to find him."

Paris stood, looked at his watch. "Okay, Michael. How can I find Manoso?"

"He has a security detail. Very trusted. Everywhere he goes, they go. If you follow them, you'll find Manoso."

Calloway slammed a hand on Shafter's shoulder and shook her head. "He's full of shit."

Paris raised a hand, trying to slow things down and, at the same time, calm his partner. "How would I find this security detail?"

Like the Cheshire cat, he spread his smile wide, teeth exposed. "I have their private cell number."

Calloway was still fuming. "Don't trust him."

Shafter rambled off the cell number and then said it again, this time slowly so Paris could write it down. "Got it? Check it out. You'll see I'm right."

An agent approached holding onto a glass of water. Calloway took it and thanked the agent. Reluctantly, she brought the glass up Shafter's lips.

Thank you," Shafter replied with politeness.

The killer was satisfied.

CHAPTER 43

"I STILL DON'T TRUST HIM." Calloway whispered her opinion but loud enough for Shafter to hear.

He sat, stone-faced on the couch, cuffed hands resting on his lap.

Paris was on the phone with Dools. They'd been bantering over whether to hold off on the other warrants. Shafter's help—if he was being truthful—could prove invaluable. The threat to Clarion and his family was still real, and until they could find Manoso and his men, the danger would never go away.

It was the right thing to do, a risk they had to take. And it was their best chance of finding him, hopefully, before he was able to bury himself deep out of sight. If that happened, God knew where and when he would turn up. For now, they agreed to hold off on the other warrants. With this new information, it was worth investigating. They had nine days to execute the others. It was agreed: if nothing came out of Shafter's information, they'd hit the other locations.

"Get a pen, trap and trace, and tracking on the security team's phone," Paris ordered Dools.

Hanging up the call, Paris saw Calloway pacing, glued to her cellphone. She felt his eyes on her, looked at him without a word. She shoved the phone into her pocket and walked over, pointing a finger at Shafter. "What do you want to do with him?"

Paris regarded his prisoner, who was taking in their every move. "I don't want to book him quite yet."

Calloway rolled her eyes but relented. She knew Paris wanted to hide him, at least for a while. "I understand," she said, looking toward the open front door, the grill of a visible patrol car. "Santiago, on the other hand, needs to see what the inside of a holding cell looks like."

Paris nodded. "I can have the black and white take him to lock-up but keep him on ice."

Calloway shook her head, obviously with another option. "I got him." She reached for her bag and hoisted it over a shoulder. "I'll ride with him downtown. It'll give me some time to get him to reconsider his options."

It made sense. "Call," he said as they exchanged waves.

Paris turned his attention to the living room table and at the collection of field reports, sealed evidence bags, and maps. He pulled the notes of his interviews, trying to see what he might have missed. He was dog-tired and his notes and drawings looked like an assortment of jumbled words, scribbled lines, and random numbers. Paris ran his thumbs across the lids of his eyes, wishing the fatigue away. It hadn't been more than a few seconds before he felt someone's presence, a slight nudge and a familiar scent.

Calloway reappeared. She was inches from his body, gently brushing against his side while arbitrarily reaching for a file folder. She didn't seem to care which folder, it appeared, thumbing through all of them at random. It was obvious it wasn't the reports that brought her back. Her right hand touched his, even paused for a moment before gliding softly across his. Her face was close, close enough that he could smell that familiar and alluring fragrance. It made his blood rush.

She spoke softly without looking up, the words meant only for him. "Thank you for being there for me."

He saw she was holding back a smile. Then she turned and walked away as if she had done what she had come back for.

An hour rolled past. It was almost two p.m. and Paris was getting antsy. Guys like Manoso wouldn't wait around to be caught, and with all the television coverage of the kidnapping, not to mention the shootout in Marin County, it would only be a matter of time before he would eliminate his connections and move on.

And that security detail cell number? It would be the first one he'd dump. Paris needed a back-up plan, one that would give him assurance, an alternative. It was essential.

Maybe there's another close associate to track?

Without a second one, he had to rely on a mid-level associate, who was far from being trustworthy. He thought about something that Shafter said.

They have common associates.

Paris reached into his pocket, pulled out his cell, and dialed Dools. It rang once before he answered.

"What?" Dools sounded frustrated.

They went over the case and what information they had so far. Paris talked about his need for a back-up plan, another associate. Dools tossed out several ideas, none of which sounded promising, at best, long shots.

Dools started to ramble before getting to the point. "You know, you've been dancing around our best chance at getting us what we need."

It only took Paris a second for him to know where he was going. Calloway's informant.

"You've got to get control of him."

Paris felt the blood drain from his head as everything started to swarm before his eyes. He knew what Dools was suggesting, what could very well destroy the trust he now felt with Calloway.

Thank you for being there for me.

Paris also knew Dools was right. Their time was short and her source was their best chance at getting Manoso.

Work over personal life.

"The tracking order," Paris said. "Find him now."

CHAPTER 44

THE RIDE WAS QUIET IN THE PATROL CAR. Santiago sat secured in the backseat, staring distantly out the side window. Every few minutes the silence would be interrupted with the sound of Calloway's cellphone vibrating.

Without looking, she would push the end button and shove it back into her pocket. The officer driving the car stopped bothering to look over after the first couple of times. It wasn't any of his business.

Heading into traffic, Calloway felt a stabbing moment of anxiousness. She leaned her head against the side window, trying to bring back her focus and not let go of control. The driver stretched out his back and rubbed his neck, the movement making his ballistic vest crackle like bubble wrap.

Calloway looked back at Santiago. She saw a man who, over the years, forged a drug trafficking network from intimidation and greed. He strong-armed the neighborhood businesses, recruited men who would do anything for a price. He collaborated with his competitors and then killed them when the opportunity presented itself. Now, he was given a chance to save his own skin—with the opportunity to do so by eliminating his primary competitor—and said no. Calloway realized why. His refusal to cooperate was a basic philosophy of survival. She knew Santiago would figure out another way to eliminate Manoso without having to cooperate with law enforcement.

Frankly, Calloway couldn't care less. She knew both would eventually end up on a corner's slab or a shallow grave. Either way, she would find satisfaction.

She turned over her shoulder, breaking Santiago's concentration. "Any sins you want to confess?"

Santiago ignored her by closing his eyes but couldn't hide his indignation over her condescending tone.

"I would ask for forgiveness now, Ramone," she said. "To cleanse your soul. That's if you have one."

Santiago said nothing, snubbing Calloway's warnings. To him, life was nothing but a series of obstacles to confront and, always, overcome. This one was no different. Arrested for drug trafficking, Ramone Santiago would hire a top attorney, do what was best for himself, and then find his way back into the game.

Calloway studied Santiago as he daydreamed out the window. He looked smug and that made her despise him even more. She was irked, trying to hide the emotions bubbling inside while she contemplated her next move.

Thirty minutes later, the officer navigated the black and white into the FBI parking lot.

"Over there," Calloway said, directing him to a blue Chevy Malibu.

The car came to a stop and Calloway wasted no time, pulling Santiago from the backseat. The driving officer came around and stood behind Calloway, awaiting instructions.

"I got this," she said.

Hesitating, he stood quiet for an instant. The car engine ticked in perfect imitation of a stopwatch as it cooled. Before he decided to turn and walk away, Calloway reached in her bag that was slung over her shoulder and retrieved a manila envelope.

"Do me a favor," she said. "Drop this off for Agent Paris."

The officer took the package and started walking toward the main entrance to the FBI office.

Calloway watched as the he walked away then pushed Santiago into the back of her Malibu, strapping his seatbelt across his chest and giving him a pat on the shoulder.

"You're all mine, Ramone."

Santiago laughed. "Talk to my attorney, Detective."

Calloway slipped the key into the ignition, fired up the Malibu, and drove out of the Bureau lot. She entered onto the freeway and held her speed at a moderate cruise, eventually cresting into downtown but then sailed past the off-ramp that would have led them toward the jail.

Santiago was familiar with the area and watched Sacramento's iconic

Tower Bridge drift past and out of his view as they continued west. "You missed our exit, Detective."

"You're not going to jail, Ramone. Like I said, you're going to pay for your past sins."

Calloway looked in her rearview mirror, saw Santiago's eyes sharpen, his focus on the back of her head. His attention was no longer about something outside the window. It was now about everything inside.

Throughout the quiet drive, Calloway kept peering back at Santiago, as if, for a split second out of her constant purview, he would vanish. But she knew that wasn't going to happen. She wouldn't allow it. For all the years she'd been chasing the ghosts of her past, her time had finally come.

That made her smile.

CHAPTER 45

NORTH AND SOUTH MEANT NOTHING.

"Am I turning right or left?" Paris's voice was gruff, his tone short with a touch of frustration.

Over the phone, Dools slowed the tempo, bringing calm to his voice. "Turn left. That'll take you into Richmond."

Dools was already with the tracking team, trying to get Paris to join in. They were close in locating Manoso's security detail, within a few blocks, hoping to pinpoint the exact spot soon.

It was difficult. Signals were bouncing off walls, giving false direction, a game of hide and seek. So long as the phone was on, they had a chance at finding it. To do this though, every so often, they had to send out a ping, like a submarine trying to find its enemy in the vast darkness of the ocean. He made it a point to keep them to a minimum.

By the time Paris caught up with Dools, the surveillance was on the move. Ending up at San Francisco's wharf, the team snaked between long commercial buildings, trying to hide their intent between large eighteen-wheelers, vans, and flatbed trucks, loaded with palletized crates and boxes.

They studied the faces of every person standing inside doorways and rollup gates, smoking, doing nothing. Maybe they were lookouts? Heavy bags were tossed into backs of vans. Could they be loaded with high-powered weapons and ballistic vests? Were these the men they were looking for?

One of the agents called out over the radio. He'd spotted two men who looked suspicious, pulling out in an SUV, driving in the opposite direction. The windows were blacked out. There could have been more people in the back. It was impossible to tell. Another agent tried to intercept the SUV but was caught behind a flatbed leaving a warehouse garage. By the time he made his way down a parallel road, the SUV was gone.

Paris parked a few blocks away down an alley.

A minute later, Dools pulled up. He squeezed his large frame out from behind the wheel, scoped out the area, and wedged himself into Paris's front passenger seat. He looked sweaty and tired. "We're close," he said. "I can feel it."

Paris considered the totality of the situation and didn't like where this was going. This wasn't only about kidnapping a child. It was also about territory, power. Revenge. Manoso was taking over the territory. "You think Manoso's starting a war?"

Dools shrugged. "Or ending one."

The dilemma: finding and following this group was their best option in locating Manoso—but letting an armed group of henchmen move freely was too big a risk to take. Losing them on surveillance could mean the difference between finding Manoso and a bloody massacre.

"How many agents do we have out here?"

Dools ran through the names in his head, keeping track with his fingers. "Ten, not counting us."

It was enough. If they came upon multiple vehicles, Paris would be able to follow or choose their best bet. Believing these guys would be armed to the teeth, Dools called the Bureau air unit and requested help. They told him it would be at least thirty minutes.

As Dools got on the radio to position the team, Paris placed a call to Calloway. The cellphone rang three times before going to voicemail. Calls going straight to voicemail meant phones were turned off. Phones that rang usually meant the person was screening their calls. Calloway was screening.

"Call me," was the only message he left.

He looked over at Dools, waiting for him to finish talking on the radio.

Dools put down the mic but didn't look Paris's way. "What?"

"Where's Calloway's informant?"

Dools leafed through a few pages in his notebook, scrolled down with a finger. "Downtown SF." Then he added, "Signals are bouncing around buildings so it's hard to say exactly where but the tracker shows he hasn't moved for quite a while."

Paris sat silent, contemplating his next move.

"You think Calloway is with him?"

Paris shrugged.

Dools was trying to be accommodating. "If you want to take off and go find her, I'll manage the team."

Paris wanted to take Dools up on his offer but worried he was making his decision for the wrong reasons. His phone vibrated. It was a number he didn't recognize. When he answered it, the voice was familiar.

"Mr. Paris?"

"Selma?"

Selma began speaking in a low hush as if trying to hide the conversation from others within earshot. Although tempered, she sounded troubled.

"I'm sorry to bother you but do you know how I can reach Miss Valerie?"

Paris explained his own failed attempts and frustrations. He rolled down the car window, suddenly feeling the need for fresh air. "What's going on?"

"Something's not right," Selma said, telling Paris about the last time Calloway was at the care facility, about Ruth Calloway's sudden emotional flare-up and her fear for her daughter's life. "She said Miss Valerie was in danger."

"I don't understand. Why does she think that?"

Selma's volume jumped. "I don't know but I think you better get down here and see for yourself."

He ended the call and turned to his partner. Paris could tell Dools heard the entire conversation. Before Paris could say anything, Dools pulled on the car handle and threw a leg out the door. "You better get going."

WHEN CALLOWAY EDGED HER CAR UP to the curb, Ramone Santiago looked out the window and took in every detail of the tall apartment building that resembled nothing like a police station.

"A planned detour, Detective?"

She didn't say a word. Instead, Calloway stepped out of the car and opened the back door, grabbing Santiago on his upper arm.

At first he hesitated, but Calloway yanked hard. A stabbing pain radiated up his side, the pinch of the flex cuff biting deep.

It didn't bother her that people were walking past, seeing her manhandle a handcuffed Santiago. Every so often, a pedestrian would watch the interaction, only to turn their attention back to their iPhones as if nothing was out of the ordinary. She and Santiago entered the building into an open area of mailboxes. Calloway shoved Santiago forward every time he would start to slow and drag his feet. Despite trying to play it cool, Santiago knew why they were bypassing formal booking for a private apartment in a gritty part of San Francisco. Detective Calloway was going to continue her interrogation—in her own way. Was she the kind of cop who would circumvent the law just to get what she wanted, no matter the cost? As hard-edged as she appeared, Calloway was still just a woman.

Santiago didn't think she had it in her. But appearances could be deceiving.

Inside, Calloway elbowed him forward, toward a narrow set of stairs. "Go on," was all she said. Santiago studied them for a second before feeling the pressure of a gun pushed up against his back. "Walk," she ordered.

Three flights up, the two turned down the hallway, toward an apartment door on their right, slightly ajar. Calloway pushed the door open while keeping her weapon pressed against Santiago. "Get in."

He took a few steps into a small room that led directly into the kitchen area. Once inside, Santiago came to an abrupt stop, causing Calloway to bump against his back. She felt Santiago body's tense, his eyes fixated at the man sitting at a small table, hands folded squarely in front. The man's eyes were looking at nothing. He didn't turn when Santiago entered, already anticipating his arrival.

"Hello, Ramone," the man said, the tone void of warmth.

Santiago had no choice but to respond. "Hello, Manoso."

CHAPTER 46

S ELMA WAS STANDING AT THE COUNTER, studying a chart when Paris entered the building. She heard the door open and looked up. Seeing Paris, she dropped the clipboard and stepped into the hallway.

As Paris approached, he saw the stress in Selma's face, knowing whatever she was going to say, it wasn't going to be good.

"This way," she instructed, indicating the two should talk in private.

They walked over to an area where there was a sink and a line of vending machines, away from the patient's rooms. The lights were dim and there was no one else around.

Selma turned and leaned against the counter, folded her arms across her chest. "She's in there mumbling something about how Miss Valerie can't do this and shouldn't do that." She shook her head. "It sounds bad, like she's in trouble."

"You mentioned, *danger.*"

"That's right. She said, *danger.*"

Paris concluded the only way to find out what Ruth Calloway meant was to talk with her, directly. That was if her mind hadn't faded back into the darkness.

"Is Mrs. Calloway awake?"

"Let's go see." Selma made an open-handed gesture, an invitation for him to lead the way. They treaded lightly down the corridor to the elevator, rode to the third floor, and stood in front of Ruth Calloway's door. Before they entered, Selma hesitated. "You know, it's White."

Not understanding, Paris stopped at the entry. "White?"

Hands resting on her hips, Selma replied, "Her name. You know it's White, not Calloway?"

Paris waited for an explanation. She saw the confusion in his face. "I thought you knew."

"Knew what?"

Selma blew out a frustrated breath. "Her past." She stared at him in disbelief. "The murder," she prompted. "Miss Valerie seeing it all and at such a young age."

Confused, the words bounced around in his head, like entering a racetrack after the cars had already taken their first lap, never giving the opportunity to catch up. "I have no idea what you're talking about."

Selma began speaking, hesitating at first with the words tumbling over each other. She was unsure how much she was allowed to say, how much she should say. Eventually, she spoke of Ruth's arrival, her need for constant care, and her diagnosis of early onset Alzheimer's. Over time Selma formed a bond with Ruth White, having late night conversations, not knowing, at times, if she was speaking from reality or imagined memories.

It was during her lucid moments when Ruth spoke of the time when she and her husband, Morgan White, lived in the rural town of Vaughn, Mississippi, with their child, Valerie. How one summer day, Ruth woke to find Morgan lying bloodied and dead in a patch of dirt alongside their home and Valerie, crumpled in a corner, forever changed. Ruth spoke of how the police came and removed Morgan in a body bag, and how they took Valerie to one psychologist after another, to find out what she saw, but, more importantly, how to make her whole.

"Who is Calloway then?" Paris was still absorbing this new revelation.

"Mother's maiden name." Selma gestured, as if drawing the assumption that everybody knew. "I understood from Miss Ruth's account of everything that happened that Miss Valerie needed a fresh start in life. She probably didn't want people knowing or asking about her past."

Paris felt a cold chill run up his spine. He placed a hand on Selma's arm. "I better speak with her now."

PARIS GUESSED RUTH FELT HIS PROXIMITY when he entered the room. He was standing quietly over her bed when her head rolled to the right and her eyes opened. Though they had a slight haze, Paris noticed the deepness in them, bright green forcing through the cloudiness.

He knew—like a light flickering on and off—Ruth was in the real world.

She reached up and gently touched Paris's arm. "You were here before," she whispered. "With Valerie."

Paris smiled and nodded. He hadn't realized she was awake and aware of his presence during the first visit. It made him wonder what else had she heard throughout long durations of closed eyes and stillness.

"You're really here, yes?" she said, as if questioning which of her two worlds she was currently in. "Do you know where my Valerie is?"

Paris felt embarrassed. "No."

"You have to find her." Ruth forced herself closer. "She found him."

Paris pulled back a few inches, seeking an insight, a foothold, a window, a clue. Answers. "Found who?"

"Him. The man that killed my husband, Morgan, Valerie's father."

Paris felt the blood rush to his head. Did Ruth slide back into her imagination? "Who killed Morgan?"

Her face was so close, he could feel each hard-won breath, could almost see the buried memories behind those eyes, beseeching. Almost feel her pain from those years long ago, a time when so much was lost to her.

Then, it was gone, and her head lolled to one side away from him.

He heard her moan. "She's going to kill him."

CHAPTER 47

B Y THE TIME CLARION FINISHED TELLING HIS WIFE, Barbara, the reason he was heading to San Francisco, he realized, his own explanation didn't make any sense.

"Why does the FBI want to talk with you now? And why in San Francisco?"

He shook his head as he exhaled a deep breath, maneuvering the BMW around a caravan of slow-moving minivans filled with what looked like high school kids, the sides painted with the words, *Go Cougars* and *Beat the Trojans*, triangle flags fluttering from the car antennas.

"The man said Agent Paris needed to speak with me right away and in person."

Barbara's voice went meek. "Is he going to arrest you?"

Clarion flinched at the question but pushed it out of his head. If Paris wanted to arrest him, he could have easily come to the house. "All I know is they say it's important and somehow involves Rachel's safety."

There was a long pause on the other end of the phone. He knew Barbara was about to unleash another dozen questions, to which he was already prepared to answer, *I don't know.* "Look, I'll call you right after I speak with the FBI," he said. "Promise."

Barbara appeared to accept his response because she simply answered with an "Okay."

He ended the call and placed the phone on his lap. His anxiety level intensified, agonizing about each minute he was not at home watching over his wife and child, worried that at any moment, Manoso would make another move to finish what he started. It would be like cancer, remaining hidden until the opportunity presented itself. Clarion believed Manoso would waste no time. He'd do it now.

In the silence of the drive, he thought about the past two days since the shooting, Rachel's rescue, and his conversation with Agent Paris. It made Clarion think about his life as a drug distributor and the chaos it brought him. About when his whole world went sideways after the first time Rachel was kidnapped. How he had been forced to look over his shoulder every day since.

He cringed, wondering if Agent Paris was right, about getting his family to a safe place. Did he make the right decision? Maybe it was his ego that made him refuse. Like his decision to deal drugs. It wasn't about making money or the national fight on legalization. He wasn't doing it on moral grounds or *for the family*.

The truth was, he liked being a drug dealer. He liked the power. Until it jeopardized his family's safety. Realizing how misguided his intentions were, Clarion wished he could do it over. Start from zero. But that wasn't going to happen. Now, he needed to fix this mess.

He looked down at the small piece of paper. He had scribbled the address given to him by the FBI dispatcher. It took him nearly an hour and a half in evening traffic before he entered the city, making his way up Market Street and over to an apartment building located somewhere in the Tenderloin District. After some searching, he found a parking spot, shoved a few quarters into the meter, and hiked up the street to the front entrance. He found it strange Agent Paris would pick such a seedy spot to meet.

Clarion entered the dark vestibule and decided to take the stairs up the three flights before knocking on the door marked in brass: thirty-four. When the door opened, Clarion stared into the green eyes of Detective Valerie Calloway.

Before he could say a word, Calloway put a hand on his chest and gently nudged him back wanting a conversation out in the hallway. Clarion glanced to each side of Calloway, then back into her eyes.

"Where's Agent Paris?"

Detective Calloway leaned against the doorframe, blocking his access, her face tense.

Clarion sensed things were not right. "What are we doing here?" he asked, taking a step back.

Calloway shook her head. "Agent Paris wasn't the one who wanted you here."

He frowned, confused.

"Over the past five years, you have never been able to stop worrying about your family," Calloway said. "Am I right?"

He didn't know how to respond.

"Tonight, I'm going to fix that." She turned around and pushed the door open. "Come on in."

Clarion slowly followed her into the small apartment, first seeing a large man standing to the side of two other men seated at a table. He recognized one of them: Manoso.

Calloway walked behind the second man and placed a hand on his shoulder. The man flinched at the unwelcome touch before he let out an angry grunt.

"This is Ramone Santiago," Calloway said in introduction, as if this situation wasn't a giant clusterfuck already. She took a few steps to her left and placed a hand on Manoso's head. "And you know our friend here."

She motioned with an open palm, pointing at an empty chair at the table. Clarion moved, as if in a dream—or nightmare.

As he got closer, he could see Santiago and Manoso's hands were resting on the table, each bound in flex cuffs. Both sat expressionless, their focus anchored on some distant spot as if already knowing the outcome.

"Why am I here?" Clarion asked. He looked up at Calloway before turning back and locking eyes with the man standing in the shadows.

He was a large man, bald. But clearly not a cop. He was, somehow, Calloway's muscle.

"As I said," Calloway began, "you're here to ensure your family will never have to worry about being harmed. Ever again. You know, sort of an insurance policy."

Manoso choked back a laugh. He looked up at Clarion. "You're nothing more than a drug dealer who doesn't pay his debts."

Clarion could feel the anger well up inside his chest. He wanted to reach over and squeeze Manoso's neck until all life drained from his eyes. "I doubt paying back a man like you would have made any difference."

Manoso glanced back at Calloway with casual disregard, before staring ahead. "Why do you care about a drug dealer's problem? It's a part of doing business."

Clarion watched Calloway lean down and place her lips close to Manoso's ear, as if she was whispering a secret. But Calloway spoke loud enough for everyone to hear. "Because my father was one of your drug dealers."

Manoso froze but refused to give Calloway the satisfaction of his surprise.

"Do you remember me, Manoso? Do you remember my father?"

Manoso finally turned his head and studied Calloway's face.

She deliberately drew back, enough for Manoso to get a better look. "Twenty three years ago," she said. "Almost to the day."

Santiago leaned forward, now riveted on Calloway. Twenty-three years ago, Ramone Santiago was Manoso's strong arm for his drug operation. Back then they controlled the South—Louisiana to Florida. In that instant, Santiago's eyes flared with recognition. It had been many years, but the young child's face still resided in the woman.

He raised his hands, still cuffed as if in prayer, and pointed in her direction. "You!"

Calloway felt the rage swell inside her body, knowing the moment she'd been waiting for most of her life had finally arrived.

"My God," Santiago continued. "You're Morgan White's daughter."

Calloway looked over at Santiago, the feeling of acid rising in her throat. "And you're the man who killed him."

Clarion pushed back his chair, getting to his feet, only to feel the large man hold him in place with a strong hand on his neck. Clarion shoved the man's hand off. "What the hell is going on?"

"These men are scum," Calloway said, her voice fighting to remain calm. "For decades, they have murdered their way to the top of the drug trade, my father being one of their victims." She pointed toward Santiago. "This one beat him with a baseball bat." With her chin, she motioned at Manoso. "This one gave the orders to do it."

"You don't understand," Manoso interjected. "Your father was a drug dealer. He refused to pay his debt," he said, as if his actions were justified.

"He had nothing to give!" Calloway responded, unable to stay calm.

"He was a drug dealer!"

Calloway stood behind the two. "You're right, Manoso. Sometimes punishment is the only answer," she continued, turning in the direction of the large man standing behind Clarion. "Alexi," she said, pointing at the large man, "has been watching Peter Kennedy for several months, waiting for you to show up, Manoso."

Manoso turned the other way.

Calloway switched her attention back to Santiago. "Then as luck would have it, you show up." She leaned in close to Santiago, savoring every detail. "I have been waiting to have you both together for a long time."

She holstered her weapon, pausing before reaching into a darkened corner. When she returned into the dim light of the lamp, Clarion saw what she held in her hands—a heavy wooden baseball bat. She wrapped both hands around the grip, as if she was judging the weight, before letting it touch ground, dragging it across the hardwood floor.

Santiago shifted, heeding the sound of the wooden bat clipping the legs of his chair. *Rumble, tap.*

"It's time, Ramone."

"Wait, let me explain."

Rumble, tap. "It's your turn."

"It was just business." Ramone's voice cracked.

Tap.

It was the last sound in the room before Calloway pulled back the bat and unleashed a full swing. The head of the man, who had brutally murdered her father, snapped hard to the right, a stream of blood exploding from his mouth before he fell from his chair onto the floor.

Clarion jumped back, slamming into the Alexi's chest. It was like striking a wall. The big man didn't budge.

Manoso grimaced and shrank to his left, turning his face away from the spray of blood.

Calloway swung again, coming straight down onto Santiago's head. It sounded like crushing two-dozen eggshells at once.

Santiago's body shuddered from the energy of the blow, involuntary reflexes. He was dead.

Calloway lifted the bat and let the tip fall onto the table, stamping a bloody mark of death. She looked down and spoke to Santiago's dead body. "I promised my father I would hunt you down for what you did."

She dragged the bat toward Manoso, eventually leading it up his chest before pressing it into his neck.

Manoso looked up with contempt at Alexi. "You said you wouldn't kill me."

Alexi smiled. "I won't." He jutted a finger at Calloway. "She will."

"Now, you, Manoso," Calloway said.

Clarion saw Santiago's blood starting to pool toward him as he stepped away. "For fuck sake," he snapped. "Why am I here?"

Calloway slowly made her way over to him while tapping the head of the bat on top of the table. She stopped in front of him and held out the bat. "This is the man who took your daughter, who will never stop hunting her. If he lives. I want to help you fix that."

She reached over and took Clarion's hand, placing the blood-soaked bat in it. Clarion instinctively took it. As if in a bad dream, he could see his fingers clenched around the bat, but he could only hear the debate, the rationalization, the regret raging inside his head.

Calloway relaxed her shoulders and stepped back. "Go on," she said. "Fix it."

At first, he stood motionless, considering what he was about to do. Adrenaline surged through his body and he felt his face flush with anger. He hoisted the bat up to eye level. Less than three days ago he made a promise to Barbara that he would resolve this threat, fix it. Now, the opportunity was right in front of him. Calloway was spot-on. She was providing him a way out, a solution. It had been five years of wondering if his family would ever be safe. At this turning point, he could finally be sure. Clarion rotated his grip around the bat, finding the perfect feel that would give him power behind his swing, knowing it would only take one. With one stroke, it would be over, his family forever safe from the likes of Manoso.

He raised the bat, letting it fall heavy on the table, once. The contact reverberated, sounding like a burst of thunder.

Manoso recoiled, fighting back the fear. "Don't do this," he said, trying to sound threatening, but the words came across more like a plea.

Clarion slowly raised the bat chest high, effectively giving Manoso a closer look at the bloodstained tip, a prelude of his inevitable demise.

The room fell silent. It gave Clarion a moment to reflect. He thought about his life and all the decisions he had made over the years that had led him here, the trail of destruction following him and his family. The consequences from those choices were devastating—each one spiraling down to the next until, eventually, he landed in this dingy room, at this defining moment.

Now he was forced to be judge, jury, executioner. To kill Manoso. Was that the answer? Would this decision result in a better outcome than those he had made in the past? As much as he wanted to take the swing, he knew doing so would be a mistake. He would forever be a murderer, just like Manoso. Clarion stopped and turned back toward Calloway, letting the bat fall from his hand.

"No," he said.

Calloway displayed a look of disappointment but then offered an unsettling smile. "Fine," she said in a comforting voice. "I gave you an opportunity and you chose not to accept it."

"Just arrest him," Clarion said, his remark sounding ludicrous, considering the circumstances. "Let the courts do their job."

Calloway shook her head as she walked back to Manoso. She leaned a hand on his shoulder while drawing her nine millimeter Glock pistol with the other, pressing the barrel of the weapon against his temple.

"I can't do that," she said. "Bat or bullet. It's all going to end here."

CHAPTER 48

W HEN THEY DEPARTED THE WAREHOUSE LOCATION, Rafael worried about surveillance. As the SUV meandered slowly between the commercial buildings, he kept a close eye on any trailing vehicles, but by the time they hit the main road into town, he relaxed, seeing nothing behind.

Less than half an hour later, they found the address given by their boss. Rafael pointed at a five-story building down the street and all eyes in the back of the van gazed up. He rubbed his chin, studying the building, watching people come and go from the front entrance.

"You think he's in there?" Sancho, a security member, asked.

Rafael frowned, his eyes continuing to study foot traffic, still on the lookout for possible tails. Without knowing Manoso's exact location, Rafael and his men would have a difficult time rescuing him, even with all the firepower they possessed. "Listen up," he said to the group.

Everyone went silent.

Rafael focused his attention on Sancho. "Take two men around the back of the building and make your way inside." He turned to the two remaining men. "Stay with me."

Sancho pulled open the side door and bounded out into the cold San Francisco air. Holding onto the side of the van he turned toward Rafael. "What are we looking for?"

"You see anyone with a gun, you screw yours into their head."

Sancho nodded.

"Make sure they tell you the location of Manoso first," Rafael barked. "Then kill them."

Sancho turned up his jacket collar and took off down the street, followed by his team.

One of the remaining members jumped up into the driver's seat, started up the van, and threw it into drive. Under Rafael's direction, the driver coasted past the next block before he swung right, slowly circling the tightly crammed buildings, looking for a place to park in case they needed to make a fast escape.

PARIS PLACED THREE CALLS TO CALLOWAY'S CELL, with each one going directly to voicemail. As in the past, her intent was clear. She didn't want to talk to anyone.

What happened? Why now? What had changed from only a few hours ago? Their last interaction was no misunderstanding. It just didn't make sense. Paris thought he knew the answer but now doubted everything he felt about Valerie Calloway. He called the jail, got the runaround until he was finally connected to the watch commander who gave Paris the bad news: Ramone Santiago was never booked in.

As quick as that call ended, his phone vibrated. Dools. After leaving the assisted living facility, Paris had filled him in on what he had learned from his conversation with Ruth White. He had ordered Dools to find out everything he could about the death of Morgan White.

"What happened?"

"Morgan White," Dools started off. "Found murdered at his farmhouse in Vaughn, Mississippi, February, 1987. Multiple blunt force trauma."

"Was the case solved?"

"Nope, but," Dools added, "DEA reported White was suspected of being a mid-level distributor. Mostly weed. They think the murder may have been over a drug payment dispute. Here's where it gets interesting." Papers rustled in the background. "Looks like White had a daughter, Valerie White, who witnessed the killing." He paused and rustled more papers. "The case languished for a couple of years without coming up with a suspect. Time passed, and mother and daughter decided to leave the area for parts unknown."

"What's Ruth White's maiden name?" Paris asked to confirm what he had learned from his conversation with Selma.

Dools knew where Paris was heading. "Calloway," he answered.

Paris took his foot off the accelerator, letting the car drift to the right, his focus on the upcoming off-ramp.

"It explains a lot," Dools said. "Working alone, obsessed with this phantom drug dealer. This whole time, she was chasing her father's killer." Then he said, "We should have never trusted her, Jack."

Paris let the last declaration slide by without biting back. "Where are you?"

"Tenderloin District," Dools responded.

Without checking his blind spots, Paris crushed the accelerator and jammed the car across three lanes of moving traffic. Car horns blared and tires screeched as he barely cleared the Hoffman Boulevard off-ramp, blowing through a major intersection and looping back onto the 580 westbound toward the city.

"We got three on foot and two still in the van," Dools continued.

"Where's Valerie's informant?" Paris asked.

He swore he could hear Dools smirk then, as if he was expecting the question. "I just checked with the office. Triangulation has him within blocks of our location."

Paris felt a rush of fear course through him. Calloway was with her source, and the two were with Santiago. Whatever had happened over twenty years ago, Paris knew Calloway was hell-bent on settling a score. And from the looks of things, Ramone Santiago was in the middle of it all. Before ending the call, Paris told Dools to keep him updated, he'd be there soon. Until then, Dools would work with the tracking team to pinpoint Calloway's informant.

Paris decided to make a last-ditch effort at contacting Calloway. More than likely, she wasn't going to pick up but maybe she was listening to his messages. As he expected, the call went straight to voicemail. He waited for the beep. "Val," he said as calmly as he could muster. "I spoke with your mother. She told me everything." He paused, trying to clear the dryness from his mouth. "I know what you're planning. I know about your father. Don't do this." Before he clicked off, Paris made a final plea. "I can fix this."

It was an offer of hope but, deep down, he knew there was little he could do. If Santiago was the person who killed her father, Calloway was going to get retribution. Paris's only prayer was to get to her before she could pull the trigger. The odds of that happening were fading by the second. And saying he could fix this was a bold face lie.

CHAPTER 49

It wasn't quite sunset but, in a city of tall buildings tightly compressed and separated by narrow alleyways, the streets of San Francisco were already dark and shadowless. Paris was unfamiliar with much of the layout, relying on his conversations with the FBI cellphone tracking team to give him guidance.

The phone to Calloway's informant was still on, but Paris worried how long that would last. Calloway had to know by now that Paris had learned Santiago was not booked into lock-up. The trackers told Paris they had a faint signal off Van Ness, on the east side on Bush Street.

That was a good sign, putting them in the same area where Dools was following Manoso's security team. Paris was already in spitting distance, driving north on Leavenworth, just south of Geary. He was now near enough to start picking up the surveillance team's radio traffic. Dools was parked in front of a drycleaners off Post and Leavenworth.

The radio crackled and the voice of an FBI agent came over the air. They had a vehicle believed to be the security detail. "Three are out of the van. Moving, eastbound through Leavenworth on Post."

Dools instructed his team to stay with the subjects on foot. The others, along with the fixed-wing, were to remain on the van.

Dools rang Paris. "I got a feeling we're close," he said over the cell. "How about you?"

Paris peered up at the street signs. "Yeah, real close."

The traffic was thick coming up Post, the intersection jammed with slow-moving pedestrians and stopped cars. The light had already changed to yellow, and unless Paris was willing to run people over, he had no choice other than to continue north, catching the next eastbound route.

He peeled around three cars waiting at the turn, nearly clipping the bumper of a pick-up truck carrying boxes of fresh vegetables, and then cleared through the cross street that had gone red, before heading north on Leavenworth. He pulled up to Sutter but found a one-way heading west. Listening to radio chatter, he could hear the surveillance agents calling out street after street, leaving Paris behind, stuck in standstill traffic. He flipped on his siren, a series of loud blips. Pedestrians jumped, cars braked.

He blew through the clearing and accelerated up Leavenworth toward Bush. Preparing to turn right at the intersection, Paris glanced up and spotted a car parked on the right side halfway up the block. A blue Chevy Malibu.

As he got closer, Paris could see a distinctive steel screen separating the front seats from the back, a dead giveaway of a police car.

He pulled up close enough to see the exempt license plates, another indication it was law enforcement and sufficient confirmation for him to know whom it belonged to.

Paris threw the car into reverse and squeezed into an open space just behind Calloway's. He got on the radio and called out to Dools.

"I'm coming your way," Dools said. "Be careful."

"FUCK ME," GROWLED ONE OF THE FBI SURVEILLANCE AGENTS.

He was on foot, exasperated over losing sight of the security team that was wandering along Bush, just east of Leavenworth. The agent, following the three suspects, was distracted, listening to Agent Paris's discovery of a car of interest, which had caused him to momentarily take his eyes off of the group. When he returned to his targets, he saw only two, the third person missing. There was an alleyway just prior to their location. Had number three gone down that way? Did he go into the nearby building? The agent informed the other team members over the radio, asking them to box off the area in an attempt to find the missing target. Until then, the agent could only hope the unaccounted-for suspect would return to the group shortly.

PARIS PUSHED EVERY CALL BUTTON on the apartment board, hoping someone would just buzz him in without asking. No one did. A few voices came over the loud speaker, none offering to help.

Finally, someone did. "Manager," came a female voice over the speaker.

"FBI," Paris replied.

There was a pause and the sound of the intercom disconnecting. A second later the lock on the metal security gate buzzed allowing Paris access into the small lobby. As he entered, there was the sound of another clank from a latch and a long squeak from a door opening.

An old woman, maybe in her late sixties, stepped into the vestibule from a blind hallway to his right. She dipped a pair of glasses down her nose and peered over the top at Paris. "Can I help you?"

He pointed out the door, toward Calloway's vehicle. "Do you know the owner of that car parked in front?"

The woman looked out the glass door and squinted, studying the car before shaking her head. "Sorry, no."

He took in a breath, trying not to look frustrated. "Do you know all your tenants?"

The woman again shook her head, looking a bit embarrassed. "I just became the manager last week."

He held out a hand. "I need to see the list of your tenants."

"You can do that without a warrant?" the manager asked.

Was that a question or a confirmation? "Yep."

The woman led Paris to her apartment, pulling out a large ledger. She opened the book and handed it to him. He scanned the list, looking for a familiar name. The renters were listed in order of apartment number.

On the third page, Paris stopped at the listing marked *Apartments thirty-four/thirty-five.* He looked up at the manager. "Do you know who's renting these?"

This time the manager nodded, smiling at finally being able to help. "Yeah, she just paid the rent. They belong to a Ms. Valerie White."

CHAPTER 50

ALEXI MOGILEVICH LOOKED DOWN at his ringing phone, seeing a number he recognized.

Nicolai.

Having Manoso and Santiago—now deceased—with him, there was no reason to answer the call. He pressed the end button, sending the call to voicemail, knowing there wouldn't be a reply. Mogilevich turned to Manoso. "It's for you," he said with a smile.

"That's my security team," Manoso proclaimed without even seeing the screen on the phone. "They're out looking for me, and they're persistent."

"They'll be too late."

Manoso scooted as far forward as the bindings would allow, the muzzle of Calloway's pistol still pressed against his skull. "Turn me over to them and I promise they will not harm you."

Mogilevich laughed. "They don't know where we are."

"They'll find us." Manoso nodded toward Calloway. "You killed the man that murdered your father. It's done."

"What about you?"

Manoso's tone was subdued, almost conciliatory. "Ramone was an idiot. I told him to collect the money. I didn't say to kill him. That was his decision."

Calloway locked her eyes on Manoso, refusing to accept what he was saying. "I don't believe you."

She pressed the muzzle harder against Manoso's head. He went rigid, squeezing his eyes shut, waiting for the inevitable blast to come.

"I won't be a witness to this!" Clarion shouted. He started for the door but Mogilevich blocked his path.

"Let him go," Calloway called out. She waved a dismissive arm and leveled her attention back on Manoso. "It doesn't matter anymore."

Mogilevich stepped aside, giving Clarion just enough room to pass. As he reached for the door handle, Clarion spoke without turning around. "You're making a mistake."

"Maybe," she said, acknowledging Clarion's warning. "So did he, twenty-three years ago."

She watched Clarion pull the door wide and step into the hallway. When he did, she caught sight of a shadowy figure just outside the entry. Calloway was able to see the man first, sizing up Clarion then looking deeper into the apartment. His gaze fell on her then on Mogilevich and, finally, Manoso. She saw the look of recognition.

Rescue party.

Before she could level her weapon toward the door, the man threw a hard right at Clarion's face. Clarion tried to block the punch but took the full force across the temple. He crashed against the doorframe and crumpled to the ground.

Mogilevich's large frame blanketed the entry. He pulled his weapon and fired twice. The intruder folded at the waist and stumbled back but not before getting off two rounds, the first striking Mogilevich in the shoulder, and the second in the throat.

Calloway pushed her way around the table and ran toward the door, seeing Mogilevich still standing, frozen in place, weapon dangling, in his hand, near his thigh. As Calloway neared, she reached out to touch him.

Mogilevich fell backward, his bulk nearly crushing Calloway as they landed in a heap. Two more rounds zipped past Calloway's right ear, striking the window frame, glass exploding into fragments. Calloway lifted her weapon, beading the shooter square in her sights. As she began to squeeze the trigger, Calloway heard someone shouting, followed by the sharp crack of more rounds being fired. The intruder's head snapped to the side, twice, blood spitting from the exit wound before he collapsed, dropping to the floor. For a moment, the room went still. Car horns honked, bus engines rumbled, and sirens blared—city noises floating up through the broken window.

Calloway pushed aside Mogilevich's dead body, keeping her weapon trained in the direction of the door and whoever might be there. Looking back, she saw Manoso pulling himself up in an attempt to flee. She swung her pistol his way now, making him understand that she wasn't done with him. She was confused, ears ringing from the gun blasts.

Her informant and an attacker were dead. How many others were out there waiting? As she tried to get a handle on the situation, she froze, hearing a familiar voice call out from the corridor.

"Valerie, it's me."

CHAPTER 51

P ARIS WAS ALREADY STANDING on the second floor landing when he heard a scuffle from above, followed by shots fired. He would have called Dools, requesting back up, but that would take too long.

He sprinted up the next flight of stairs, the firefight growing louder, more out of control, more shooting, the sound of bodies crashing into walls, falling to the ground.

On the third floor, Paris darted left and spotted a man twenty feet in front of him. He was in a crouched position, shooting into an apartment door. Paris could see he was wounded. His right hand, covered in blood, pressed hard against his abdomen.

Paris dropped back into a kneeling position, using the side of the wall as partial cover, drew his Glock, and pushed it forward. "FBI, Drop your weapon!"

The shooter spun, weapon aimed at Paris. Before he could squeeze the trigger, Paris squared his site and fired twice. The man's head snapped back, then he fell to the floor.

Jumping up, Paris ran straight to the doorway, weapon directed at the entry. As he approached, he saw blood seeping from two small holes in the dead man's head, eyes still open. Another man lay sideways, half-way in the doorway. This second man groaned and rolled onto his back, showing his face. Paris saw it was Clarion.

Paris peeked through the door and saw Calloway kneeling next to a man, who he assumed was dead, given the blood around his skull. Her weapon was trained on another man Paris did not recognize.

It was the calm after the storm. No one was shooting, no one made any aggressive movements.

Paris tried to take in everything, understand what was happening, and, mostly, stop any more carnage. He leaned into the doorframe, close enough for Calloway to recognize his voice, hoping there was still a chance he could bring this situation to an end without more death.

That, he thought, *is going to be a tall order.*

CHAPTER 52

"DON'T COME IN!" CALLOWAY SHOUTED IT TWICE, even after Paris promised he only wanted to talk.

Her head was pounding, and she couldn't concentrate. Her plan had gone terribly wrong. In her mind, no one else was supposed to be involved, no one else was supposed to get hurt. This was her promise to keep, hers alone.

"She's crazy!" Manoso shouted, pleading for Paris to stop Calloway from finishing what she'd started.

Calloway shifted her weapon back at Manoso and slid her finger over the trigger. He curled up in a ball and braced for what came next.

"It's just me, Val," Paris called back. "Let me come in and talk."

Tears welled up, blurring her vision. She wiped them away with her forearm but kept her gun trained on Manoso. No matter what happened, she was going to fulfill her promise.

When her eyesight cleared, Calloway saw movement at the door. Slowly, she saw Paris lean farther into view, his hands out, free of any weapons. He hesitated—unsure, but committed—standing in plain view, filling the doorway.

"I promised you," he said. "I would be here for you."

Calloway swung her weapon around and squared the sights on Paris. She saw him flinch but he refused to move. He stood in her line of fire.

"Go away," she pleaded.

He paused then shook his head. "No."

This was not the way it was supposed to end. It had taken decades for each puzzle piece to be twisted this way and that, to fit into the right spot. She'd sacrificed everything to find the men who murdered her father. The memories floated in and out of her consciousness, a constant reminder of her promise. His smile and love. Stolen. He never got the chance to see her grow up, go to college, have her first boyfriend. They never got the chance to talk about her career, a wedding, about grandchildren. She never got the opportunity to hug him and thank him for taking care of her and her mother. To keep them safe. To grow old. She would never be able to have these memories.

"Do something!" Manoso demanded.

Through more tears, Calloway shouted back. "Shut up."

Paris motioned with both hands, indicating everyone should calm down. He cautiously stepped over Clarion who was lying soundless on the floor. Three steps brought him fifteen feet from where Calloway stood. "I spoke with your mother. She cares about you, Val. She needs you. She wants you back."

Calloway emphatically shook her head in denial. "No, I can't." She started to shuffle back toward Manoso, expanding the distance between her and Paris, now twenty feet away.

"Don't do this," he pleaded as he continued to step forward. Ten feet away. "I promise, we can fix this together."

"Stop her!" Manoso hollered.

"Shut up!" she shouted back.

"Put down the gun, Val," Paris said.

Five feet away.

Calloway now stood next to Manoso, her jaw clenched so tight, she could barely hear past the ringing in her head. She looked at Paris, thought about their time together, secretly wishing for that life—one without deception and obsession. But it was too late. Her shoulders sagged. "Why do you care?"

She saw him searching for the right words. A second passed before he looked into her eyes, as if the answer was obvious. "Because I need you."

He'd said it. The words hit Calloway hard, like a wave washing over her. Since the beginning of their involvement, she'd known he was drawn to her. She'd just denied it. But the fact that he'd said it made it all the more real. Something she had never heard from another man.

In that ephemeral sliver of time, she felt her head spin, confused, now questioning her direction.

As if all the hate and pain in her soul had exited her body, Calloway went limp as she lowered her weapon from Manoso's head.

Maybe there is a chance to fix this.

Paris stepped back and relaxed.

Then she heard what sounded like soft laughter coming from Manoso. He tilted his head up, delivering a winning grin. At once, the hate flooded back and so did the memories. The promise. She raised her weapon and pressed it against his temple. This time she wasn't going to hesitate.

"No!" Paris screamed.

Calloway pulled the trigger. Jagged flames leapt from the barrel. The bullet penetrated Manoso's head and exited on the right side, trailing a spray of crimson and bone.

Paris moved forward but Calloway took a step back.

"Don't," she said.

He stopped. "Please, Val. Put down the gun."

Calloway felt tired. There would be no more decisions to make, no more second guessing. The visions of hate that had resided in her for all those years would now be gone, finally giving her respite.

She raised her weapon, this time placing the muzzle to her own head. "It's over." Her voice caught. "I did what I promised I'd do."

Struggling for the right words, Paris pleaded, telling her he would find a way to make things right. He would stand by her side. She could see he was being sincere, that he really cared. But she knew it wasn't possible. Her life was beyond salvageable. Avenging what Manoso and Santiago did to her father was the endgame and the ultimate sacrifice. *It's over.*

Calloway slid her finger onto the trigger as her eyes bounced in a daydream state. In flashes, she caught sight of Paris running forward, hands extended, grabbing for her gun. But he was too late, too slow to reach her.

She pulled the trigger. Brilliant light erupted, followed by a bullet moving faster than the speed of sound, spinning, flying, penetrating.

It was just a fleeting pain. Then, nothing.

The entire world slowed down to a crawl before coming to a stop.

The spent shell casing ejected from the port and skipped across the floor to a dark corner of the room.

As Calloway fell, the gold chain around her neck twisted and danced into view, a tiny rabbit charm attached. It bounced twice on her neck before slowly disappearing under her now-bloodied blouse.

CHAPTER 53

Today:

THE MORNING SUN HAD FINALLY TURNED THE SKY BLUE. Clouds drifted high. The air felt cleansed of hate and revenge, but the heaviness was still present. The automatic coffee pot clicked on and began dripping, allowing steam to rise from the glass carafe.

Paris forced himself to get off the couch. He poured a cup, before sitting down at the kitchen table, and wrapped his hands around the mug, letting the aroma hit his face.

Morning light reflected off the white case file covers like a beacon, greeting him once again, rooted there with worn tabs that displayed the names of their victims. Like wandering tendrils, curling up at the edges, photographs peered from the file folders, taunting him to peruse them once more, still hiding the gore that waited inside.

It had taken a week since the shooting for Paris to finally listen to the tape she left, hoping it would offer some justifiable reason behind her actions. It did but it didn't.

Hearing the details of the events leading up to her father's death was tragic but it didn't compare, in Paris's mind, to the psychological devastation it brought Valerie Calloway. All those years, she was unwavering, glued to a perilous promise to avenge her father's murder—a promise that delivered her deeper into despair. Her unconditional single focus isolated her from everyone, everything, where she sank into a world void of human connection, shared memories, and any chance of happiness.

It cost her valuable time with her mother that could never be recaptured, relived, or repaired. She was blind to the wake that spread out behind her, never realizing that the time she spent disconnected and distant caused just as much suffering as that summer morning.

Calloway was right when she said her life ended the day her father died. She just didn't realize her mother's did too. Could Paris have saved Calloway? Could he have changed her mind? *That would have been a fantasy,* he mused, *to have seen this, acted on it, saved her from residing deep in a well of desolation, especially because we met so late in the game.*

He wished their interactions, their intimacy, could have been enough, but her destination was already prearranged, her path set. She had made her decision, and nothing Paris did could have changed her course. The promise she had made was not meant to be broken.

There was a knock at the front door, followed by the sound of a key inserted into the lock. Paris didn't have to look to see who it was.

It was Dools.

Paris had given him a key long ago, in case he needed to retrieve a file, check on the place when Paris was traveling, or simply have a place to crash when he had nowhere to go. Dools was also separated.

He walked into the living room, spotted Paris, and waved to announce his entrance. Heading straight to the coffee pot, he poured himself a cup. He sat across from Paris, pushing the stack of files off to the side so he could have a clear view of him.

Paris watched out the back window lost in thought.

Dools pointed at the tape. "You find what you were looking for?"

Paris shrugged. "Her reason why she did what she did."

Dools shook his head. "All those years, just to become a cop so she could hunt down the two responsible for her father's murder."

"She made a promise."

"We all did."

He was right. Promises were made by everyone—Calloway, to avenge her father's murder; Clarion, to end the threat to his daughter; and Paris, to keep the Clarion family safe. They'd all made promises, each one with their own reasons and justifications.

We all make promises. There was one more. The last thing he told Calloway the night of the shooting, something he would always remember. *I promise, we can fix this together.*

That was a promise he couldn't keep.

He looked back and saw Dools out of his seat, now standing in the living room. He had the padded envelope that contained the tape, his hand rummaging around inside, and removed a small glass figure. Dools walked over to Paris and placed the object, a porcelain rabbit, on top of the stack of case files. The black dots for eyes looked as if they were staring right at him, unblinking.

Paris picked it up and studied the rabbit. Two chips spoiled the painted surface.

"A curiosity piece," Dools said.

"From a cabinet of curiosities," Paris replied, remembering his conversation with Calloway. "That's who we are, Dools. Pieces of curiosity."

CHAPTER 54

THE FRONT DOOR WAS BRIGHT WHITE—cathedral style—with a brass handle and glass-winged windows on both sides. Paris stared from his car at Clarion's house from across the street. The neighborhood was quiet. Tall oak trees running the length of the street rustled with the summer breeze.

A minivan drove by, full of soccer-bound children, a mother behind the wheel, her window rolled down. Everyday life. Like a Norman Rockwell painting. He stepped out of his car, walked to the door and knocked. He waited, imagining a police officer to quickly approach, asking him what he was doing there.

But that wasn't going to happen. There was no longer a threat to Rachel, to the Clarion family. The protection detail called off. It had ended with Manoso meeting the deadly end of a pistol, all because he couldn't walk away from a bad debt and being disrespected half a decade prior.

Had he not come back after Clarion, would Manoso still be the king-pin of the territory? Maybe so. Then again, he didn't consider the rami-fications of killing Morgan White all those years earlier, didn't count on the promise of a heartbroken daughter.

The door was pulled wide. Clarion had seen him through the side window. He stood silent, giving no sign of a welcome, not even a smile.

"How's Rachel?" Paris asked.

Clarion stepped out the door, gently closing it, as if he didn't want anyone inside to hear them speaking. He tilted his head, implying every-thing was fine.

"I spoke to the prosecutor," Paris added. "She's in agreement with my position. No charges will be filed." He spread his arms away from his side. "You're clear."

Clarion broke into a grin, joy siphoning anxiety away. He leaned against the door and crossed his arms. "I never wanted any of this to happen."

What could Paris add to that?

"I love my daughter, I love my wife . . ." Clarion's voice trailed off. "You married? Kids?"

Paris forced himself not to wince, didn't want to give any hint of his unease.

"I can't change the pain I caused my family because of my past," Clarion said. "I can only try and make it right."

"I wish you would have come to us, instead of trying to deal with it yourself."

Clarion looked down, kicked the toe of his shoe on his welcome mat. "What I did in the past was all my fault. My job to fix."

"What are you saying?"

Clarion looked directly into Paris's eyes. "To make it right, I'd do it again."

There it was. A father's commitment. Could Paris blame him? Robert Clarion was a man who, early on, had confused his priorities and forgotten what he was striving for in life—the result inflicting irrevocable emotional scars on his wife and daughter.

How does one walk away from that responsibility? Would Paris have done the same thing? Was he the only one who could correct the mistakes made? Trusting others to make right what you had made wrong? It wasn't in either of their DNAs.

Clarion relaxed, as if he had found comfort in his admission. He reached back and opened the front door, turned, and started in. "Don't take this personally, Agent Paris," he said as he cleared the threshold of his front door. "But I hope I never see you again."

PARIS WALKED BACK TO HIS CAR and took one last look at Clarion's house. It was quiet, peaceful, the past never to return. A small amount of satisfaction washed over Paris's body but his thoughts were already being invaded by the blowing winds of the other unsolved cases. All the others lying in wait, stacks on his living room table. Like uninvited guests. They were calling for him. Quietly waiting for his return home.

ABOUT THE AUTHOR

GEORGE FONG SPENT TWENTY-SEVEN YEARS as a special agent with the FBI, investigating kidnappings, serial killings, white collar, gangs, bank robberies, drug trafficking, and other violent crimes. He was also a lead instructor at the FBI's International Law Enforcement Academy in Budapest, Hungary, presenting on organized crime, undercover techniques, informant development, and electronic surveillance.

In 2002, Fong was promoted to supervisory special agent, managing the Violent Crimes and Major Offenders squad in Sacramento, to include the undercover program and the Forensic Evidence Response team. In 2007, he was again promoted as the Unit Chief, overseeing the FBI's National Violent Gang Program at FBI Headquarters in Washington DC.

He became an assistant inspector during his last year in the bureau before retiring. Currently, he is ESPN's Director of Security and Safety for the western half of the US and Pacific Rim countries.

He is married with two children. His sidekick, Sparky has since passed. His new dog is Scout.